KIRA SLAPPED AT HER COMM BADGE SO HARD SHE WAS SURE IT WOULD BRUISE HER PALM.

"Kira to Bashir."

Furious at her own stupidity, more furious still at her embarrassment when nothing but silence echoed back across subspace.

"Kira to Bashir!"

Nothing. No doctor, no wayward Klingon, not even an open channel to hint that Bashir's communicator still existed. The doctor was gone.

The Klingon Rekan Vrag was the first to break the silence, and although there was triumph in her voice, its icy chill told Kira it wasn't a triumph she was proud of. "You have given up another hostage," she said accusingly. "Now do you begin to see what an abomination is a Klingon without Honor?"

STAR TREK
DEEP SPACE NINE®
ARMAGEDDON SKY
DAY OF HONOR
BOOK TWO OF FOUR

L. A. GRAF

POCKET BOOKS
New York   London   Toronto   Sydney   Tokyo   Singapore

This book is a work of fiction. Names, characters, places and incidents are products of the author's imagination or are used fictitiously. Any resemblance to actual events or locales or persons, living or dead, is entirely coincidental.

An *Original* Publication of POCKET BOOKS

POCKET BOOKS, a division of Simon & Schuster Inc.
1230 Avenue of the Americas, New York, NY 10020

A VIACOM COMPANY

STAR TREK is a Registered Trademark of Paramount Pictures.

This book is published by Pocket Books, a division of Simon & Schuster Inc., under exclusive license from Paramount Pictures.

ISBN: 0-671-00675-4

First Pocket Books printing September 1997

10 9 8 7 6 5 4 3 2 1

POCKET and colophon are registered trademarks of Simon & Schuster Inc.

Printed in the U.S.A.

To all you bonobos,
wherever you are.

ARMAGEDDON SKY

CHAPTER
1

KIRA ARCHED PERILOUSLY backward to dodge her opponent's *bat'leth,* scraping her heel on the edge of one carved bone step. She stumbled and felt her way up the irregular steps with one hand thrust out behind her. From both above and below, the ancient Klingon courtyard echoed with the sounds of fierce and bloody combat: metallic crashes, ground-shaking thuds, and occasional curses spat out in the dozen languages Dax spoke fluently. At least one of those had been Bajoran, and from its breathless invocation of Prophetic aid, Kira gathered the battle on the courtyard's floor wasn't going well at all. Neither was the battle on the shivering balcony above her—the thunder of booted footsteps across it exploded abruptly into shattered bone balustrade and splintered crystal floor tiles. The

1

cascade of debris startled Kira so much that she almost missed the spectacle of Odo whirling to the courtyard floor in a splash of effluvium.

In retrospect, she realized she should have expected it. The constable had been all but forced into joining Dax's holographic "defense of honor"; during the preliminary arming ceremonies he'd grumbled non-stop that the Trill's insistence on authentic medieval Klingon armor was going to exhaust his shape-changing abilities before his duty shift even began that night. Odo might not have been able to withstand Dax's wheedling any more than Kira, but since he'd only agreed to participate if he wasn't forced to use a *bat'leth,* he was too pragmatic not to avail himself of the first opportunity to remove himself from the combat.

Unfortunately, flinging herself into glorious, bloody death was not exactly an option for Kira. Tearing her eyes away from the still-rippling evidence of Odo's demise, she refocused her attention on the battle just in time to catch an armored elbow in the face. The holographic Klingon warrior who had backed her up the stairs might have been carefully programmed by Worf to match her fighting skills, but it hadn't been given her ability to be distracted—or her underlying impatience with this ridiculous ritual challenge.

It wasn't a full-force blow—Kira could have avoided it if she'd been paying attention—but it was enough to stagger her off the stairs and back down into the courtyard. She chased her balance with two backward steps, then felt her heel come down in something slick and rubbery. She realized what—*who*—it was an instant before her foot whisked out from under her.

Odo's gelatinous flinch had to have been more from sympathy than any need on his part. Kira pinwheeled to land without use of her hands, worried for one absurd moment that she might crush him. The jolt of discomfort that thumped up her spine was enough to inspire a curse of her own, this time so vile that even the Klingon looming over her blinked in surprise.

"That's it." She heaved her *bat'leth* toward the open courtyard and called out, "Program: delete 'Kira,'" just to watch the weapon evaporate before it could hit the ground. "I quit."

Dax, chestnut hair loose and wild about her armor-plated shoulders, threw Kira an irritated scowl as she whirled to avoid a downward lunge from Odo's former opponent, nimbly kicking him in the teeth as she did so. "You can't quit!" she complained, to both Kira and her own former adversary, now leaning down to help Kira to her feet. "What about the insult to my honor?"

Odo rippled with what might have been a snort if he'd had the nose and lungs to produce it. He extruded a rudimentary head big enough to remark, "Either it doesn't require as much defense as you thought, or you've picked the wrong warriors to help defend it." The platter of gel under Kira's hand twitched testily. "Major, if you don't mind . . ."

"Oh . . . sorry." Kira shifted her weight as best she could, ignoring the clench of indignant muscles across the small of her back. Odo oozed out from under one hand, then the other. The bulge at the top of the gelatin pool glided smoothly into a humanoid outline, then sketched in its own details of color, texture, and form.

"Come on, you guys." Dax's *bat'leth* struck holo-

3

graphic sparks off holographic armor as she swung around to confront Kira's former attacker. Deprived by the holo-suite computer of their programmed targets, both of Worf's seconds were now closing in on the Trill. She seemed more exasperated than intimidated by this development. "You can't just walk away from our *Suv'batlh!*"

Worf fastened a huge hand around Kira's elbow. "It is not *our Suv'batlh,*" he rumbled. His expression, always somewhat grim by Bajoran standards, all but smoldered beneath the shadows of his lacquered facemask. Kira fitted her hand between a seam in his armor's vambrace, and tried to take at least some of her own weight as the big Klingon heaved her to her feet. "This is not any *Suv'batlh* at all."

If Dax appreciated the thunder on Worf's dark face, Kira saw no sign of it. "Speak for yourself," she countered, knocking the second holographic Klingon onto his back with a fierce swing of her *bat'leth,* then thumping Worf in the small of his back with the rounded edge of her weapon. "I'm not going to stand by while you tell me where I can and can't go, like I was one of your courtesans."

Worf spun on her, growling with all the fury of a *ghar*-wolf as he seized her *bat'leth* in both hands. In that instant, Kira appreciated how much of his Klingon nature he hid from them every moment of every day. "Computer: End program!"

A polite, nonintrusive chime wafted through the burning air of the DuHoH desert, rippling the edges of *meO* trees and Klingon-hewn stone until it seemed the whole world was melting in the heat. By the time the computer informed them, "Program ended," their slice of ancient Klingon history had dissolved down to four black walls and a gridwork of intersecting lines. Kira felt the same startling press of claustrophobia that always swarmed over her when the holo-suite's illusion of openness was over.

"You make a mockery of an honorable tradition." His words were accusatory, but Worf's tone sounded more disappointed than angry. He released Dax's weapon with a snarl. "I should not have accepted your challenge."

Dax shook her hair back from her face, exposing the very unKlingonlike spattering of freckles at each temple. "I'm not trying to mock anything." She looked tall and lanky in her exoskeleton of Klingon armor; the intricate structure of both *rantou* lacquer and *bat'leth* stood out in even greater relief now that the holo-suite's walls were all that surrounded them. "You knew that going with the *Victoria Adams* was important to me." Kira had heard this argument in every permutation ever since the Terran science vessel left the station two days ago, but the indignation in Dax's voice still sounded freshly minted. "Do you have any idea how many thousands of years it's going to be until I get another chance to witness a cometary deluge like this one?"

"The rarity of an astronomical event does not make it imperative that every science officer in Starfleet view it," Worf informed her bluntly. "As station tactical officer, I determined that your primary duty is here. On DS9."

Sighing, Kira wearily popped the straps at the knee joints of her armor and settled to the floor to wait out the debate.

Dax grounded her *bat'leth* with a thump that rang painful echoes off the bare holo-suite walls. "On DS9,

Commander Worf, my *duty* is to document all scientific phenomena in and around this region of space."

"Not when a Starfleet research vessel has already been dispatched expressly for the purpose of observing that phenomenon," Worf snarled back. "In that case, your duty consists of—"

"I know, I know." The Trill's voice sizzled with a level of annoyance that didn't quite match the wry glint in her grey eyes. "Making sure the station is prepared for all the possible scientific emergencies that might arise. Emergencies that *you* felt the need to enumerate in a four-page report that convinced Benjamin he couldn't afford to let me go!"

"It is important for a commanding officer to know all the strategic considerations that might influence his decision. And the current situation with the Klingons—"

"No matter how many Klingons may or may not be violating the Neutral Zone, the *Victoria Adams* is no less likely to be attacked just because *I'm* not on board." A hint of youthful petulance crept into Dax's voice. "And I *wanted* to watch the comets fall."

Worf scowled, not yielding. "The danger to the *Victoria Adams* is beside the point. As a senior science officer, you are too valuable to this station to risk yourself on frivolous scientific tourist excursions."

"How about frivolous Honor Combats?" Dax retorted, giving her *bat'leth* a twirl.

The tactical officer grunted, and Kira almost thought she saw him flush. "Precisely why I should not have accepted your challenge."

That gruff admission was apparently retreat enough for Dax. Her resilient, puckish humor returned with a fierce smile. "Admit it," she cajoled, dancing forward a step to chuck his arm with the side of her *bat'leth*. "With the Day of Honor coming up, you thought a little *Suv'batlh* might be a fun way to celebrate the holiday."

Worf stiffened, but didn't pull away. "Honor is not meant to be fun. And the *Batlh Jaj* is not a *holiday*. It is the occasion on which true Klingons re-affirm their own sense of honor and commemorate the honor of their most esteemed enemies."

"Like Captain James T. Kirk of the first *Enterprise,*" Dax said, with a mischievous smile. "My old friend Kor used to demonstrate the esteem he felt for Kirk by drinking an extra keg of blood wine on every *Batlh Jaj.*"

"That," said Worf repressively, "is *not* the correct way to celebrate the Day of Honor."

"Neither is increasing the number of provocative intrusions into the Klingon-Cardassian Neutral Zone, if you ask me." Odo folded his hands atop updrawn knees in unconscious mimicry of Kira. "It makes me wonder if your people still believe in celebrating the honor of their enemies, Commander."

"Not all enemies *have* honor," Worf growled. "To those that do not, the Klingons owe no commemoration of *Batlh Jaj.*"

Odo snorted. "From the response we've been getting to this holiday of yours, I'd say the Humans feel exactly the same way about the Klingons."

Kira found herself forced to agree with that. While she thought the observance of *any* Klingon holiday within the Federation a dubious practice, considering the recent tensions that had flared between the two former enemies, she certainly hadn't expected the violent antipathy that had ignited throughout the Alpha Quadrant as preparations for the Day of Honor drew near. On DS9—which had acknowledged the holiday for as long as the Federation had kept a presence there—there'd been a distinct increase in racist grumbling. As the grumbling increased, they'd gradually phased out plans for a display of locally owned Klingon art, then the Klingon food festival, and finally even the re-enactment of the Klingons' traditional Honor Combat—*Suv'batlh*—for fear of how station personnel would respond to the Klingon costumes and weapons.

Worf shoved off his lacquered battle-mask to reveal a grim face streaked with rivulets of sweat. Dax might not have been winning their face-to-face combat, but she'd certainly managed to press the Klingon warrior to his limits. "I advised Captain Sisko that to commemorate the Day of Honor so soon after the invasion of Cardassia might be unwise."

"I don't think it's the Cardassians who are the problem," Kira said soberly.

"No," Dax agreed. "The problem is that the Day of Honor is supposed to celebrate a time when Humans and Klingons united against a common enemy, even while they were fighting each other. And now, when we're facing a common enemy greater than any we've encountered before—"

"My people," Odo interjected, with the bitter resignation that always soured his voice when he spoke those words.

"—the Klingons have endangered the entire Alpha Quadrant by dividing it rather than uniting it. It makes the Day of Honor—"

She broke off again, this time slanting Worf a wary look. However, the Klingon tactical officer finished the thought for her with the ruthless lack of self-pity Kira found so characteristic of his race.

"—a mockery of what it is supposed to represent." His dark eyes slitted down to angry lines of frustration. "Which is why I cannot even challenge those who spit upon *my* honor with their signs and their curses!"

Kira winced at the snarling tone of repressed fury, and wondered if, all along, this holographic combat hadn't just been Dax's Trill-clever way to give Worf's bottled rage a safe place to erupt. The fact that this possibility had just occurred to her now, she thought wryly, was a testimony to her own naiveté about the conflict brewing between the Klingons and the Federation.

Kira hadn't known any Humans until after the Cardassian Occupation ended, didn't even really know what a Klingon was except for having heard their name and practices invoked in Cardassian threats. When she'd first been forced to work with Humans in the rebuilding years after the Occupation, she'd found them incomprehensibly diplomatic, infuriatingly even-tempered, and maddeningly dense. The first Klingons she encountered—staunch allies of the Federation for what had seemed, at the time, an eternity—had struck her as being even less understandable, despite their refreshingly straightforward lack of Human manners. They'd comprised different facets of her indoctrination into galactic culture. And, after four years' immersion on board Deep Space Nine, she'd learned to appreciate—even like—Humans, if still not completely understand them. The Klingons, however, still completely eluded her.

They were a hard people, in many ways more complicated than the simplicity of their behavior suggested. Their separation from the Federation and all its friendship meant had seemed irrational to Kira. She saw their sudden, aggressive expansion into every border star system that couldn't drive them off as being no more forgivable than anything the Cardassians had ever done. In the months that followed, she heard the Humans around her speak in ways she'd never expected. Of populations battered to extinction, starbases brutalized, grandparents or uncles or even older siblings tortured to death by an enemy too different, too barbaric to ever trust or understand. They'd sounded like they were talking about demonic creatures of such supernatural evil that they threatened the very existence of the universe. Instead, they were talking about the Klingons. That was how Kira found out about the world before the Khitomer Accords.

Venerable Human politeness had prevented the Federation from lingering over the fact that they'd been mortal enemies with the Klingons for generations longer than they'd ever been friends. They'd graciously granted the Klingons their cultural differences, learned not to take offense at the aggressiveness Klingons tended to fling around them like spittle, prided themselves on their respect for Klingon history and tradition. In return, the Klingons endeavored to be less obvious in their disdain for Federation bureaucracy, and stopped bullying Starfleet officers. Apparently, everyone had thought this great progress at the time.

But from Kira's point of view it had seemed to be progress built more on tolerance than respect, and doomed to fail because of that. For a comparatively short period of time, it had looked like the Klingons and the Federation needed each other—two vast giants coming to grips with the fact that even the greatest behemoth needed someone to guard its farthest edges. Maybe if their peace had lasted longer they would have eased into a more lasting symbiosis. As it was, their fledgling romance hadn't lasted past the first cultural spat. Borders slammed, families remembered all the atrocities and fears passed down from beloved grandfolk and historical texts, and the comfortable shackles of hatred slipped back into place, as though no one had ever loosened them.

"It's not you." She hadn't really meant to say anything—if there was one thing she'd come to understand about Worf since he joined the crew, it was that he was proud, and intensely private. But the words popped out as though tumbling directly off her thoughts. She knew when he turned his frown on her that she'd trapped herself into completing her observation, whether Worf would appreciate it or not. "The people here—they're not even seeing *you*. They're seeing political battles that are keeping them from getting letters to their loved ones, or spare parts for the atmospheric propagators." She lifted one shoulder in a somewhat apologetic shrug, even though she wasn't sure what she herself had to apologize for. "Don't take it personally."

Worf gave her a sharp frown, as if her words had translated into a threat rather than the friendly advice she'd intended. More proof that Kira still didn't understand Klingons. "Hatred is always personal," he told her bleakly. "It is only the face of your enemy that changes."

There didn't seem to be anything she could say in response to that; Kira was glad when her comm badge chirped and gave her an excuse to look away. "Sisko to Kira."

She fumbled with latches on her armor with one hand as she answered, anticipating. "Kira here."

"Major—" Sisko's deep voice was hard to read, colored over by the busy sounds of Ops in his background. "I believe you're with Commander Dax and the Constable."

Kira glanced reflexively at the officers surrounding her. "And Commander Worf," she said, rolling carefully to her knees. Then, in response to the tension in his tone, "Is there a problem?"

"Why don't we discuss that here in Ops?" The captain had an unnerving way of sounding his most calm when things were approaching their most perilous. "Right now, we're facing either a delicate rescue operation or a full-scale Klingon war. I thought I'd collect a few second opinions before I decide."

Benjamin Sisko could still remember precisely what he'd felt three months ago, in the moment he'd heard about the breaking of the Khitomer Accords. A single icy spike of disbelief, then an explosion of frustrated anger at the success of the Dominion's divide-and-conquer tactics. Despite all the later emotions that had knitted themselves into the tangled tapestry of his feelings toward the Klingons— betrayal, annoyance, even unexpected sympathy for Worf's impossible position in Starfleet—the sharp memory of that initial reaction had never faded. Great moments in history did that to the people who lived through them—crystallized a single day's events inside the shifting smoke of memory the way a supernova hammered a permanent singularity through the fabric of space and time. Sisko sometimes wondered if those shock-carved memories weren't the truest imprint of history, more real and indelible than any datachip's video record.

Unfortunately, not enough time had passed since that day for his deep-seated rage to be relegated entirely to memory. The embers of it still smoldered, banked beneath the accumulated worries and stress of the hundred intervening days. And the disrupted emergency transmission he had just watched flicker across the main screen of Ops hadn't done a thing to quench it.

The turbolift platform hissed into sight, rising far too slowly, as it always seemed to do in tense situations like these. When it finally arrived, what looked like a medieval Klingon melee poured out into Ops, making one of the junior officers gasp and another stifle a laugh. Sisko lifted an eyebrow as he recognized the senior officers who made up the core of his tactical analysis team beneath the sweat and jangle of lacquered armor. Kira shot him a rueful glance of apology, while Worf just looked stoic. Dax went to her science console as if reporting for duty in ancient Klingon fighting garb were something she'd done a dozen times before. Knowing Curzon, that might even be true.

"We got a report in from the *Victoria Adams* already?" she asked, reading the signature frequency of the transmission on her display before Sisko could even open his mouth to brief them. "But they can't have had time to gather much data on the cometary event. They were only scheduled to arrive in the KDZ-E25F system a few hours ago."

"It's not a scientific report." Sisko crossed Ops to join her in front of the panel, frowning at the digital gibberish that scrolled across her screen. "Unfortunately, right now that's all I'm sure of. The message was so badly disrupted that all we could make out was that Captain Marsters encountered Klingons and an emergency situation had developed. Can you sift through the interference and clean the signal up, old man?"

"I can try." Dax handed him her *bat'leth* and pulled back her unruly mane of hair, then focused on her data display with the kind of instant intensity that only a joined Trill symbiont and host could summon. Sisko took a step back and reined his simmering impatience in with an effort. Badgering Dax for results right now would only slow her down.

Instead, he wrapped his fingers tight around the

traditional Klingon weapon he'd been given, feeling the deep warmth of the metal blade radiating through its sweaty leather grip. Whatever archaic Klingon ritual his senior officers had been re-creating down in Quark's holo-suite, their battle gear hadn't just been donned for authenticity. Only a long and hard-fought battle could have soaked so much of Dax's body heat into her weapon. Sisko raised an eyebrow at Kira, and saw his first officer drop her hand almost guiltily from the sore shoulder she'd been massaging.

"Could you reconstruct the *Victoria Adams*'s coordinates at the time of transmission?" the major asked, clearly determined to ward off any questions about her fitness for duty. "If they veered off course toward one of the areas the Klingons have claimed as theirs—"

Sisko shook his head. "The signal tracked right back to the E25F system. That's nowhere near any of the disputed territory."

Worf frowned over his armored shoulder. "Still, there has been a significant increase in Klingon incursions throughout the entire demilitarized zone in the last few months," he reminded Sisko. "If you recall my warnings on the possible dangers of this scientific observation mission—"

Sisko winced. It had been easy at the time the *Victoria Adams* had departed to dismiss Worf's warnings as Klingon paranoia. No incidents, other than a few distant sightings of warships and smugglers, had disturbed the uneasy peace of that part of the Klingon-Cardassian demilitarized zone. And there had been nothing special about the KDZ-E25F system—aside from its unfortunate ownership of a disintegrating giant comet—to attract the attention of either the Cardassian or Klingon empires. "Limited landmass, no significant resources, and utterly impassable vegetation" was how the ancient Starfleet survey charts had summarized the system's single Class-M planet. It had seemed a safe enough place for a small shipload of planetary scientists and retired Starfleet officers to go to view a cosmic fireworks show.

"This isn't deliberate signal-jamming," Dax said abruptly, saving Sisko from having to answer his tactical officer. "The interference cuts randomly across the entire subspace spectrum."

"Couldn't the noise be coming from all those comet impacts the *Victoria Adams* went to observe?" O'Brien inquired.

Dax shook her head. "Not unless the comet fragments in that shower are made of dilithium instead of ice. The electromagnetic noise generated by bolide impacts on a Class-M planet might very well contaminate the radio and visible bands, but it shouldn't touch subspace frequencies. Not even to mask—"

Her voice broke off without warning, and her fingers began to fly across the computer panel. Sisko shot a frowning glance at her data output screen, but saw nothing he could recognize as a significant change in the random display of noise.

"What is it, old man?"

Dax looked up, her eyes crackling with sudden realization. "This interference we're seeing—it's not a generated signal at all, natural or artificial. It never adds to any wavelength of the *Victoria Adams*'s subspace signal, it only decreases it to a greater or lesser extent. In the places where the transmission's nearly wiped out, there's no static in its place. Just *nothing.*"

"What does that mean?" Kira asked.

"It means the *Victoria Adams*'s subspace signal has been filtered through a massive depolarizing field."

A rumble too fierce for a groan and too wordless for a curse emerged from somewhere deep in Worf's chest. Sisko shot a questioning look at him, and saw the bared-teeth grimace that said his chief tactical officer didn't like what he was going to have to say.

"There is only one way to create that kind of field in open space." Worf's voice deepened in a bleak mixture of vindication and regret. "Massive Klingon disruptor fire."

"Yes," Dax agreed. "The *Victoria Adams* must have been under Klingon attack when she sent this message."

For a moment, the only sound in Ops was the beep and hum of computers handling the routine business of the space station. The machines were the only ones oblivious to the military and political crisis crashing down upon them. Then Sisko grunted and allowed three months of stifled anger to escape in a cascade of orders.

"Dax, get me the best resolution you can on that transmission. I want to know as much as we can about what happened out there." He swung to face the rest of his crew. "Major Kira, put in a high-priority call to Starfleet and brief Admiral Nechayev about the attack on the *Victoria Adams.* Commander Worf, I want an updated report from Intelligence on all known and suspected Klingon forces in the demilitarized zone. O'Brien, get the *Defiant* ready for immediate departure and notify Dr. Bashir to assemble an emergency medical team."

"Yes, sir." The cadet-sharp response from the whole crew told Sisko he was probably letting a little too much of his temper spill into his voice. He took a deep breath, but it didn't do much to ease his tension. Bad enough that the Klingons had decided to spit in the face of the Federation by attacking a civilian ship. But to have that ship be the defenseless research vessel *Victoria Adams* with its load of vacationing Starfleet retirees—it made Sisko's gut burn with a rage fierce enough to scorch any remnant of hesitation from his mind.

The familiar, gravelly sound of a throat being cleared brought his narrowed gaze around to the one senior officer to whom he had issued no orders. Odo gazed back with a quizzical expression in his not-quite-human eyes, his eyebrows arched in wordless inquiry.

"Is there a problem, Constable?"

"I don't know. *You* certainly seem to think so."

Kira snorted without looking up from her communications panel. "The Klingons just declared war on the Federation, Odo. You don't call that a problem?"

"Did they?" the Changeling asked dryly. "It's not as if the *Victoria Adams* was in Federation space when she was attacked. Maquis and Cardassian ships have been getting fired on and chased out of the Klingon demilitarized zone for the past three months. We knew there was a risk the same thing would happen to the *Victoria Adams*. Wasn't that why Commander Worf recommended our science officer not join the expedition?"

"True," Sisko agreed. "But that doesn't mean the Federation can turn a blind eye to the destruction of an unarmed research vessel on a scientific mission."

"Or that we can ignore a Federation vessel's distress call, and leave its survivors to die, just because we are afraid of Klingon retaliation," Worf added grimly.

"Ah." Odo tilted his head, an ironic glitter in his pale eyes. "No doubt you all learned that lesson at the Academy, from that Starfleet training exercise—the *Kobayashi Maru.*"

Sisko exchanged frowning looks with his chief tactical officer. "This is *not* a no-win situation, Constable," he said at last. "If we can get to the E25F system in time to rescue the crew of the *Victoria Adams*, we might be able to avert a diplomatic crisis—"

"—over a misunderstanding that could be resolved just as easily by negotiation between the Federation and the Klingon Empire," Odo pointed out, with the same unerring logic that made him such an impartial arbiter of merchant disputes on the Promenade. "The loss of a small research vessel—"

"—might be smoothed over," Sisko agreed. "But the loss of the last two surviving officers from the long-range explorer *Glimmerglass*, the only captain to take her ship successfully through the Chienozen passage, the science officer who established contact with the first inhabited neutron star, the diplomatic liaison who—"

Odo held up a hand, giving Sisko the stiff nod he used to acknowledge his mistakes. "You're saying we have to interfere because the Starfleet veterans who went along for the comet show were unusually important—"

"No, they weren't," Sisko said bluntly. "Except for one or two, they were just the normal run of Starfleet retirees. What I'm saying, Constable, is that the loss of *anyone* who served in uniform as long and as honorably as those people did is going to poison Starfleet's relations with the Klingons for years to come. No matter what the Federation diplomats may say or do."

"Enhanced transmission coming up on the main screen." Dax broke into the argument without ceremony. "I managed to extrapolate an additional seventy percent of the signal from the fragments that got through. Be prepared—we're still going to lose the end."

The main screen of Ops blanked, then exploded into a signal so brilliantly over-enhanced that Sisko had to squint to make out the burned-in shadows of the *Victoria Adams*'s bridge. Dax frowned and adjusted some control on her screen, muting the stilled image down to more bearable levels of brightness. The colors of deck and uniforms and bridge stations remained artificially monotone, however, a computer's extrapolation rather than the varied tints and shadings of real life. A single rawboned figure occupied the captain's chair. Dax's enhancements hadn't

changed the tense set of his lantern jaw or erased his
scowl, but they had brought into finer focus the sweat
that beaded his face. He looked out across time and
space with intent eyes, making Sisko once again feel
that the man was making eye contact directly with
him.

"This is Captain Charles Marsters of the Federation research vessel *Victoria Adams,*" said a clipped,
precise voice. Sisko barely recognized it as the same
static-fuzzed drawl he'd managed to decipher only a
few words from fifteen minutes ago. "Request urgent
assistance from Deep Space Nine. We've encountered
an armed Klingon blockade around the planet KDZ-
E25F." A blast rocked the science vessel, staggering
the captain and momentarily knocking the image
back to glittering white nothingness.

"Blockade?" Kira demanded incredulously.

Sisko grunted. "I thought that was what he said
before, but I couldn't be sure. This was where we lost
the audio feed."

Dax adjusted something on her panel, and the
Victoria Adams's bridge did a slow fade back into
existence on the screen. "—attacked us for not leaving fast enough," Marsters said, still sounding calm
despite the crackle of on-board fire beneath his words.
"Hull and warp core integrity are holding, but we lost
all life support systems in the initial attack. We're
running on limited emergency backup now. All passengers and nonessential crew have—" The transmission shattered into nothingness again, presumably
due to another close-range disruptor blast. This time,
when the visual feed coalesced back into existence, it
looked more ghostly and snowed over than before.

And although Marsters's lips were still moving, no sound emerged.

Sisko cursed in fierce disappointment. "That's the best you can do, old man? We still don't know exactly what happened."

"The subtractive effects of the disruptor fire were worst in the audio portion of the signal. I can't extrapolate something from nothing, Benjamin."

"They evacuated the rest of the crew and passengers in a large planetary sampling shuttle," Odo said unexpectedly. "The *Victoria Adams* is going to cover their departure by leading the Klingons as far out of the system as possible."

Sisko swung around, startled. His chief security officer stared so intently at the screen that he didn't even blink at the final, blinding explosion of white nothingness. It was at times like this that Sisko remembered Odo's humanoid shape was merely assumed, and not hampered by any biological limitations.

"Constable, how do you know that?"

"I can read lips." Odo's pale eyes swung over to him, irony washing through them like a chill of frost across a windowpane. "It's a valuable skill to have when you're watching Ferengi make illegal bargains across a noisy bar."

Sisko lifted an eyebrow, but it was with respect, not skepticism. His years of experience had taught him that the Constable never claimed to have skills he didn't possess. "Did Captain Marsters say where the shuttle went after it left the ship?"

"Down to the planet," Odo said promptly. "I believe he said something about deliberately taking a depowered entry path, to make it look to Klingon sensors as though they were a falling comet fragment."

Dax frowned. "But in a thick Class-M atmosphere like that, a steep entry path could destabilize the shuttle and force them into a crash landing. It seems like such a risk—"

"Not as much of a risk as staying on the *Victoria Adams*, with the Klingons in pursuit and life support failing." Sisko felt his jaw tighten around the next question he had to ask. "Was that final explosion the ship blowing up, Dax?"

She surprised him with a shake of her head. "I don't think so. The signal strength was actually fading compared to the disruptor depolarization toward the end. I'd say the *Victoria Adams* was actually pulling away from her pursuers."

"I just hope they pulled all the Klingons away with them," O'Brien said. "That would leave the system clear for us to go in."

"Yes." Sisko turned to pin Kira with a frowning glance. "Any reply yet from Starfleet Command?"

Kira grimaced. "Regional headquarters acknowledged our hail, but says Admiral Nechayev is in a crucial meeting with representatives from the Vorta. She left orders that all emergency situations be handled under the protocol of sector commander recognizance."

Sisko's breath hissed through his teeth, but it was in satisfaction, not annoyance. "That means that, for now, the decision is up to us. Recommendations?"

"Go," said O'Brien curtly.

"Go," Dax agreed.

"Go now!" growled Worf.

That was the Starfleet side of his mixed command crew, reacting exactly as Sisko had expected. Their majority vote essentially settled the question, but Sisko forced himself to look over at his Bajoran second-in-command, trying to make sure he wasn't allowing service loyalties to overrule his better judgment. He got back a look of crackling impatience.

"Of course, we *have* to go," Kira said. "Give the Klingons a research ship in the demilitarized zone, and they'll take a starship in the Alpha Quadrant. If we don't stop them now, we'll just have to deal with them later."

"Constable, do you agree?"

Odo snorted. "I think we're going to start exactly the war we're trying to prevent. But since I appear to be the only one who feels that way, I'll save my energy for saying 'I told you so' a few days from now."

"I appreciate that," Sisko said dryly. "In the meantime, could you assemble a skeleton security squad for the *Defiant?* I want to take minimal crew, so we'll have enough room to evacuate all survivors." He glanced over at Dax. "Do you remember how many passengers and crew the *Victoria Adams* carried?"

"Fifteen scientists, ten ship's crew, and twelve passengers," Worf said before the science officer could reply.

"If they were on emergency life support, the captain couldn't have taken more than four of the crew with him when he tried leading the Klingons away," O'Brien added.

"Then we'll need to have room to evacuate at least thirty-two." Sisko scrubbed a hand across his face, mentally counting out the crew he could spare. "Dr. Bashir will still have to take a full medical team, which means we cut down ship's crew to fifteen. Agreed?"

Dax gave him a somber look. "I don't think we need to be that conservative. You're assuming all the survivors we rescue are going to be healthy. If the medical bay is filled, we'll end up with five empty bunks that could have held ship's crew."

"All right, twenty. Staff all sectors accordingly and assemble in docking bay five in fifteen minutes." Sisko vaulted out of the central hub of Ops and headed for the turbolift that would take him to his ship, reining in his impatience just long enough to let his five senior officers board the lift with him. "Promenade," he told the computer, confident he would find Bashir and his team already waiting to join them. "O'Brien, will you brief the doctor on what injuries he can expect to find in the crash survivors?"

His chief engineer shot him a startled look across the crowded turbolift platform. "Why me?"

Sisko lifted an eyebrow at him. "I assumed you'd know what kind of space-drive the planetary sampling shuttle had, so Dr. Bashir could know whether he needs to deal with radiation damage or plasma burns."

O'Brien grunted. "Crash damage is probably the least of the survivors' worries, Captain."

"What do you mean?"

"Well, nobody told that giant comet out there to stop disintegrating just because the Klingons fired on our research vessel. The survivors from the *Victoria Adams* are taking shelter on a planet where fire is raining out of the sky and the days are as dark as the nights—"

"And tsunami shock waves are coming in from any impacts that happen to hit the ocean." Dax sounded more wistful than worried. "It must be like—"

"Hell," Worf suggested.

"Not hell, *sylshessa*." Kira saw their questioning looks and shook her head until her earring tinkled, obviously at a loss to translate the Bajoran word into English. "It's an old legend from Tal Province, about a future time when the sky burns and the earth explodes and the waters of the sea crash together—"

"Armageddon," Sisko said softly. "That's the Human version of the prophesy."

Odo grunted. "And in your version, is Armageddon the utter end of everything?"

"No," Sisko said grimly. "It's the beginning of war."

CHAPTER 2

AT FIRST GLANCE, it didn't look much different from any other planetary system. A saffron yellow star spit out a normal amount of heat, light, and solar wind; three gas giants circled in far-flung orbits. But where the inner rocky planets should have spun in the star's golden glow, an ominous parabola of dust and ice enshrouded half the system. Dax's long-range scanners detected two small, airless planets orbiting outside that haze, one swung out beyond its perigee and the other caught between the curving arms of debris. Magnification of their sun-baked surfaces revealed a crazy quilt of craters and impact scars from past orbital swings through the comet track.

Dax stored the surface images for later analysis, then ran a quick check on the extrapolated orbital parameters for both inner and outer planets. As she'd suspected, all of them showed perturbations from a third, rocky inner planet, whose orbital diameter should have put it midway between the other two. It must be somewhere inside the remnants of the disintegrated giant comet. She turned her attention to the difficult task of filtering interference out of the sensor beams as they refracted through the debris.

"Major Kira, any sign of Klingon ship activity?" Sisko watched the main screen with a frown. Devoid of sensor enhancements, all that could be seen of their destination was the central twinkle of its star and a frosty trail of debris. That crescent of scattered gauze didn't look anywhere near as threatening in real life as it did on her sensor scans. Unfortunately, Dax knew her computer-enhanced version was closer to the truth.

The Bajoran shook her head without looking away from her output screens. "I've jacked up the sensitivity of our ion detectors as high as they can go, but they're showing no trace of any cloaked vessels in the vicinity." She pursed her lips as though considering, then added, "No sign of uncloaked activity, either." Meaning the *Victoria Adams*.

"That's a good sign. It means Captain Marsters got away and took the Klingons with him." Sisko frowned at the *Defiant*'s main viewscreen. "I'd like to know what's on the surface of those planets. There's a chance the planetary shuttle might have landed there. Dax, can you enhance the display?"

"I can, but sensor scans show no sign of a recent landing on either planet." She transferred her two stored images up to the main screen, assigning them to their proper locations around Armageddon's golden sun. "Computer analysis of their orbital parameters, however, indicates there's a third inner system planet inside the cometary debris cloud. I haven't been able to image it yet." She glanced across at Sisko, reading his impatience in his drumming fingers. "But it's the most likely location for the shuttle to land, since it's the planet the *Victoria Adams* went to study. Unfortunately, it's also the one that's being most heavily bombarded by cometary impacts—at least once every two or three days."

O'Brien frowned over his shoulder at her. "Just what is going on in this system, Commander? Why did the *Victoria Adams* come here to begin with?"

"Because it's one of the few planetary systems in this quadrant whose Oort cloud agglomerated into a single body, too fluffy to be a planet but much too big to be a comet. It got kicked into an inner-system orbit fifteen thousand years or so ago when another star grazed past this one. The stresses of that new orbit kept tearing it apart, scattering debris along its path, until it finally disintegrated completely on its last solar swing, just last year. What you're seeing are its final remains." She shot a vexed look across the bridge at Worf. "It's a perfect re-creation of the kind of event that we think caused a mass extinction on the Trill home-world. Observing it would have been a once-in-a-lifetime opportunity, even for a Trill."

"Had you gone with the *Victoria Adams,* you might have found it the last-in-a-lifetime opportunity," the Klingon tactical officer reminded her. He looked up from the pilot's console he'd taken over while Dax concentrated on her sensor scans. "Can you obtain a rough fix on the planet's position using the curvature of its gravity well? I need to plot a course."

"And I'd like a visual image," Sisko added.

"I can fix the third planet's position, but I can't image it through all the interference. This is the best I can do." Dax sent the blotched gray image she had captured to the main viewscreen. It looked even worse when it was magnified, so vaguely outlined that it could have been the veiled halo of a comet as easily as a planet. "Chief, can you give me any more resolution on my sensor beam?"

O'Brien tapped a scan into his control panel and grunted. "I can give you a sixty-five percent increase in beam confinement, Commander, but only for a few minutes. On your mark."

Dax carefully delimited her scanning range to the exact coordinates of the planet to avoid wasting sensor power. "Mark."

The image on the screen slowly swam into focus as the tightened beam scanned across it. Its blurred outer edge became the hazy smudge of an atmospheric layer, as oxide-browned as a heavily industrialized planet's. But its nightside showed no signs of urban lights, and the isolated sprawl of island archipelagos dotting its blue-green oceans seemed too small to support any kind of machine-based civilization. There was only one larger landmass in view, half-hidden by the planet's terminus. Dax thought she saw the hint of a massive impact crater in that shadowed twilight edge, but the resolution faded back to fuzzy gray before she could confirm it. She hoped it had been a comet that made that scar.

"Sorry, Commander," O'Brien sighed. "That was all the power I could jack in without burning out the sensor array."

"That's all right. I can't confirm impact structures, but that brown color means there's been a lot of dust and ash kicked into the stratosphere recently. We'll have to get a lot closer before I can tell you if there's a crash site."

Worf glanced back across his shoulder at Sisko. "Shall I lay in an orbit, Captain?"

Sisko rubbed his chin. "Can we navigate safely through all that cometary debris?"

"Our shields should take care of the smaller debris," Kira pointed out. "And we can program short-range sensors to alert us to any imminent collisions with larger fragments."

Worf frowned at her. "Given the political situation, I strongly recommend that we remain under cloak at all times on this mission. If we were to fire at an oncoming comet fragment, we would give away our presence to the Klingons."

"Assuming there are any Klingons here to give it away to," Kira retorted. "I'm still getting no trace of ion trails anywhere in the system."

"But that doesn't mean we can assume they aren't here. The Klingons might have already come back from chasing the *Victoria Adams,* and dropped into a Lagrangian orbit around the planet to conserve power." Sisko drummed his fingers on the arm of his command chair, looking intensely thoughtful. "O'Brien, can we recalibrate our shields to an angle that will deflect any oncoming debris fragments without disturbing our cloaking effect?"

"We can try." The chief engineer hunched over his panel as he ran the calculations. "But we're not going to have full power as long as we're under cloak. It looks like we should be able to deflect about ninety percent of the debris we encounter without any significant change in vector. The rest will hit at such a direct angle that we'll feel the impact, even through shields. It shouldn't cause any real damage, but if someone was watching us closely, they might notice the fragment bouncing off." He glanced up unhappily. "It also means I can't promise we'll maintain shield integrity under a disruptor hit."

"That's a chance we'll have to take." Sisko turned back to the pilot's console. "Mr. Worf, as soon as the shields are recalibrated, take us into a circumpolar orbit at minimum impulse power. That should give us an opportunity to scan the whole planet without having our signals or our ion trail picked up by anyone who might be watching."

"Aye-aye, sir."

Sisko swung his command chair back in the other direction. "Major Kira, as we come in, I want you to concentrate your ion detection scans on the planet's Lagrange points. If there *are* Klingon vessels present, we may be able to pick up some minor leakage from their warp cores. Dax, I want full scans of the planet's surface, calibrated for humanoid life signs, as soon as we hit orbit."

"It may take longer than usual with all that atmospheric pollution," she warned. It didn't seem worth adding that the racial diversity of *Victoria Adams*'s crew would also add unique convolutions to the readings.

"Understood." Sisko stood and paced down to the front of the *Defiant*'s bridge, as if physical proximity to the fuzzy planet displayed there would show him something he hadn't already seen. "I wonder why the Klingons would risk attacking a civilian ship all the way out here? What's in this system that they don't want us interfering with?"

"Besides generic Klingon aggression?" Kira asked. "You don't think that's reason enough for them to sweep their borders clean?"

Sisko made an impatient gesture with his hands. "Maybe. But I can't see any tactical advantage to this. Something about it just doesn't feel right."

"That is because it is not honorable to wage war on a weakened enemy," Worf said stiffly. "And all Klingons know that scientists are the weakest warriors of all."

"Oh, are they?" O'Brien raised his eyebrows toward Dax, and she rewarded him with an amused smile.

"That's a prejudice that's cost them a lot of battles in the past," she assured him.

The bridge doors hissed apart before Worf could do more than glower at her joke. Bashir and Odo came through them together, the doctor glancing curiously up at the viewscreen while the security officer went to join Kira at the weapons station. "Any sign of Klingons yet?" Odo asked.

"Not an ion's worth." Kira yielded the panel to him, stretching as she turned to look up at the main screen.

"What about survivors?" Bashir followed Kira's gaze, drifting almost unconsciously toward Dax. The gauzy veil of debris had resolved into hazy streaks and glowing gas streamers while they approached it, a tangled braid of cometary fragments trapped and melting in the heat of Armageddon's saffron sun.

"We're still working on that," Dax assured the doctor. "Worf's taking us in for a closer look."

A worried frown settled over his lean face, but Sisko silenced any protest he might have voiced with a single raised finger and a calmly spoken, "Patience, doctor." He nodded down at Dax in a clear gesture of redirection. "Dax, how can this much ice exist in such close proximity to the star?"

"It can't," Dax admitted. "That's why the whole debris belt looks so fuzzy with vapor. But there's enough debris from the ice giant to last for quite a while."

"So comet fragments will continue to bombard the inner planets for years." Kira shook her head, looking somber. "I wouldn't wish that fate on *any* inhabited world."

"At least they don't have to suffer it all year round," O'Brien pointed out. "They have an 'impact season' while they're inside the debris field, but then they can recover during the time they spend outside it."

"That doesn't seem to have helped the two smallest planets in the system," Dax said. "They've suffered such intense bombardment in the past that they don't have an atmosphere or hydrosphere left. It's all been blasted into space."

"Let's hope the escape shuttle actually made it to the Class-M, then." Bashir folded his arms as though to hide the nervous clenching and unclenching of his hands. "What was it called again? KPZ-E20-something?"

"KDZ-E25F," Odo said precisely. "Not exactly a memorable designation."

"No," Dax agreed. "In my science notes, I've started calling it Armageddon."

"You would," Bashir said, more in resignation than disgust.

"Why not *sylshessa?*" Kira demanded.

"Because there already is a planet called Sylshessa. It's a Tellarite colony near Vulcan." Dax threw a cautious look at the captain, knowing her odd Trill sense of humor didn't always sit well with him at times of tension. The glint in his dark eyes encouraged her to add, "At least Armageddon is a better name than Splat. That's what the crew of the *Victoria Adams* was calling the Class-M planet."

"Let's hope neither of those names becomes a self-fulfilling prophecy, old man," Sisko retorted. "For us or for the survivors."

"We are entering the cometary debris field now, Captain." The deep tone of Worf's voice never varied under pressure, but Dax knew him well enough now to read the strain in his carefully clipped syllables. She felt the *Defiant* lurch a little as a large ice fragment impacted its newly angled shields. "Our shields appear to be deflecting most of the debris, but we are losing some directional control to friction."

"Lower speed to warp one and compensate for course deviations." Sisko resumed his command seat, staring up at the viewscreen with the fierce attention he usually reserved for opponents in battle. The image of the Class-M planet slowly resolved as they drew closer, condensing back into the dust-stained, blue-green sphere they'd caught a glimpse of before. The terminator had crept slightly westward, exposing more of the long, oblong gouge scarring the one large landmass.

"Is that the crash site?" Bashir asked.

"No." The increased magnification of her science panel showed Dax the scatter of smaller craters trailing away from the main one, each surrounded by a starburst of exploded rock and soil. "It's a cometary strike—looks like a large bolide shattered just before impact. There's almost no erosion on the debris fans. I'm guessing it happened within the last few weeks."

"We are entering circumpolar orbit now, Captain."

"Very good. Dax, begin scanning for life-signs."

"Yes, sir." She punched in extra sensitivity filters for humanoid vital signs, then paused to read the flickering output from her sensors. "I'm showing a standard oxygen-nitrogen atmosphere, with traces of methane, carbon dioxide, and argon."

"Also methyl iodide at a level indicative of marine-dominant photosynthesis." Bashir leaned over her shoulder to point at the telltale spike on her spectrographic display. "The ocean's still full of life, despite getting blasted by rocks from outer space. Are you picking up any life-signs on land?"

"Yes. A surprising amount, actually." Dax read through her scanner output again, to make sure she hadn't misinterpreted the unusual readings it gave her. "According to this, the main continent is pretty much desolate in the interior, but swarming with native life around its edges. Thick vegetative cover of some kind is showing up on IR, both on the coast and on the islands. I suspect there are several types of higher vertebrates still inhabiting the surface, many of them exhibiting herding or pack behavior."

Sisko waved a hand, impatient as always with the dry basics of biology and planetology. "What about the escape shuttle? Any sign of it?"

"Not so far." The *Defiant* cruised slowly over the planet's unglaciated polar region, then down across its other hemisphere. Here, night was falling across a second enormous blue-green sea, this one even more thickly laced with surf-fringed tropical islands. "Life-sign scans are still showing only native vertebrates and marine life—no, wait . . . We've got a hit!"

"The crew?" Kira demanded.

"I don't know . . ." Dax flicked her eyes back and forth across her panel, trying to absorb every reading at once. "I'm showing about twenty life-signs on one of the small islands in that central archipelago. They're masked by some kind of phased energy field—I think it might be the shield generator from the shuttle."

"What about the shuttle itself?" Sisko asked.

Dax shook her head at her display. "I'm not picking up any kind of equipment or power-source reading at all. Just the field interference and the—" A flutter in the readings distracted her. "Julian, come take a look at this." She leaned to one side to let the doctor bend over her shoulder. "Is this a problem with my scanning filters, or are almost all of these life-forms injured?"

Bashir tapped a query on her computer, cursing softly at the response he saw. "There's nothing wrong with your filters. These are humanoid readings, and at least thirteen of them are injured, seven critically. Three of them are nearly dead."

A grim silence fell over the *Defiant* while everyone stared at Armageddon's unrevealing freckled oceans as if they could somehow answer all their questions. "That must be the *Victoria Adams*'s crew," O'Brien said at last, voicing the conclusion that none of them wanted to reach.

"But there were thirty-two passengers and crew on the *Victoria Adams,*" Kira protested. "You're saying half of them are dead or dying?"

"I'm saying they're in urgent need of medical help, whoever they are." Bashir glanced across at O'Brien. "Chief, can we transport them straight to the medical bay?"

"Not as long as that shield generator is going. And I doubt they're going to drop it—they're probably using it to try and ward off comet impacts."

"Very well." Bashir straightened and turned toward Sisko, suddenly wearing the innate dignity that his strong sense of medical ethics could bestow on him despite his youth and *joie de vivre*. "Captain, request permission to take an emergency medical team to the planet's surface."

"Granted," Sisko said without hesitation. "Major Kira, go with him. And Dax"—he fixed her with a not-entirely humorous glower—"this had better be the end of your complaining about not going on the *Victoria Adams,* old man." Dax winced, but the acidic comment couldn't entirely quench the scientific enthusiasm bubbling through her.

Worf glanced over his shoulder, furrowed brow drawn into tighter lines than usual. "Captain, I am the obvious choice to accompany Dr. Bashir as protection. As chief tactical officer—"

"I'm going to need you here in case the Klingons show up and challenge us," Sisko returned. "Don't worry, Mr. Worf. I'm sure Dax and the major can take care of themselves."

The Klingon grunted and threw Dax the severely reproving look she was never quite sure how to interpret. "Under normal circumstances, I would agree," he said grimly.

"How reassuring." Dax set her sensors on autoscan until her replacement could arrive on the bridge. Kira was already accompanying Bashir to the turbolift, leaving Odo in sole command of her console. As she turned to follow them, Dax paused only long enough to blow Worf a facetious kiss. It made him wince and look away, just as she'd expected. "You be careful, too. You're going to be getting bombarded by as many comet fragments as I am."

The chief tactical officer growled up at the viewscreen, although Dax didn't think it was the view that had enraged him. "Somehow," he said between his teeth, "I think the comets are going to be the least of our problems."

Bashir's first impression of Armageddon was that it stank like a butchery.

The stench slapped over them with a force completely overriding any images of dust-shrouded sun, crystal blue ocean, or pearlescent sand. Bashir brought his arm up to shield his nose and mouth. He

39

knew it was pointless, a blind make-work instinct, even as his left hand scrambled to open his medical kit and dig out the tube of olfacan by feel.

He'd carried olfacan in every medkit, and stored some in half a dozen sick bay drawers, ever since his first medical school autopsy. Logic understood that illness could be ugly. Sight could be trained to see the person beyond radiation burns, to understand the pathology of trauma and disease. But smell spoke directly to those most primitive places of one's brain; it simply refused to be reasoned with. Still, after half a lifetime of downplaying his own assets for the sake of peer acceptance, it had taken him by surprise to discover a weakness he hadn't suspected. Later, he would try to convince himself that it was his super-naturally acute sense of smell that had betrayed him. At the time, his stomach gave in to a fight-or-flight reflex that no amount of intellectual resistance could override, and he'd fled the autopsy theatre in an effort to minimize his humiliation. It was afterward that an older resident introduced him to the joys of an anesthetized olfactory nerve—a fingerful of colorless ointment across the upper lip, and even Bashir's keen sense of smell faded into blissful nonexistence for a good two to three hours. Years later, he still greeted the cessation of smell with a kind of guilty relief; the animal mind at work again, convincing him that no one with a half-million credits worth of biological enhancements should need something so trivial as protection from unpleasant odors. But the guilt didn't stop him from using it.

Warded against his baser instincts, he extended the tube to his physician's assistant, Heiser. The young lieutenant took a grateful smear with one index finger and passed half along to nurse LeDonne. Bashir twisted to include Dax and Kira in his offer, explaining, "It's a nasal anesthetic. It'll help block out the smell."

Kira gave a wry little snort. It was one of many sounds Bashir had learned to associate with the major's private conviction that he had the intestinal fortitude of a sand flea. "No, thanks. I learned to ignore worse than this a long time ago."

Of course. There was little Starfleet could expose her to that was as bad as Cardassian prison camps. Bashir wondered if she'd ever considered that the ability to tolerate something unpleasant didn't obligate you to do so. Or maybe that was more of what she labeled sand flea thinking, and not even worth mentioning.

He slipped the olfacan back into its protective sleeve and worked loose his tricorder instead. "My God . . ." He may not have been able to smell, but his eyes still stung; he felt like he was going to sneeze. "How many crew members did *Victoria Adams* carry?"

"Smells like thousands." Heiser scrubbed at his sparse blond mustache as though trying to help the olfacan work. "Should we do a reconnoiter?"

"No." Dax glanced up from her own singing tricorder in response to Bashir's startled glance. "Those aren't dead bodies," she clarified, dipping a nod toward her scan results. "Not humanoid dead bodies, at least. If the *Victoria Adams* crashed here, she did it too recently to allow for this level of putrefaction. Besides, we aren't close enough to the source of that

41

shield generator to be smelling any corpses from that site." She snapped shut her tricorder and repositioned it on her belt, pinching at her nose again despite the olfacan. "Let's get going before this smell makes me vomit."

But the stench got worse instead of better as they made their way down the long curve of beach. Smooth, white sand—so fine that it packed almost as solidly as soil where the waves shushed up to dampen it—made a level shelf more than thirty meters wide for as far as Bashir could see. To his right, tropical blue water undulated like a platter of softened glass, bending itself into mountains, valleys, and gently stroking tongues of wave. On his left, what looked to be a wall of woven sticks and vines rose to more than twice his height, its seaward side decorated by draperies of mummified kelp and tangles of long-dead detritus. Some sort of weather wall to protect against ocean storms? Erected by—who? The crash survivors? The natives? No, there was too much greenery beyond it, just as high and twisted as the wall fronting the shore, and stretching as far to that direction as the ocean stretched in the other. And Armageddon's volatile local environment made the possibility of sentient natives more than just highly unlikely. It was some sort of natural vegetative feature, then—the planet's attempt to defend itself against itself.

At first, Bashir thought perhaps the rotten odor originated with this littered hedge. He and his assistants were sufficiently shielded by the olfacan to no longer notice what smells surrounded them. But Trills apparently didn't respond as well to the anesthetic, and Kira had refused it from the outset. Bashir rather

42

easily tracked the strength of the stench through the simple expedient of watching the women's faces. Dax squinted to protect her eyes from the fumes, and Kira's already wrinkled nose wrinkled even further in disgust. It wasn't until they stepped in front of a gaping rent in the wall of brush that whatever they'd been smelling must have rolled out in force: Dax grunted a little sound of disgust, and Kira jerked away from the opening as though she'd been slapped. Even Bashir imagined he detected a pungent belch of stench too strong for the olfacan to fully counter. Still, it was the tacky blaze of clotted blood darkening broken foliage that jolted his heart up into his throat. It was already too old and rotten to tell if it had come from any familiar species. Touching a hand to his tricorder as though it were a talisman, he stepped gingerly into the crushed-down path and forced himself to keep a measured pace until he reached the end.

"Julian!"

The passage widened abruptly into a lidless natural amphitheater, its sides as smashed and shattered as the corridor. He meant to call back a reassurance to Dax. Instead, he looked up at the mountain of gore in front of him and coughed abruptly into one hand. There was a horrible moment in which he thought he'd be sick even with his immunity to the fetor, but he managed to swallow his stomach under control just as Kira trotted up from behind. He heard something that might have been a stunted sneeze, then the major croaked softly, "Maybe I'll take a noseful of that stuff after all."

In all his life, Bashir could not remember imagining something so wretchedly horrific. Carcasses—each

43

easily three tons even with skins and half their internal organs removed—lay piled within a veil of buzzing flies and decomposition gases. They'd been stacked higher than Bashir's own head, but the combined weight of the upper layers had crushed the bodies on the bottom until only shattered bone ends and the occasional rotting hock jutted up from the bloody mud into which they'd been pressed. Some clinically detached segment of his brain noted the internal structures that said they were probably mammalian, and the flat, cylindrical teeth which suggested they were herbivorous. Some more emotional part of him struggled to pin a number on how many bodies one needed to build a pile of carnage five meters high and perhaps another twenty meters long.

He felt the warmth of someone close on his left elbow several moments before noticing a science tricorder's distinctive warble. "In case it matters," Dax said quietly, "I was right—these carcasses are definitely too old to have anything to do with the *Victoria Adams.*"

It was no consolation at all, and Bashir bitterly envied Dax the lifetimes of experience that let her face something like this without losing composure. "If not the survivors, then what?" Relief throbbed in his stomach when he finally dragged his eyes from the slaughter. "The comet impacts?"

Dax shook her head. "Even the nearest comet damage is too recent."

"What else could have killed so many animals at one time?"

"Spears."

He didn't want to look at Kira—he'd have to glimpse the mutilated pile as he turned, and everything inside him wanted to avoid that more than he was comfortable admitting. Dax rescued him by tossing a silent question at the major over Bashir's shoulder, then looking where Kira apparently gestured. "And somebody field-dressed them, too," the major went on. "I don't think they normally come with exposed organs and no hair."

Dax nodded slowly, thoughtfully. "You're right . . ."

"Do you think it was natives?" Bashir asked. Partly because the question of intelligent life brought to mind his original thoughts about the weather wall, and partly because he didn't want to seem so completely weak-kneed that he wasn't even following their conversation.

Dax glanced at him with a scholarly frown, as though prepared to debate all aspects of that question in the interests of science. Then something in his face softened her expression. Bashir suspected it was his waxen pallor, or perhaps the first hint of nauseated tears in his eyes. Whatever the cause, she slipped her arm across his shoulders and turned him back toward the beach with its virginal stretch of bright white sand.

"I don't know enough about the planet yet to even take a guess," she said, voice smooth with equal parts consideration and sympathy. "We'll ask the survivors about it when we find them."

By the time they reached the survivors' settlement, natives were the last thing on Bashir's mind.

"Cholegh'a' chIm ghobDu'wI'!"

Dax's voice—raised and roughened to bark the words with what Bashir assumed was either authority or challenge—fell flat amongst wreckage no longer tall enough to encourage echoes. From inside the shimmer of force field, swarthy, chiseled faces lifted, turned to them with no particular malice or interest. They'd apparently finished salvaging hours ago; by now, adult and sub-adult males clustered with adult females in the meager shade of the weather wall, well away from the shield's humming margins yet well protected by its umbrella. Their bodies were lowered into deep squats, their hands balanced on their knees as though prepared to spring into action despite the weariness etched into all their faces. Klingon faces. Bruised and weary and creased with despair, but still undeniably *Klingon klingon sapiens*. Bashir counted less than ten scattered about the tumbles of debris, standing or sitting. Judging from the bright blossoms of Klingon blood splashed across every survivor's clothing, there were at least that many again wounded or already dead. He saw no sign of Humans.

"NgliS Hol Sajatlh'a'?"

It hadn't been a big village even before its devastation. A row of strongly woven huts, opposing ends open to the air, seemed to have been extruded directly from the weather wall. They were little more than a scatter of twisted sticks now. The shield's irridescent bubble covered only the centermost sections of the camp, leaving exposed blankets and racks that had no doubt filled the tiny hovels only a few days before. The blurry touch of Armageddon's sun warmed

46

hoops of braided vine and their circles of stretched hide, while hammocks of dessicating organ meat slowly dried beside what looked like racks of some frothy yellow gland. It was an impressive collection of foodstuffs, obviously the bounty from the hunting 'scraps' the landing party had already found. This was certainly no temporary castaways' camp, and couldn't have been erected in the short time since *Victoria Adams* had reported Klingons in the area.

Dax halted with her toes just brushing the terminal margin of the shield. *"Devwi'ra 'Iv?"* Tiny sparks skittered in the sand between her boots.

Bashir wasn't sure if it was the Trill's words that ignited the flutter of interest among the silent Klingons, or the distinctly Klingon bravura of her approach. Whichever it was, something passed from Klingon to Klingon on a chain of turning heads until one of them rose to his feet from amidst a ring of other adult males. Bashir thought he recognized the arrogance of a Klingon commander despite the warrior's limping stride.

He didn't even stand as tall as Dax, but the broadness of his chest and limbs betrayed a strength easily a match for the entire landing party. Shoulder-length hair, still curling and black with Klingon vigor, went well with an equally vigorous beard but not so well with the bruise-deep shadows of exhaustion beneath his eyes. Despite that, and despite the swollen foot that he favored when he walked, Bashir saw none of the gauntness of long-term starvation in the warrior. The absence of traditional Klingon armor only accentuated the ripple and bunch of his muscles, the smoothly filled planes of his broad face. It was clear why his crew felt secure enough to waste so much of the animals they'd hunted and killed, rather than utilizing the whole.

Bashir made an effort to push that last bitter thought away. For all he knew, the meat was inedible and the skin and glands were the only parts the Klingons could use. Besides, the entire planet would probably be blasted clear of life in just another few days. It hardly seemed reasonable to hold ecological grudges.

The bandy-legged commander looked as though he might split the seams of his dusty civilian tunic when he halted just opposite the shield from Dax and flexed his shoulders. "I never believed I would someday be happy to stand unarmed among Starfleet officers." His Standard was clear, though heavily accented. If he'd meant his greeting as a joke, it didn't sound like a happy one. Thumping one fist against his chest, he rumbled, "I am Gordek, of the House of Gordek."

Dax lifted one eyebrow in what Bashir took to be surprise, but said nothing to expound on her gesture. "Lieutenant Commander Dax, from space station Deep Space Nine." She apparently felt no need to reciprocate Gordek's theatrical physicality. Bashir was just as glad. "This is Major Kira. And Dr. Bashir, Lieutenant Heiser, and Ensign Le-Donne."

The Klingon's onyx-chip gaze leapt instantly to Bashir, but skidded away again before allowing interpretation. "You are here because of the Federation shuttle that crashed yesterday, out in the *tuq'mor.*"

48

His deep voice made it a statement rather than a question.

"Yes." Dax never broke her own gaze away from Gordek's. "Did you find any survivors at the wreckage site?"

"None," said the Klingon curtly. Bashir's rush of bitter disappointment was sliced off unexpectedly by Gordek's next words. "We found no bodies, either. We had to hike several miles of *tuq'mor* to reach that ship. Whoever rode in it left long before we got there."

Kira frowned at him. "Are you the ones who made it crash?"

A throaty rumble of what might have been Klingon threat or Klingon laughter. Bashir always found it hard to tell the difference. "Yes, of course. We attacked a Federation ship and destroyed it, then immediately beamed ourselves down and built this village, threw away all our technology, armed ourselves with spears, and then waited for a comet to destroy us." The points of his teeth gnashed when he grinned, but Bashir still wasn't sure if he was amused or angered. "Is that what you wanted to hear?"

"What she wants to hear," Dax said clearly, "is whether you are the reason that the ship was attacked, not whether you are the ones who attacked it."

"Ah." Gordek's gaze swung back to the Trill, his oddly angry amusement fading to a more recognizable emotion. Surprise. "You know what we are, then?"

"I think so," she said calmly. "Will you tell me, or are you going to make me guess?"

"Guess." The Klingon spat over one shoulder as casually as a Human might gesture with one hand.

Dax said something long and intricate in Klingon, something that made a muscle jerk in Gordek's cheek, as though something had stung him. "Vrag," he said reluctantly, and the Trill nodded as though that single word had brought enlightenment. She took a step back from the glittering shield, looking for all the world as if she expected it to drop now. Bashir and Kira followed her back to where Heiser and LeDonne had waited for them, wearing matching looks of concern and bafflement.

"What did you just say?" Bashir demanded. "Are they going to let us in to treat the wounded, or are they sending us away?"

"They'll let us in." Dax sounded more somber than usual. "They may not be happy about it, but they don't have anywhere else to turn for help. They're *ada'ven*—political exiles from the Klingon Empire, sent here to live out the rest of their lives in isolation from their society."

There was a long silence, filled only with the muffled groans and stirrings from the wounded. Gordek was limping over to the central firepit, beyond which Bashir could just see the actual shield generator. Its glittering duranium husk was roughly cobbled to an equally out-of-place portable power supply. Both looked like standard Federation issue to Bashir.

"How did you know?" Kira asked at last, while Gordek fiddled with the field controls. The wall of force that separated them from the Klingons began to waver and ripple, as if an unfelt wind was blowing through it.

Dax sighed again. "I didn't recognize the House of Gordek as any traditional Klingon clan. Starfleet intelligence has noticed that for the past year any small Klingon house that comes into conflict with Chancellor Gowron quickly disappears from view. I think Gowron's decided to put his past experience with the House of Mogh to use by duplicating it on other politically inconvenient families. All I did was name those houses, until I came to one that made him blink."

"Vrag," Kira repeated.

"Yes. Unfortunately, of all the exiled houses, that's the one I know the least about. They could have been thrown out for being pacifists or for wanting to start an outright attack on the Federation. We should be—"

The shield rippled one last time, then vanished. Bashir promptly crossed into the center of the Klingon encampment, drawn by the universal sounds of suffering that he could now hear clearly.

"—careful," Dax finished behind him, ruefully. He could hear her and Kira following along, but his attention now was locked to his medical tricorder and the flickering vital signs it guided him toward.

The little alcove trampled into the brush wall was more just a place to dump the wounded than any real attempt at an infirmary. Bashir covered the last meter with a few quick strides and knelt beside the first in what seemed an impossibly long line of patients.

Heiser had already headed for the other end of the line, tricorder and medkit in hand, while LeDonne positioned herself near the middle. Bashir would suddenly have given an arm for another dozen medics, all of them only half as good as these two.

The female now laid out before him was still young by Klingon standards. Her brow ridges were fully carved, but twelfth-year incisors only showed perhaps five or six years' worth of wear. A depressed skull fracture had been bandaged with only a single strip of fine-weave cloth, and not even so much as a half-cured hide had been spread over her to keep out the chill. Of course not—Klingons should be strong enough not to require coddling. Even when they were more than half dead. Grey matter in the tangle of her hair, and no reflexive response from either pupil. Bashir closed her eyes with a gentleness he suspected she wouldn't appreciate, and moved on to the next body in line.

Gordek circled behind the doctor, limping to a stop just outside Bashir's range of vision. Bashir could feel the Klingon's stare on him as he compiled tricorder readings on the patient, a burning itch on the back of his skull. "What happened here?" he asked, more to tell the Klingon he knew he was being watched than because he really needed to know.

That gained him only another streak of spittle, this one landing distressingly close to his tricorder. "What do you think? You must have seen the sky as you came here."

"Comet impact," Kira translated. It sounded as if she spoke through clenched teeth, and Bashir was oddly glad to know he wasn't the only one reacting badly to Gordek's blend of anger, aggression, and reserve. "When did it happen?"

"Three days ago, just at sunset. We saw a streak across the sky, but we have seen many such streaks in the last few months. This one was different. This light came down further into the sky, then exploded around us, like a photon torpedo."

"Lower atmosphere burst," Dax said. "The most damaging kind of impact."

Gordek grunted. "Several of my house were killed outright. Others have died since. But there are still enough of us left to survive." The statement was almost defiant, as if he thought they might have some reason to question. "After we found the wrecked Federation ship, I knew we would be fine. The shield will keep us safe from any more explosions in the sky."

Straightening carefully, Bashir took a moment to sterilize his hands before he moved on to the next critical patient. Dax watched in silence while he knitted ribs and sutured the punctures they had made in the skin. Klingon physiology was remarkable in many respects, not the least of which was their ability to stoically endure damage that would have killed a human or a Trill within hours.

It was Kira who resumed the interrogation. "When you were stripping the wreckage, did you see any evidence of where the crash survivors might have gone?"

Gordek spat again, this time in her direction. It was apparently an all-purpose expression of scorn rather than a personal comment. "Following tracks in the *tuq'mor* is a fool's errand. There was a trail close to where your ship crashed, one that I followed north-west from here. It continues another half-day's walk to the main settlement."

"Main settlement?" Dax inquired, while Bashir reached the last patient in his third of the row. He had added an open pelvic fracture and lateral pneumotho-rax to his list of casualties, and reached to tip first Heiser's, then LeDonne's tricorder screen to a read-able angle so he could add their lists to his before Gordek answered the Trill's question.

"It is where the *epetai* keeps those loyal to her, a warren of burrows in the middle of the *tuq'mor*." He spat again, more fiercely this time and in a direction away from them. "All underground, the better to rot and die where they stand!"

Bashir exchanged enlightened glances with Dax. "No wonder you got so few humanoid readings on this planet," he said softly. She dipped a single thoughtful nod in agreement.

Kira pushed in front of Gordek, either oblivious to or determined to ignore his growing belligerence. "Could the survivors from the crashed Federation vessel be at this main settlement?"

"They might." Gordek stepped back, his broad face emotionless but his onyx-cold eyes skipping from one to another of them with a look of unexpected calcula-tion. "If I tell you how to find it," he said, "will you send down phasers and a permanent power generator for our new shield?"

"You want to stay here?" Bashir tried not to sound too appalled by this loyalty to any planet that had doled out such ruthless punishment for crimes that were none of its affair. He couldn't help noticing

54

Dax's matching frown of surprise. "You've got at least six critical injuries so far, plus another four who might not die but who need bones regrown or limbs regenerated." He glanced behind him, and was only half-startled to find both Dax and Gordek so close that he bumped them with his shoulder when he turned. "I'd like to beam them up to the ship right away."

"You have doctors on your ship who can tend to Klingon warriors?"

Bashir made himself scowl back into Gordek's accusing glower. "No. But we have stasis facilities that can keep them alive until we get to a better equipped sick bay." Although he found it hard to believe this Klingon cared overmuch how many of his people did or didn't survive the journey. Thinking of the first young woman with her brain in her hair, he offered more gently, "We also have a morgue, if you'd—"

Gordek waved off the suggestion with a whuff of disgust. "The dead are dead." He looked as though the sight of his dead people annoyed him. "Leave them."

"There will be more dead," Dax warned him. "Even with the shield, you can't survive a direct comet strike."

The Klingon leader's glossy black head lifted in a faint echo of Worf's towering pride in his heritage. "I prefer to die under a killing sky than to accept mercy from my enemy. You may transport my people to your ship for treatment," he added to Bashir arrogantly. "But you will beam them down again along with the power generator I have asked for. Is it a bargain?"

"Yes." Kira overrode Dax's more tentative response with the crisp confidence of someone who'd been a field commander for longer than she'd been an adult. "You have my word of honor as a Bajoran."

The thick muscle of Gordek's cheek spasmed again, but whatever had startled him apparently wasn't worth commenting on. "I accept that," he said promptly. "And you have the word of honor of one who will be *epetai* someday."

CHAPTER
3

KIRA FELT THE difference in this new Klingon encampment even before the transporter had fully released her. Sunlight—harder and hotter, with no ocean breeze to mitigate its strength—cut patchwork patterns through shadow too woven and deep to come from trees; peaty-smelling mud leveled the ground with flaccid puddles; and the volume and snarl of the voices crowding about her reminded her abruptly that, even on the best of days, Federation personnel had no reason to expect a warm reception from Klingons.

Unfortunately, it was a little late to voice that kind of pithy observation. Solidity raced through her limbs with an almost electric shock. With it came the full return of sight and sound and movement. She had barely jerked away from the first Klingon who lunged to grab her arm when Dax's shout took over where the transporter had left off. "Kira, don't! Julian, don't fight them!"

Not that they had much choice—one thick, stone-hard arm snaked around Kira's middle while some-one else seized her wrist and pinioned it between two hands. She couldn't even see Bashir, only hear his thin hiss of pain somewhere behind her. Her teeth gnashed so hard they hurt, but she didn't use her free hand to gouge anybody's eyeballs. She thought Dax should at least appreciate the heroic proportions of that restraint, considering how incomprehensible Kira found the whole concept of passivity.

She estimated more than four dozen Klingons just within the sweep of her eyes, most of them drifting in menacing orbit around her, Dax, and Bashir. Another unseen handful held them all immobile. Bandages, rough splints, even a pair of crutches lashed together from twists of local wood. Nothing in sight like the massive injuries they'd left LeDonne and Heiser to tend at Gordek's camp, but also hardly representative of this encampment's entire populace. Although sur-rounded by the same tangled brush growth that had bordered the shoreline, this campsite was many times larger and obviously more permanent. What might have been trees, except that they'd been planted upside down, punctuated the huge clearing, dotting the edges and even marching a way into the brush. Klingons sat comfortably atop arching roots-that-should-have-been branches, emerged curiously from the cavernous hollows dug under the enormous barrel trunks, looked up from where they etched intricate symbols into the still-growing wood to expand on patterns already months—if not years—old.

A tall, white-haired female climbed with unhurried dignity from the depths of the largest tree-cavern. Her head plates braided into an elegant arch from the bridge of her nose to the peak of her skull, and hair that must have been longer than she stood tall had been coiled and woven into a regal coronet. Kira didn't think she'd ever seen a Klingon so obviously old, or so impressive.

Striding through the corridor that suddenly appeared before her in the press of bodies, the matriarch halted less than an arm's length from the prisoners to fold her hands in front of her polished bronze belt. She regarded them with aristocratic reproach. *"TlhIngan Hol Dajatlh'a'?"*

"Yes." Dax spoke up without waiting for either of the others to ask for a translation. "But my friends speak only Standard."

The Klingon measured Kira and Bashir together with a single flick of her eyes, the way a hunter casts off unnecessary tissue with a single sweep of his knife. "There is no honor in exploiting your enemy's confusion." She managed to convey a wealth of disdain, even in her graciousness. "I am Rekan, *epetai* of the House of Vrag."

Not the House of Gordek, Kira noticed, and was not too surprised by that.

Rekan *epetai* Vrag listened to Dax's introductions with an almost Vulcan stoicism, only tipping her head once with interest when the lieutenant commander said her own name. "You are a Trill."

Even Kira could tell that wasn't a question. Dax nodded.

"Were you once called by the host-name Curzon?"

The Trill seemed to weigh her answer carefully, studying Rekan's face as though looking for her words in that queenly sculpting of planes and angles. "I'm sorry," she said at last. "I'm sure Curzon would have remembered such a striking female."

If Rekan found the remark as condescendingly masculine as Kira did, she didn't show it. "I never had the honor of meeting Curzon Dax while he was among us. But he was said to be an extraordinary man." She delivered a short, glancing blow to whoever stood behind Kira, the way a *ghar*-wolf cuffs at its offspring. Just that quickly, the grip on Kira's throat and arm was released. Rekan *epetai* Vrag stepped back, but only far enough to prevent physical contact between herself and the outsiders, not far enough to suggest a retreat. "You have come to retrieve your soldier."

Kira glanced sideways at Dax, and was relieved to see the Trill more concerned with the health of her tricorder than her own rough handling. Bashir rubbed gingerly at one biceps, but seemed none the worse for wear. Neither of them seemed to have noticed the odd nature of that statement. Kira frowned and turned back toward the older Klingon female. "Soldier?"

"From your crashed ship," Rekan said calmly. "We have been waiting for you to come retrieve him."

"There's only one?" Bashir's dismay roughened his

normally smooth voice. "There should have been over thirty, most of them scientists and older people."

The Klingon leader shook her majestically silvered head. "We have seen none of those. We have only one young male Human, wounded." Her mouth compressed in a smile that showed none of Gordek's aggressive baring of teeth. "And all he will tell us is his name, rank, and identification number. He says he is a communications officer. We assumed he was from a downed warship."

Kira frowned back at her. "He's from a Federation research vessel, sent here to observe the comet fall," she informed the exiled Klingon leader. "Your people shot it down."

"My people?" The Klingon matriarch lifted her chin in either interest or amusement, Kira wasn't sure which. "Look around you. We have no ability to shoot anyone down."

"But if it wasn't for you—"

Bashir interrupted with the sidelong scowl that Kira knew meant he'd had enough of unproductive truculence. "Can we have this discussion later, please? I'd like to see my patient."

"Ah." Rekan nodded as if something had been vaguely puzzling her but was now resolved. "You are a doctor. I understand now. Follow me."

Bashir did so without pause, leaving Kira hesitating in the center of the main exile colony. Dax gave her a wordless nod, but that didn't do much to reassure her. After all, this was the same Trill who thought coming down to this comet-battered planet was a once-in-a-lifetime treat. Still, when Dax swung past her to catch up to Rekan's long, purposeful strides, the barrage of hostile glances Kira could feel pouring out of the myriad hollows and caves was enough to speed her steps as she followed.

Rekan Vrag had threaded her hands into her sleeves, a gesture that must have dated from a time when she wore the more elegantly draped robes of the Klingon military aristocracy. Somehow, even dressed in drab utilitarian brown, the gesture did not demean or humble her. "Enter," she said simply, pausing at the threshold of one small overhang. Kira's warning instincts rose to full clamor when she saw the featureless, dim interior. But when Dax snapped on a belt-lamp and used it to pick out the single slim figure huddled against the far wall, Kira was the next one in after Bashir. At least these Klingons had spared him the luxury of a blanket.

The survivor stirred when Bashir started his examination, his hands rising in a move Kira recognized as a standard defense technique taught at Starfleet Academy. She caught his hands back easily from Bashir's oblivious throat, feeling them shake with frustrated weakness between her own.

"It's all right," she said, hearing her voice drop to the crooning hush she'd used to soothe younger children in the camps during attacks. "You're safe."

"Safe." The young man licked dry lips, barely able to say the words past them. He peered up at her puzzledly, then his gaze moved to Bashir's familiar uniform and eased. "Starfleet . . . ?"

"That's right." It didn't seem worth pointing out

that Kira was with the Bajoran military, not Starfleet. She suspected that just not being Klingon would have been enough to reassure him. "I'm Major Kira. This is Lieutenant Commander Dax and Dr. Bashir."

"I'm . . . my name's Alex, Alex Boughamer. How did you know I was here?"

Kira tossed a warning glance at Dax, inclining her head toward the tall and rail-thin shadow that still slanted across the mouth of this deep overhang. Dax nodded back at her soundlessly, then answered. "We picked up the *Victoria Adams*'s distress call at Deep Space Nine yesterday." She paused, carefully eying the pale face below them. "Alex, did anyone else survive?"

Boughamer startled Kira with a breathless chuckle. "Hell, *all* of us survived, Lieutenant. In fact, I'm the worst off. Captain Marsters packed us three deep in the sampling shuttle—you should have heard the geologists bitch about that—and one of the . . ." His drifting words sliced off abruptly, as if he'd just recollected that he was still among Klingons. ". . . um, an older guy among the passengers who used to be a pilot or something—he piloted us down. He was amazing. We took some bumps in the comet field—that's when the spectrometer fell on me—but otherwise we made it down pretty much in one piece. I couldn't believe it." His blue eyes sharpened to a more crystalline alertness as Bashir's bone regenerator skated across his ribs. "What about the *Vicky A*, Major? You said you got a distress call. Did she make it out okay?"

"We don't know," Dax said, in the gentle voice she

usually reserved for hopeless causes and untimely deaths. "So far, there's no word."

Boughamer's face seemed to crumple in on itself for a moment, then firmed up again. "That's okay. We knew—Captain Marsters knew she might not make it. He just wanted to make sure we got away, and we did. He'd be glad about that."

They were silent for a moment, listening to the hum of the deep-tissue regenerator that Bashir scanned across Boughamer's abdomen. The daylight slanting in from outside seemed too bright, now that Kira's eyes had adjusted to the darkness. She restrained an urge to ask Rekan to step closer to the mouth of the overhang to provide more shade.

Dax touched Boughamer's shoulder to get back his drifting attention. "You said all the other survivors were alive. Where are they?"

"With the Klingons," he said simply.

Kira glanced out at Rekan's silhouetted figure and frowned. *"Which* Klingons? There's no one here but you."

Boughamer shook his head, then groaned and dropped his head back to the ground. "Not here. They caught us at the crash site and took us someplace far away. It was dark . . . we were in a cave, I think. Deeper and colder than this—more wind blowing through. But I don't know—" He started to shake his head again, but desisted when Bashir laid a gently restraining hand across his forehead. "They had me blindfolded part of the time, and I was passed out the other half. All I remember is waking up and being in some kind of vehicle—something that lurched a lot, like a big landhopper or all-terrain crawler. I was there for what seemed like forever, then I was here. That's all I know."

Kira fell silent again, this time in sizzling frustration over the lack of clues she could follow to the missing survivors. She lifted an eyebrow at Dax to see if the Trill had any other questions.

"Alex," Dax said, "the Klingons who found you after you crashed—what did they look like?"

"Was one of them a heavy guy, long black beard and hair?" Kira put in.

"No." Boughamer's eyes closed, but his voice sounded so much clearer now that Kira guessed he was doing it to better remember. "They were too young to be a ship's crew, no armor, nobody in charge. And they've lived there, wherever we were, for a while. I could smell that—the smoke smell and the food smells and the Klingon smells."

"Why did they take the rest of the crew and passengers back to the caves with them? Why didn't they bring them all here?" Bashir asked.

Boughamer's eyes flashed open, looking startled and oddly angry. "Didn't I tell you already?" He cursed when he saw their heads shake. "I'm sorry, I thought I had—I've been repeating it over and over in my head until I wasn't sure what I'd said and what I'd just thought. It's what they sent me here to tell you, it's *why* they sent me. They knew someone would come to look for us, and this is what they want you to do."

He took a deep breath, then launched himself into a message so singsong and practiced that its original

Klingon cadences could scarcely be heard anymore. "You are from Starfleet who listen to this, and you have come to rescue your people from the comets. But there are people on this planet that you haven't come to rescue, and to us their lives are more valuable than these are to you. So we say to you, we who live on this planet and for this planet and with this planet, that we will not release these people of yours from the threat of the comets until you have released our people from it, too, forever. If you do not, then the comets will release us all." Boughamer's breath whistled out of him in near-exhaustion, but his eyes were already anxiously turning from Kira to Dax to Bashir. "I really said it that time, didn't I? I didn't just imagine that I did?"

"You really said it." It was a good thing at least one of the Trill's brains could still form words, because judging from the arrested expression on his face, Bashir had been thumped as speechless as Kira. "The rest of the survivors from the *Victoria Adams* are being held hostage by a group of Klingons. They'll be released only when we've managed to protect the entire planet from the comets. Otherwise—"

"—otherwise they hang on to the hostages until *sylshessa,*" Kira said grimly. "Until Armageddon, when everybody dies."

It was the mark of a mission going bad, Sisko thought ruefully, when your first instinct upon being hailed by your sector commander was to have your communications officer tell her you'd beamed down with your away team. Had it only been a few hours ago that he'd felt utterly confident that he could swoop into the Armageddon system, elude the Klingon blockade, beam up the survivors from the *Victoria Adams,* and be back at the station before Admiral Nechayev had finished conferring with her Vorta equivalents? Now that he was orbiting high above this comet-scorched planet, his sensors blinded by impact debris, his ship in imminent danger of detection by a returning Klingon blockade, and his away team stymied by Klingon ecological activists—of all the unlikely antagonists!—he wasn't sure Nechayev was even going to believe his progress report, much less endorse his continuing mission. And he could tell from the surreptitiously sympathetic glances he was getting from O'Brien and Worf that they shared all of his doubts.

With a resigned sigh, Sisko nodded at the young ensign who'd taken Dax's place on the bridge. "Put the admiral through."

"Captain Sisko." Interference from the comet field fuzzed the high-security channel, making Nechayev's image waver. As usual, though, the admiral's polished steel voice cut through the background hum with ease. "Do you know what's going on right now?"

"We're still trying to locate the survivors from the *Victoria Adams,"* he said. "We've gotten proof that most of them are alive, but—"

Nechayev waved his explanation to an unexpected stop, her carved face tightening with an emotion too cold to be anger and too tense to be irritation. "Let me update you on the larger situation. Twenty minutes ago, the *Victoria Adams*—and the Klingon ship she appeared to be traveling with—were destroyed by a Cardassian military outpost at KDZ-A17J. The Cardassians claim it was an act of self-defense."

"What?" The shout resounded so loudly around the *Defiant*'s bridge that Sisko knew it hadn't just been his voice raised in unconscious protest. "How could Captain Marsters attack a Cardassian outpost? The *Victoria Adams* wasn't armed!"

Nechayev frowned. "According to the Cardassians, Marsters came into the system at high speed and made a suicide run straight at their outpost. When they destroyed the *Victoria Adams* to prevent the impact, a cloaked Klingon vessel that was shadowing her—or pursuing her—returned their fire. The ensuing battle took down two Cardassian warships and half the station's defense system before the Klingons were destroyed."

Sisko whistled softly. He'd only met Marsters once, and although he'd been impressed with the research captain's intelligence and good judgement, he would never have expected a Vulcan Science Academy graduate to display such reckless courage in defense of his passengers and crew. "He deliberately incited that battle to keep the Klingons from returning here," he told Necheyev without hesitation. "He must have known it was the only way he could stop them."

Worf let out a rumble of Klingon respect. "That was the act of a great warrior."

"You know that, and I know that," Nechayev snapped back. "But all the Cardassians know is that they've been attacked by what looked like a joint Federation-Klingon force. It's taking all the diplomatic pressure we can muster to keep open war from breaking out all along the border."

"Look at the bright side," O'Brien offered. "At least we won't have to worry about the Klingon blockade for a while. They'll be so busy shoring up their border patrols—"

"I disagree," Worf interrupted. "If the Klingons blockading this system were willing to fire on an unarmed Starfleet vessel and pursue her into the teeth of a Cardassian outpost, there is something of immense importance to them in this system. I do not believe they will abandon it."

Nechayev's image fractured into hissing rainbow prisms as a chunk of cometary ice rebounded against the *Defiant*'s angled shields, then reformed into an ironic frown. "For once, our diplomatic corps agrees with you, Commander Worf. They tried to make some subtle inquiries about this KDZ-E25F planet of yours, but couldn't get their usual Klingon informants to spill so much as a word. The best guess our tactical analysts can make is that it was the site of some heroic Klingon military action in the Cardassian invasion."

"Unlikely," said Worf. "The only battlefields sacred to Klingons are those where a single warrior or ship held off an overwhelmingly superior force. The Cardassians were never that."

Nechayev's frown deepened. "Then what's *your* explanation, Commander? Do you really believe the Klingons are shooting down Federation science vessels just to keep the cometary fireworks show to themselves?"

"No." If he felt discomfited at having drawn the needling attention of their sector commander, Worf didn't show it in either voice or expression. "What we are seeing is most likely an internal Klingon dispute of some kind, with the *Victoria Adams* inadvertently caught in the middle. The presence of only a single house among the Klingons stranded on the planet—"

"What Klingons stranded on the planet?" Nechayev blinked in surprise.

Sisko cleared his throat to draw the transmitter's autofocus back to him. "I started to tell you that our crash survivors are being held hostage by one of three groups of Klingons who say they have been stranded on this planet."

Nechayev's eyes narrowed. "And the fact that all these stranded Klingons come from a single house makes you think they might be political exiles? Imprisoned in the neutral zone because of some power struggle in the Klingon High Command?"

"Yes." The glint of Worf's dark eyes now held surprise and discomfiture in equal quantities. Sisko could have told him not to underestimate Nechayev's intelligence. He might not always like her strategic decisions, but he had to admit that the admiral had a raptor-swift grasp of salient facts. "However, since we do not yet know why or how these Klingons came to be marooned here, I cannot speculate as to the exact nature of the dispute."

Nechayev's thin, pale brows arched. "It could be anything. With all the recent unrest and turmoil he just quelled in the Klingon High Council, Chancellor Gowron could be unwilling to let *any* hint of internal dissension get out."

"Agreed," said Worf. "It will thus be a point of

great honor to the Klingons to keep the blockade manned, to prevent the dishonored ones from escaping their sentence of exile."

"Which is now," Sisko pointed out, "a sentence of death."

"Because of the comet disintegration." Nechayev followed his logic as easily as she had followed Worf's. "Are the Klingons demanding evacuation to safe haven in return for releasing the crash survivors?"

"No." Sisko tried to mask the exasperation in his voice, but suspected he didn't do a very good job. "Most want us to just leave them alone to die. A few want us to give them enough technology to let them survive the bombardment. But the ones who actually have custody of the survivors from the *Victoria Adams* want us to save the entire planetary ecosystem by sweeping the comet debris out of the system."

Sisko had rarely seen Admiral Nechayev taken by surprise, and never seen her speechless. Until now. The arctic blue of her eyes glittered at him for a long moment, but only the background sizzle and thrum of small ice particles vaporizing off their shields filled the stunned silence.

"The Klingons want you to protect the planet they were stranded on against their will?" Her words were so filled with disbelief that they sizzled almost as much as the melting ice. *"Why?"*

Sisko took a deep breath. "We don't know. We haven't even made direct contact with them yet. So far, my away team has gotten all of its information from the *Victoria Adams*'s communications officer. He was sent to the main exile camp to deliver the ultimatum, but he was wounded too badly to identify where he was brought from. Major Kira and Commander Dax are interrogating the other Klingon exiles now in an attempt to locate where this splinter group might be hiding."

"Do they really think the other Klingons will betray them?"

"They might, if Dax can convince them it's the honorable thing to do. Even if she can't, we can always divert a few of the oncoming fragments, to convince them of our good intentions for long enough to evacuate the crash survivors. After that—"

"After that, it's not our problem," Nechayev said bluntly. "Are we absolutely sure the rest of the *Victoria Adams* crew and passengers are still alive?"

"Yes." He wasn't, but had a feeling it wouldn't be wise to admit that to Nechayev.

"Then your orders, Captain, are to negotiate their release as soon as possible. If you don't succeed before the Klingons reestablish their blockade, I suggest you clear the area at that time."

"You *suggest?*" Sisko cocked a startled look at his commander. "You're not making that an order?"

Nechayev grimaced. "God knows, I'd like to. I'd rather not lose the best ship in my sector—not to mention the entire staff of a space station that isn't exactly the most requested post in Starfleet—over a few damned chunks of comet." She fell silent and her lips tightened, as if it was difficult for her to decide how to phrase the next part of her transmission. "There is a retired officer among the tourist party who under no circumstances must fall into the hands of the Klingon High Council. *Under—no—*

circumstances." She repeated it with enough emphasis to make Sisko's eyebrows lift.

"Can you tell me——"

"No," said Nechayev flatly. "Even the knowledge of his whereabouts is classified information. If the Federation Diplomatic Service ever found out that he risked his life just to see some comets crash into KDZ-E26—I mean E25——"

"We've been calling it Armageddon," Odo informed her.

"Appropriate," said Nechayev dryly. "Considering the hell there's going to be to pay if we lose the *Defiant* as well as the *Victoria Adams* there. Not to mention starting a three-way war between the Federation, the Cardassian Empire, and the Klingons."

"But if we manage to evade the Klingon blockade long enough to rescue our crash survivors——" Sisko let the sentence trail off, eying his commander closely for signs of disapproval.

The admiral regarded him with cold eyes, but allowed an ironic slice of smile to appear. "In that case, Captain, I might just be willing to overlook your blatant disregard for my opinion."

Sisko nodded. "Understood."

Nechayev reached forward to cut the contact, then paused to give him a last icy look. "One more thing. If you get a confirmed report from your away team that the *Victoria Adams*'s survivors have been killed, either by comet impact or by your Klingon activists, I want you out of that death trap immediately. And *that*'s an order."

Sisko scowled up at the viewscreen for a long moment after the admiral's image snapped out of existence, but it wasn't the dusty skies of Armageddon that were aggravating him. He now had breathing space in which to find a solution to his unexpected hostage crisis, but it was breathing space with an enormous price tag attached. What he needed was a way to protect the scorched planet below him from further cometary damage, and he needed it soon enough to get his crash survivors freed before the *Defiant* started an interplanetary war.

"Commander Worf," Sisko said abruptly. "If we angle and disperse our shields to sweep up as many comets as possible, how many trips across the debris tail will we have to make to protect the planet from impact for the next few days?"

The Klingon officer tapped a query into Dax's piloting console and scowled at the results. "Approximately two hundred and seventeen," he said unhappily. "The maneuver will take almost two days to complete."

"Too slow," O'Brien warned. "And too risky. There's bound to be a couple of comets that sneak past us while we're sweeping up the rest."

"And if a Klingon ship arrives to resume the blockade, there's too much chance they'll catch us only partially shielded. That's not good enough." Sisko strode up and down the length of the bridge, ignoring the wary look he got from his replacement science officer. No doubt the young man was wondering if his commanding officer's legendary temper was about to erupt. "We need another strategy, gentlemen, and we need it fast. We have to convince those Klingons down there that we're making good on our promise—"

"—without actually making good on it?" Odo lifted a caustic eyebrow.

Sisko favored his security officer with an impatient look. "Constable, if you have a better way to get rid of all those comets out there—"

"Why don't we just shoot them?"

It could have been a mocking question, but the steady intensity of Odo's gaze told Sisko he was serious. He paused with his mouth half-open to snap a dismissive reply, then slanted a glance at his chief tactical officer. "Is that feasible?"

This time, Worf didn't have to consult the computer to answer. "There is a limit to how wide a spread we can achieve without losing the ability to vaporize, but cometary ice has such low density that it does not present a significant constraint. However, when any kind of debris is clustered this closely in space, phaser beams tend to be diffracted by the leading edge and leave the interior of the debris cloud untouched."

"So we can't do broad-beam destruction," Sisko concluded. "What about point and shoot?"

"Selecting just the largest and most threatening fragments?" Worf nodded as if to answer his own question. "If we keep the phaser beam narrowly focused, it will not diffract. We can target almost any fragment in the tail for destruction."

Sisko grunted. "Then all we need to know is which fragments have the highest probability of impacting with the planet's surface." He paused, glancing over at the young ensign manning the science station. "Ensign Farabaugh?" he prodded, when he got no response.

"Sir?" The young man glanced back at him worriedly, alert but obviously unsure of exactly what was needed.

Sisko tried not to let too much impatience show in his voice. It wasn't Farabaugh's fault that Dax would have already realized what he wanted and programmed her scan accordingly. "Have the computer mark and track all fragments with an eighty-five percent probability of impact over the next five days. Concentrate on the most dangerous fragments—the large ones within a ten thousand kilometer range."

"Aye, sir." Looking relieved to be assigned a specific task, Farabaugh bent over his console, punching in the scanning parameters. "Um—I'll probably need to run a probabilistic vector model to account for fragment interactions. First results might take about seven minutes."

"Very well." Sisko swung back to eye the remainder of his bridge crew, smiling for the first time in what seemed like a long while. He always felt better when he had some immediate goal to pursue. "I think we could all stand to brush up on our manual track-and-fire skills, don't you, Commander? Who wants to go first?"

"Not me," Odo assured him. "I don't find blowing up inanimate objects as pleasurable an activity as you humanoids appear to."

"That's all right, Constable. I need you to keep an eye on the entire system, watching for ion trails." Sisko glanced over his shoulder. "Ready with tracking coordinates, Mr. Farabaugh?"

"Almost, sir. I still need to plot—" The young science officer broke off, staring down at something on his screen. "Captain Sisko, we've just been hailed by a

Cardassian battle cruiser! I'm putting it on-screen now."

The dust-stained oceans of Armageddon vanished, replaced by a deeply furrowed Cardassian face. "Captain Sisko of the U.S.S. *Defiant,* this is *Gul* Hidret of the Cardassian war-cruiser *Olxinder.*" It was unusual to see such an elderly soldier still serving as a *gul,* but the shrewd glitter in Hidret's eyes told Sisko he wasn't dealing with some political appointee or recalled reserve officer. "If you wish to avoid a conflict, please acknowledge this hail at once."

Sisko flexed his fingers on the arms of his command chair, hard enough to feel the duranium core beneath the padding. "Whatever you do, Mr. Farabaugh," he said through his teeth, "do *not* acknowledge that hail." He swung to scowl at Odo. "Constable, why the hell didn't you detect the Cardassians' arrival in the system?"

"For the very good reason that they haven't arrived yet," the Changeling shot back, unintimidated. "There are no uncloaked vessels present within the entire scanning range of my sensors."

"The communicator signal's red-shift indicates the Cardassians are hailing us from at least eighteen light-years out," Farabaugh volunteered. "It's so distant, I can't even tell for sure if they're heading our way or not."

Sisko's scowl swung back to the image of *Gul* Hidret, now waiting in confident silence for a reply. "Then how in God's name did they detect our presence?"

"They didn't," O'Brien said. "They're beaming a directed wide-cast over the entire Armageddon system. They just suspect we're here." The engineer looked up from his console, baffled. "What I want to know is how they learned our travel plans. That information sure didn't come from Starfleet."

"No doubt Cardassian High Command has its sources." Sisko tapped a reflective finger across his chin, debating pros and cons. Although it was tempting to remain silent and shatter *Gul* Hidret's smug sureness about the *Defiant*'s presence here, this wasn't a decision he could entrust to gut feelings. "Gentlemen, give me your opinions," he said abruptly. "Do we respond or not?"

Odo turned to give him a quizzical look. "Our orders from Admiral Nechayev were to refrain from starting a war. I assume that means she'd prefer that no one know we're here. Am I missing something?"

"The fact that the Cardassians already *know* we're here," O'Brien retorted. "If we don't warn them away, they might tangle with the Klingon blockade and start the war that way."

"True," agreed Worf. "But I do not advise we reply. The Cardassian battle cruiser is at least eighteen hours away, but there may be other Cardassian ships in the area who can backtrack our communications signal."

Sisko let out a frustrated breath. "And I want to know what *Gul* Hidret is up to. Deadlock."

Ensign Farabaugh cleared his throat, looking tentatively back and forth between them. "Would it help if we could respond to the Cardassians with a ricochet signal?"

Sisko swung to face his youngest bridge officer. "A

signal that can't be traced back to the *Defiant?* Can you do that?"

He got a shy grin in response. "With all the comets around here, Captain? No problem. The signal quality will degrade a lot when it bounces, but it should still get through."

"Do it." Sisko turned back to face the waiting image of *Gul* Hidret, summoning up all his self-control for the next few minutes. "Notify me when we're on-line."

"Hang on, sir, I'm working out a three-way bounce . . . scanning for target . . . All right, we're connected. Go ahead, Captain."

"Gul Hidret of the *Olxinder,* this is Captain Benjamin Sisko of the *Defiant.* Can you read me?"

"Barely." Judging from the squeal of feedback and the way Hidret squinted at his viewscreen, the Cardassian wasn't lying. "Are you engaged in battle with the Klingons?"

Sisko lifted one eyebrow, knowing the gesture probably couldn't be detected by his counterpart. Had there been a slightly hopeful tone in that question? "We're just experiencing some cometary interference, *Gul* Hidret. What do you want?"

"To save Cardassia," Hidret snapped back, brusquely enough to make Sisko's gut tighten with apprehension. When a *gul* dispensed with sly innuendo and circumspect hints, you knew you were in trouble. "We know the system you are in is under Klingon control. If you aren't fighting them, I'll have to assume you're in league with them and proceed accordingly."

Sisko grimaced. *"Gul* Hidret, there *are* no Klingons in this system right now." Sisko ignored Worf's frown and Odo's disapproving look. He knew a Federation diplomat would probably have fainted to hear him dish out that information so generously, but there was a method to his madness. "And our own presence here is only temporary. As soon as we locate some Federation crash survivors—"

"—you'll abandon the system?" *Gul* Hidret snorted in deep suspicion, the lines in his face deepening. "Forgive me if I doubt you. The Federation *cannot* be ignorant of the reason the Klingons have set up a blockade around such a worthless old scar of a planet."

"You mean the political exiles they stranded here?"

That innocent question turned the engraved lines in the old Cardassian's face from crevasses to ravines. "So they say! If you ask me, it's just an convenient excuse to claim they control the system."

Sisko exchanged baffled looks with his bridge crew. None of them, not even Odo, looked as if the *gul*'s comment made any more sense to them than it did to Sisko. But the shrewd glint of dark eyes on the screen assured him that, no matter how preposterous his story sounded, this old officer wasn't senile yet.

"Gul Hidret, you just finished telling us how worthless this planet is. Why would the Klingons need an excuse to claim it?"

That got him the bared teeth of a more normally unctuous Cardassian smile. "I expect because it's the source of all Cardassia's *geset.*" Even through the bounced and fuzzy signal, he must have seen Sisko's incomprehension. "It is the only known cure for *ptarvo* fever, a disease that decimates our young," he elaborated. "And it's only available in quantity from that dead and blasted planet you now orbit."

That comment, so apparently reasonable on the surface, sparked a snort of pure derision from Odo. Sisko shot him a quick glance, and the Changeling emphasized his skepticism by smacking a palm down to cut the audio channel on his communications board before he spoke.

"*Gul* Hidret is either a remarkably incompetent liar, or doesn't have much respect for our intelligence," he told the captain bluntly.

"What makes you say that, Constable?"

"*Ptarvo* fever is a colloquial term for the first stirrings of *paltegen* hormones in young Cardassian males. What Humans might call 'spring fever.'" Odo inclined his head at the *gul*, now mouthing unheard words at the viewscreen. "He's hiding something."

Sisko grunted, and motioned him to open the audio channel again. He didn't waste any time responding to the *gul*'s indignant accusations. "If *ptarvo* fever is such an emergency, why aren't you bringing a scientific and medical ship to study the *geset* and learn how to synthesize it? Why send in a military vessel?"

Hidret heaved a patently exaggerated sigh. "Precisely what we were planning to do, Captain, before the Klingons arrived and set up their illegal blockade. Since then, the Empire has been biding its time, hoping the Klingons would leave—but finding out that the Federation is now on the side of our old enemies was too much. The High Command decreed that it was time to intervene, before the vital secret of *geset* was lost to us forever."

"We're not on the side of the Klingons," Sisko said impatiently. "In fact, we couldn't be further from it."

"Then why have they allowed you to stay in a system that they have chased all of our scouts and warships away from?"

Sisko groaned. That was exactly the kind of flawed reasoning that could lead to military confrontation. But how could he correct Hidret's assumptions without opening up awkward questions about his own foolhardy presence in this system? Somehow, he didn't think Nechayev would approve of telling the Cardassian High Command about the strategically important Starfleet veteran who had crashed with the other survivors.

Fortunately, Worf took that decision out of his hands. "Why do you think the Klingons on the planet are not truly exiles?"

"Because when we first detected their presence, we offered to evacuate them," *Gul* Hidret retorted. "And they flatly refused. If they had been sent to that comet-blasted planet against their will, why would they not want to leave?"

Worf's low rumble echoed across the squealing feedback from the bounced signal. "It is a matter of honor. That is why you cannot possibly understand it."

"Ah, the excuse Klingons always use to disguise their covert activities!" Hidret snapped back. "I feel confident that whatever those so-called exiles are doing on that planet, it is far from honorable—and it is probably aimed at destroying the Cardassian Empire!"

"And I feel confident that you are lying through your teeth," muttered Worf, before Sisko waved him into silence.

Fortunately, the squeals of feedback must have distorted the tactical officer's words enough to mask them. *Gul* Hidret screwed his face into a squint again. "What did you say?"

Sisko took a deep breath. A reckless plan, kindled from equal parts desperation and cynicism, had assembled itself in his brain while Worf and the *gul* had been talking. He saw no reason to delay putting it into action. "I said you can easily discover whether those exiles are working against your government. Why don't you ask them to let you harvest *geset* in return for protecting them against the comets that are hitting the planet? Your battle cruiser's big enough to sweep the debris away just by recalibrating and diffusing your shields. That way, even if the exiles refused your terms, you would at least protect your source of *geset* from destruction."

"What?" He couldn't tell if it was anger, loathing, or just sheer surprise that bleached out Hidret's face to the color of old wax, but the reaction was even more vehement than he'd expected. "You expect me to de-power my shields and risk the safety of my ship just to save the lives of some *Klingons?*"

"No," Sisko said silkily. "I expect you to risk your ship to save the lives of your children."

The old Cardassian's face tightened, showing stubborn bones beneath his sagging wrinkles, but he gave no other sign of having had his bluff called. "A valiant try, Captain. Unlike Klingons, you Humans do occasionally manage to create battle strategies almost devious enough to be interesting. But your attempt to render me helpless is a little on the transparent side. If I agreed to play janitor to your cometary debris, no doubt I'd soon find myself under attack from you and your Klingon allies."

Sisko didn't bother to deny that, since he was sure his Klingon "allies" would have been only too happy to fulfill Hidret's prophecy. "Then I strongly suggest you keep away from this system, *Gul* Hidret."

"And tell your children with *ptarvo* fever to try a cold shower instead of *geset*," Odo added, in an even more sardonic voice than usual.

"So much for Federation mercy and fairness!" All pretense of affability vaporized under a boiling rage that turned Hidret's wrinkled face copper brown. "We will see who ends up in control of this system in the end, after the Klingons return and find you in it!"

Sisko smiled, buoyed up by the grim satisfaction of having forced a Cardassian to admit to something resembling the truth. "Ah, but don't forget," he said pleasantly. "The Klingons are now our allies."

With one last howl that could have been retransmitted static or pure Cardassian rage, the connection between them went black. Sisko took a deep breath, then glanced across at Odo. "Well, Constable? Does *Gul* Hidret really think we're allied with the Klingons?"

Odo's face might not have been very expressive, but he made up for that by the depth of disgust he could express in a single snort. "What *Gul* Hidret thinks is that we're going to get massacred by the Klingon blockade. Right now, he's just positioning himself to come in after the battle's over."

"Then let us hope he miscalculates and arrives early," Worf said fiercely. "Because if there is a choice between us and the Cardassians when the Klingon blockade reforms, I know which of us will be the first target."

CHAPTER
4

IN HIS LONG years of Starfleet service, Benjamin Sisko had seen sulfur ice moons torn apart and neutron stars lashed into turmoil by passing cosmic strings. As a young ensign, he'd once watched a red giant star go nova; as a much older and wiser commander, he'd not only discovered the Bajoran wormhole, but had been the first Human to travel through it. In all his years and parsecs of passage through the galaxy, however, he'd never seen the effects of a comet impact on a Class-M planet.

Until now.

There had not even been a flare of comet tail across the field of the *Defiant*'s vision to alert them. Five minutes after *Gul* Hidret's apoplectic face had cut to black and Ensign Farabaugh had hurriedly transferred Armageddon's rusty image back up on the viewscreen, a brilliant white explosion spasmed over the planet's sea-covered northern pole. Sisko jerked back from the glare, even though he knew they were orbiting far above the planet's stratosphere. He swung instinctively toward the weapons console. "Report!"

"Sensors have detected a seventeen gigajoule explosion at planetary coordinates seventy-three point five by one-twenty-four point nine," his security officer said. "The radiation signal shows only natural thermal decay, no evidence of ionized plasma or radioactivity."

"That's a comet impact." O'Brien sent Sisko a grim look from engineering. "And it's only a few hundred kilometers from our away team at the main Klingon outpost."

"Four-hundred-and-ninety-seven kilometers, to be precise," Worf clarified in a stiffly proper voice. "However, vital signs on all away team members appear stable."

Sisko didn't bother asking why the Klingon had programmed that information—ordinarily the responsibility of the *Defiant*'s science officer—to route through his piloting console. Instead, he turned his frown on Dax's young replacement. "Ensign Farabaugh, I asked you to locate the most threatening fragments in the cometary field. What happened?"

"Nothing, sir."

Worf slewed around at his pilot's station to bestow an even fiercer scowl on the young man. "Seventeen gigajoules is equivalent to the force of nine photon torpedoes! Would you call that nothing if *you* were down on that planet?"

Farabaugh's eyes widened slightly, but his sincere

look never wavered. "The explosion was thirty-seven kilometers up in the atmosphere, Commander Worf. I doubt our away team even heard a rumble of thunder from it."

"Lucky for them," O'Brien commented. "And for us. What are the odds the one comet we miss intercepting is the one that explodes prematurely?"

"We didn't miss that comet, sir," Farabaugh said in mild surprise. "The computer noted its trajectory ten minutes ago, while the captain was talking to *Gul* Hidret. It just didn't trigger an alarm."

Sisko lifted an eyebrow at his young science officer. "You knew that fragment was going to disintegrate too high to cause any damage? How?"

"Relative velocity, sir." Farabaugh punched a series of commands into his science console, and the fading afterglow of the comet impact on Armageddon disappeared. The starless black screen that replaced it told Sisko this was a computer simulation, rather than a real sensor view. Multicolored streaks swam and spiraled across the black background like minnows in a chaotic school, leaving faint, glowing trails behind them. "After I scanned the comet field to find the ones most likely to collide with Armageddon, I ran impact simulations for each of them. You can see from the white and blue streaks that most of the ice fragments are moving at extremely or moderately high velocity relative to the orbital motion of Armageddon."

"And those are the most threatening ones?" O'Brien guessed.

"Actually, no, sir. Any comets that hit the planet's atmosphere fast are subjected to enormous crushing forces. Given the low density of cometary ice, almost all the fast-moving fragments detonate high in the stratosphere. Only the ones over seventy kilometers in diameter will survive long enough to affect the surface." Farabaugh tapped another command into his panel, and a few dozen comet fragments lit up in reds and yellows. "These are the dangerous fragments—the ones that are either big enough or slow enough to survive their passage through the atmosphere. They're the ones we have to worry about."

"Will they also crash into the planet with no warning?" Worf demanded.

Odo sent him a sardonic glance. "Comets are not Klingon warriors, Commander. You can hardly expect them to issue a proper challenge before they attack."

"No." Despite his agreement, however, Sisko noticed the Klingon sat scowling up at the screen, as if he could somehow intimidate the comets into more honorable behavior.

"How much leeway do we have before an impact event, Mr. Farabaugh?" Sisko asked.

"I've programmed the computer to issue a priority-one alarm half an hour before each projected impact." The young science officer glanced back at him uncertainly. "Will that be long enough?"

"That depends on what preventive action we're going to take." Odo glanced across at Sisko. "Which was what I believe we were discussing before we were so rudely interrupted by the Cardassians."

"I don't think there's much left to discuss." Sisko

sat back in his command chair and steepled his fingers. "Phasers are ready and the coast is clear. Which of these comets do you want us to shoot first, Mr. Farabaugh?"

"Um—actually, Captain, there's something I wanted to tell you about that." The young officer cleared his throat diffidently. "I'd rather we didn't shoot any of them, if you don't mind."

Sisko saw Worf turn to scowl again at the beleaguered ensign, and waved the Klingon into fuming silence. "All right, Mr. Farabaugh. Explain."

"Actually, sir, I think I know what he means," O'Brien said before Farabaugh could gather himself together. "We learned about this in planetary engineering. If you explode a comet that's threatening to strike a planet, all you do is increase the area of devastation by turning it from one big impactor into a whole bunch of medium-sized ones."

"Exactly," Farabaugh said, looking relieved. "The destruction quotient goes up anywhere from four to ten times, depending on the number of fragments and their trajectories. And since a phaser blast would tend to selectively refract through cracks and fissures in the comet, it would be almost impossible not to break it into fragments."

Worf's scowl faded into a more thoughtful frown. "What if we increased dispersion and decreased intensity on the phasers? That should vaporize the whole comet even if it breaks apart."

"Except it will also create a radiating impulse wave that will disturb other comets in the cloud into new orbits," O'Brien said. "Which means we might add one or two more major threats for every one we remove."

"And there's no way to know that without running the tracking program all over again every time we vaporize," added Farabaugh.

"Too risky. We might bunt a comet at the planet before we even knew we did it." Sisko tapped his steepled fingers against his chin, considering his rapidly dwindling alternatives. "Well, the one thing we agree on is that we can't just sit here and let Armageddon happen. So we'll have to find something we *can* do." He shot an inquiring glance at his chief engineer. "You must remember something else from that planetary engineering class of yours, Chief. What were the recommended ways of dealing with an imminent comet impact?"

"Deflection by modulated photon torpedo blast," O'Brien said promptly. "The idea was not to break it up, just alter its trajectory enough to turn the hit into a miss."

"And the photon blast probably stripped off just enough of the dust mantle to vaporize a layer of interior ice," Farabaugh guessed. "Then the gas spurt would push the comet in the opposite direction."

"Right." O'Brien waved a hand at the multitude of colored streaks on the main viewscreen. "The problem is, there's a lot more red and yellow blobs up there than we have torpedoes. And even quantum torpedoes aren't strong enough to reach more than one or two comets at a time."

"Can we achieve the same effect by modulating our phaser array?" Worf demanded.

The chief engineer shook his sandy head. "We'd have to remodulate it for each blast, and you know how many hours that would take."

"Not to mention the fact that it would make the phasers inoperable for defensive purposes," Odo commented. "And considering that I've just detected the ion trail of a cloaked vessel entering the system—"

"Location, velocity, estimated size?" Sisko demanded. For all the implicit trust he felt in Odo and Kira, there were times when the captain would have given anything for them to have had Starfleet training. "Extrapolated destination?"

Odo scanned his panel. "Cloaked vessel is currently two-hundred-and-fifty thousand kilometers out from system center, traveling at seventy-five percent impulse speed and slowing rapidly. It appeared to be a *Jfolokh*-class vessel, but with the ion trail dissipating as it slows, the computer can't be sure. Extrapolated destination is an equatorial orbit around Armageddon." He looked up at Sisko. "If I had to guess, Captain, I'd say the Klingon blockade was back in town."

Sisko grunted. "Mr. Worf, notify the away team that from now on, all communications are on secure channels only. And tell them they either beam up soon or not for a while." He turned toward his chief engineer. "I don't care how you do it, Chief, but I want the *Defiant*'s emissions down as close to zero as you can manage for the next few hours. I don't want those Klingons to get even a sniff of our presence here until we've located the survivors and are ready to beam them out."

O'Brien grimaced. "I don't know about zero, sir. I can recirculate the ship's thermal output and put a magnetic bottle around our warp exhaust, but there's not too much I can do about the diffuse ionization off the shields. And with all the comets bumbling through our current orbit—"

"—we can't turn shields off," Sisko finished for him. "But we may be able to lower the transfer charge without compromising our deflection capacity. Do the best you can, Chief."

"Aye, sir." O'Brien scrambled out of his chair, pausing only long enough to tap open his direct channel down to the Engineering deck. "Frantz, cap the warp exhaust, *now*. Ornsdorf and Frisinger, start recycling our waste heat through the impulse baffles to equalize it with ambient."

"Aye, sir." The competent calmness of that reply was so obviously modeled after O'Brien's own legendary composure that Sisko had to smile. "Desired delta on the heat output?"

"As close to planetary infrared output as possible," O'Brien said. "And I'm coming down to recalibrate the power circuits for the shields, so get all those lines stripped and ready for modulation."

"Aye, sir."

Satisfied that his ship was going to be as invisible as any able-bodied vessel could be, Sisko turned his attention back to Worf. "Any response from the away team, Commander?"

The Klingon's glum look told him the answer before he even began to speak. "Dr. Bashir says he is not finished evaluating casualties among the new Klingon encampment, Captain. They appear to have experienced at least three impact events, although none were as direct and damaging as the one that affected the first settlement. He has asked me to beam Ensign LeDonne into the new camp to aid him."

"Is the Klingon ship still out of short-range sensor detection limit?" Sisko asked his security officer. When Odo assented with a grunt, he nodded his approval back to Worf. "Tell the doctor this will be his last chance to reassign his team, or to beam any Klingons aboard for medical treatment. What progress have the others made in locating the hostages?"

"Commander Dax has sent a full report on the interrogations she and Major Kira have conducted so far, but says they have been unable to convince any among this group of exiles to cooperate with them as Gordek did. She is no closer to identifying who the hostage-takers are, much less what their location might be. She has also transmitted the data she has collected on the planet's environmental conditions, to be attached to your logs."

"Hmm." Rather than reassuring him, that news made Sisko's skin crawl with apprehension. The only time Dax went out of her way to keep him informed of her scientific discoveries was when she thought she might not be coming back to explain them in glorious detail herself. "Keep a high-security communications channel available for the away team to use at all times, Mr. Worf. And keep a close eye on their vital signs. We still don't know if the exiles they're dealing with are any more trustworthy than the ones who found the *Victoria Adams*."

Worf grunted curt approval of that policy. "I have already programmed an automated linkage between the shields and the main transporter controls. We can have the away team aboard with only a moment's loss in defensive capability."

"Good work, Commander." Sisko saw the irritated look Ensign Farabaugh threw Worf, and shook his head warningly at the younger man. It was true that Worf's preemptive action had usurped some of the science officer's traditional responsibilities, but the end result was all that mattered right now, not how it was achieved. He distracted Farabaugh with a wave of his hand at the viewscreen. "As long as we've got a computer simulation running up there, can we add the Klingons' estimated course-heading to it?"

"Yes, sir. All I need is the tracking data from Mr. Odo's station."

"I'm transferring it to you now. And for your information, young man, I am not *Mister* Odo."

"Yes, sir. Sorry, sir." Farabaugh ducked his head over his panel, and, a moment later, a bright green disk appeared at the far edge of the viewscreen. Even if he hadn't known it was the ion-trace of the cloaked Klingon vessel, Sisko's space-trained eyes would have been caught by its unusual rate of deceleration and its erratic slalom swings through the comet field. "The Klingon vessel isn't deflecting the comet debris, Captain," Farabaugh said unnecessarily. "It's taking evasive action."

"I can see that." Sisko could admire the fierce jerks and swoops of the unknown vessel, even while he pitied any Klingons aboard with weak stomachs. No inertial dampener in the galaxy could cope with shifts that rapid. "Interpretation, Mr. Worf?"

"I am not sure, Captain." Worf squinted up at the

screen as if he could visualize the Klingon ship better that way. "Perhaps they are practicing battle maneuvers. If so, they are not standard ones."

"If I didn't know any better," Odo said drily, "I would say they were out glee-riding."

"Glee-riding?" Worf repeated.

"It's what Bajoran adolescents call careening as close as they can to the rocks when they're out icesailing. Personally, I call it trying to kill themselves just for the fun of it."

Watching the green disk swing wildly out of its way to needle between two closely orbiting comet fragments, Sisko had to admit that Odo's description did seem apt. "If that really is a *Jfolokh*-class vessel, it's running damn close to its operating tolerances. The pilot's either very good or very foolish."

"Or both," Worf said grimly. "I find it difficult to believe that this ship has been sent to resume the official Klingon embargo."

"They don't know that we're here," Sisko reminded him. "And they've probably sent all their better ships to man the Cardassian border. No matter how it's getting here, it's certainly headed for the orbit I'd expect a blockading ship to take up."

"True." Worf glanced back over his shoulder. "In that case, sir, I suggest continuous passive scanning to be sure the Klingon vessel does not attempt to beam anyone to or from the planet surface."

Sisko nodded at Farabaugh. "Do it. And monitor their communications, too. I doubt they'll be saying much on open channels, but it never hurts to listen."

"Aye, sir."

The green disk that was the cloaked Klingon vessel made one last swashbuckling swoop around a spiraling comet fragment, then settled reluctantly on station around the glowing amber sphere representing Armageddon in the computer simulation. Sisko lifted an eyebrow, noticing that the skimmed comet fragment had been blasted into a different direction by the encounter with the Klingon's warp exhaust.

"Looks like you'd better rerun your impact prediction model, too, Mr. Farabaugh," he said. "After all those close encounters with the Klingons—" He broke off, sitting straighter in his command chair. *That's* what we can do!"

Odo gave him a caustic look. "Have a close encounter with the Klingons?"

"No—with any comet that looks like it's going to hit the planet." Sisko leaped out of his chair and began pacing, trying to gather together his whirling thoughts. "We'll have to uncap our warp core exhaust, at least long enough to alter the orbit of the fragment we want to intercept. It's either that or vent some of the thermal waste stored in the impulse engines."

"Either way, we would leave a clear trail for the Klingons to see," Worf pointed out. The tactical officer did not sound negative, just thoughtful. "If we plotted our course carefully, however, we could use the planet's gravitational field to loop us toward the comet with just a one- or two-second impulse thrust. Then we would only need to graze the comet with our angled shields in order to deflect it."

Farabaugh looked up from his science console. "Can we plot a course that won't affect the other comets in the field, Commander? That way, our collision models won't need to be rerun every time we interfere."

"We can if we wait until the comet is just about to enter Armageddon's gravity well." Sisko came to a halt in front of the viewscreen and pointed at the halo of clear space around the planet. "All we'll need to do is adjust the velocity of our circumpolar orbit to be sure we're close to the comet's projected entry point."

Odo snorted. "And you don't think the Klingons will notice when a comet suddenly bounces off of empty space?"

"Not if they are on the opposite side of the planet at the time," Worf said simply.

"But that means solving some intricate orbital mechanics equations—" Sisko came to a halt in the center of his bridge, stymied once again by the absence of Dax at the science station. There was no way he could expect a single-brained human to do all the monitoring, modeling, and scanning his Trill science officer could have handled with ease. "Mr. Farabaugh, who else on the *Defiant*'s crew has had science officer training?"

"Um—well, I went to the Academy with Ensign Osgood down in the main weapons bay, sir. I know she aced all her celestial mechanics courses. And I think there's an engineering tech named Thornton who did a stint on a science research vessel. He's also an expert on sensor systems."

"Good. Contact Thornton and tell him to come up and man your station. His job will be to scan the Klingons and report back to you on any changes in their orbit. You and Osgood commandeer one of the science labs and a sector of the main computer, and set up a full-scale model of the comet belt. I don't just want to know when every comet's going to hit this planet, I want to know far enough in advance to adjust our orbit, so we can intersect and deflect it while it's still on the Klingon's blind side. Is that clear?"

"Aye, sir!"

"I want your first report by—" Sisko glanced at the shipboard clock to estimate a reasonable deadline, and only then realized why his eyes felt like he was squinting past sand. From the time they'd left Deep Space Nine yesterday until now, he'd put in seventeen straight hours on duty. And so had the rest of his original bridge crew, with the exception of Odo, who had been forced to return to his cabin and regenerate several hours ago. "—oh-three-hundred hours. Odo, you have the conn. Commander Worf, call up replacements for your station and Chief O'Brien's."

He got the scowl he'd expected from the Klingon. "Captain—"

"No buts, Mr. Worf," Sisko said crisply. "I refuse to take the *Defiant* slow-dancing with comets unless my pilot is fit and rested. Report back to the bridge by oh-four-hundred. I assume we won't be looking to deflect any impacts before then, Mr. Farabaugh?"

"No, sir."

"Unless the Klingons start up some target practice of their own." Odo's ability to find a cloud in every silver lining would have amused Sisko if his chief of security wasn't right so depressingly often.

"Let's hope that doesn't happen, Constable." Sisko cast a sardonic look at the viewscreen. "Although if our glee-riding friends over there do decide to start shooting, with any luck they'll either be too drunk or too motion-sick to aim straight."

The first dull crash jerked Kira's head around so fast she nearly tumbled off the tall root she'd been straddling. A puff of dust—or dislodged vapor?—belched skyward like volcanic ejecta above the impenetrable tract of plant life before her. A tree just like the one on which she sat shuddered dully where it poked up through the brush a dozen meters away. Another unhurried tremor; she felt this one vibrate through her bones, and clenched at the roots underneath her as a flock of silent, grey-green primates scattered away from the rumble like startled pigeons.

For just an instant, she thought about calling out in alarm. She'd never heard anything like this, couldn't scramble up any kind of mental image to scare away more dire thoughts. The closest thing memory could offer was the Cardassians' giant mining drones, crunching their way through everything that wasn't the ores they sought. But there were no ores here, and presumably no Cardassians, either, so her mind leapt to the only other thing this alien environment had to offer: a comet.

The very ridiculousness of that mental leap blew the rest of her fears into silence. Back toward the main expanse of clearing, dark Klingon figures slunk moodily from place to place. Quiet yet surly, biding the time leading up to their destruction with what no doubt constituted a Klingon display of good grace. While their lack of alarm helped solidify her suspicion that no murderous rain of ice was imminent, it also made her scowl in private disgust.

In the years since Bajor had won its independence from Cardassia, Kira had spent a great deal of effort trying to free herself of what seemed unavoidable racism. In her youth, fierce pride in her Bajoran heritage had been the only thing that let her justify the anger and bloodshed saturating her life as an antiCardassian terrorist. It wasn't until she worked side by side with Humans and Trills and Ferengi and Vulcans every day that she became aware of how much her hatred of Cardassians had slipped over into hatred of anything not Bajoran.

The realization had proved unexpectedly painful. Disgust and loathing for the race who tortured your people to near extinction had always seemed fair and right. To forgive was the first step in forgetting, and forgetting was a dishonor to the millions of Bajorans who had died under Cardassian rule. She'd taken a private satisfaction in flaunting the Prophets' warning, "Hatred poisons the soil so that nothing but more hatred can grow there." Her hatred was different. Her hatred was just.

And her impatience with the Humans? Her distrust of the Ferengi? Her disbelief in the Vulcans' sincerity? Her secret suspicion that Trills did something immoral by sharing themselves with a symbiont? It took her many months to accept that all her fears, dislikes, suspicions, and disdain were simply fruits of the soil she'd let her just hatred poison. After that, she'd begun the long task of redemption. She'd even allowed herself the vanity of believing she'd made brilliant progress in learning to embrace the values offered by other worlds and cultures.

Until today.

She'd spent the better part of the last two hours trying to wrap her mind around the concept that being thumped, spat on, and snarled at by scowling Klingons was little more than exchanging social pleasantries. Not that she was any sort of expert in their cultural ways. Still, her gut instincts just didn't seem able to align themselves with what amounted to a cultural habit of aggression.

And I thought I *was a barbarian,* she admitted with a sigh. Picking her way carefully up the tree's rough bark, she found a handhold above the tallest knee of root and used that to hike herself almost a full meter higher in an effort to improve her view. *My problem is, I just can't pretend I don't feel what I feel.* Dax's careful, rational explanations aside, Kira found it hard to silence those old instincts just for the sake of pretending she respected any society that functioned more on intimidation and posturing than on any kind of true merit. Sympathy kept running aground on the basic reality that every interview she and Dax conducted had someone shouting and growling as though eager to encourage a fight. If Dax hadn't suggested that Kira spend some time off on her own—to "cool off"—the major might just have precipitated a political situation of her own.

A slow, chuffing grumble crack-crashed its way closer through the stand of brush to her left. Kira craned up on tiptoes to steal a glimpse of the topmost surface of the foliage, and instead caught only a methane-tangy belch of breath in the face when the creature making its way toward her finally smashed its languorous way out of the undergrowth.

By the time her brain released some of its processing capabilities from the act of bolting straight up the tree, she was perhaps another two meters farther from the clearing floor. She peered down—at least slightly down—at the peaceful behemoth now stripping bark from the woody growth it had just muscled through.

Not a Cardassian mining drone, but easily a hefty second in both mass and size. It towered a good four meters at the shoulder, with a huge, blunt head that sloped down and forward to give it the look of a crashball guardsman. A flare of bony plate ridged the back of its skull like a tiara, angling to fit almost seamlessly with the armorlike skin encasing the rest of its bulk; necessary, no doubt, to protect against whips and thorns and brambles as it plowed its way through the hostile overgrowth that Dax and Kira had reluctantly deemed impossible to move through. The eyes it turned up toward Kira were gentle, if stupid, and it paid her no more attention than it took to fondle her toe with the tip of its mobile upper lip before seeking out more edible fare among the tree's scrubby leaves.

"Don't worry—she's harmless."

Kira twisted a look toward the voice, trying to look more annoyed than embarrassed. "I was just climbing up for a better view." Then she realized how awkwardly she'd wrapped herself around a limb too narrow to truly hold her weight, and couldn't hold back her blush. "I guess I wasn't expecting company," she finally managed.

The Klingon girl smiled—a smile remarkably free

of Klingon disdain, for all that it came and went like a shooting star. Tossing a coil of woven plant fiber onto one shoulder, the girl picked her way across the top of the undisturbed brush-forest with an ease almost rivaling that of the silent primates who still danced back and forth across the large pachyderm's trail. Even the bloody bandage cinched around her thigh didn't seem to slow her much. She was easily the youngest Klingon Kira had seen here at the Vrag main camp, maybe a year or two past puberty, the equivalent of a Bajoran fourteen-year-old. She'd braided her glossy black hair into a queue more severe even than Worf habitually wore, but managed to offset that austerity with simple formfitting clothes and not so much as a suggestion of the armor and metalwork normally incorporated into even the most casual Klingon attire. She trailed one hand lightly down the huge animal's side as she passed. The gesture reminded Kira of nothing so much as the Bajoran farmers of her youth, dropping unconscious touches here and there as they walked among their herds, lest the clumsy creatures forget a fragile humanoid moved among them.

"It's not like you couldn't have heard her coming," the girl remarked as she stepped from brush-tops to tree and offered Kira her hand. *"Banchory* aren't very good at sneaking up on anyone."

Kira was surprised to recognize the Klingon word for *war wagon.* She cast another nervous look at the beast now languidly splintering a branch the size of her thigh, and it occurred to her that "war wagon" wasn't a bad description for these animals.

Gingerly lowering one foot toward the brace the girl created with her fist against the tree, Kira did her best to unwind herself from her perch in something resembling a dignified manner. "So did you bring these . . ." She tried to remember exactly how the girl had pronounced the word. ". . . these *banchory* from Qo'noS with you?"

The girl shook her head, caught Kira's other foot against her shoulder before the major could lose her balance, and guided her to the relative safety of the roots with a strength that would have been disproportionate in a Bajoran girl her age. "No, the *banchory* are native to Cha'Xirrac. There used to be thousands of them." She watched the *banchory* near them strip a long peel of bark from one of the other trees, turning it over, around, and inside out using nothing but the delicate manipulations of its lips and tongue. A flash of what might have been anger darkened the young girl's face. "They once used this clearing in the *tuq'mor* as an overnight spot, but they pretty much avoid us now."

By now, Kira had come to understand that *"tuq'mor"* meant the impossibly thick snarl of vines, bushes, trees, and ferns that seemed to cover every inch of Armageddon's surface. It occurred to Kira that she should have known that even Klingons couldn't beat out a clearing the size of this one without some kind of assistance.

Kira forced herself to sit without flinching when the *banchory* turned to examine the other side of its newly made clearing, all but brushing Kira with its stubby tail as it lumbered past. "So why do they stay away now?" she asked, as much to distract herself as because she really cared for an answer. She remembered the pile of mammoth carcasses by the sea. "Is it because you hunt them?"

"Because Gordek and the other men hunt them." The bitterness in her young voice startled Kira. She clutched the rope over her shoulder as though it were a precious *bat'leth,* defiantly meeting Kira's gaze. "Grandmother thinks we can do whatever we want because everyone on Cha'Xirrac will soon be dead. Gordek thinks we can do whatever we want just because we can." A peculiarly childlike frustration pursed the girl's lips. "I thought honor was about more than just how long your conduct was remembered, or what you could force others to do."

Kira's comm badge chirped before she could think of how best to respond to such a comment. "Dax to Kira." The Trill's voice sounded stiff with frustration. "Could you join me and *epetai* Vrag?"

"I'll be right there." She tapped off her badge, then managed a smile for the girl with less effort than she'd expected. "It was a pleasure to meet you—"

"K'Taran." She thrust out her hand with charmingly Human exuberance, but performed the actual handshake with a certain clumsiness that told Kira she'd never actually performed the social ritual before. "Any pleasure belongs to me," she said with deep sincerity. "The adults say that you are the one who brought a doctor, to help relieve our suffering while we wait for the end."

"Yes, we did." Kira felt abruptly stupid. Here she was chatting about local wildlife when it seemed almost everyone and everything in the House of Vrag could benefit from medical attention. "He was over in the children's billet earlier, but probably has time to look at your leg." She pointed out the trio of dugouts where she'd last seen Bashir, as though K'Taran might not know which ones they were. "He's slim and dark, with dark hair." Then she remembered the awkward Human handshake, and realized the girl might have mistaken her for Human despite her distinctly Bajoran features. If recognizing more subtle racial differences was challenging for Klingons, she didn't want to think about how hard it might be for the girl to tell Human male from Human female. Especially when the female was as tall and strong-boned as Dax. "He's the one with short hair, and no freckles."

"Thank you." For a moment, she looked like she might try the handshake again, but instead defaulted to one fist against her chest in the Klingon equivalent. "The concern you show for my people is honorable."

Kira watched her clamber off across the *tuq'mor,* marveling again at the complexity of any word that so many people could use to mean so many different things. That there could be so many different forms of Klingon pleasantry seemed only slightly more remarkable.

The dugout tree-cave currently hosting the Vrag Household conference didn't look appreciably different than when Kira had fled it more than an hour ago. Still too dark, still too humid, still crammed with snarling, snapping Klingons battling over yet another gradation in the definition of "honor." Roots snaked and intertwined so tightly through the walls that it was impossible to tell what had been naturally eroded into hollows by dripping water and what the Klingons had excavated themselves. All their attempts to personalize the dank, formless space—all their tapestries and sculptures and crudely fashioned furniture—only accentuated what a dark, dirty, pitiful hovel the dugout really was.

"Kira . . ."

Dax seemed to appear out of nowhere, her soft summons coalescing her figure from the shadows just inside the dugout's low door. She stood beside a rickety table, toying with the handle of a simple water jug and watching the Klingons as they argued. "We've got a problem."

Kira nodded. "You mean besides a shipload of missing Starfleet retirees and rocks the size of space stations falling on our heads?"

The humor seemed to break through Dax's pensiveness, and she turned away from the discussion with a crooked smile. "In addition to that." She dropped her voice to a more conspiratorial tone. "The Klingon blockade is back. Captain Sisko's going to cloak the *Defiant* and try to avoid detection."

Kira felt a little clench in her stomach. "What about the away team? Can we beam out?"

"Only if we leave now. No guarantees if the *Defiant* is discovered."

Because then the ship would have to raise shields, and there'd be no telling when they could lower them again. Kira paced in a slow circle, rubbing at her eyes. "That would mean leaving without the *Victoria Adams*'s crew." Prophets, what time was it back on board the *Defiant?* She felt as though she hadn't slept in weeks. "And we'll have to drag Bashir out by the hair. He won't leave as long as there are casualties."

"But if we don't leave now," Dax pointed out, ruthlessly nonpartisan, "we might not leave at all."

"Then you will simply be equal to the rest of us."

Kira tossed a glance over her shoulder, surprised to find what had seemed a truly apocalyptic argument now lulled enough for Rekan to eavesdrop. The others arrayed beyond her, waiting; Kira couldn't tell how much of their sour expressions were aimed at their *epetai* and how much at her. "We're not completely equal." Kira turned to face them squarely. She'd be damned if she'd let anyone claim the moral high ground, least of all a band of defeatist Klingon exiles. "We intend to survive."

Epetai Vrag lifted her lip in a civilized snarl. "Fighting a pointless battle does not add to your honor. The comets grow more thick daily. The longer you are here, the greater the likelihood you will be involved in a large-scale strike." She reached out with almost prim disapproval and flicked Dax's hand away from the water jug. "You would better serve yourselves by accepting the inevitable and preparing your spirits for their passage, or taking the one soldier you have found and leaving now."

Kira forced herself not to slap the jug to the floor. "I'm not ready to ignore all our options just yet." She turned pointedly to Dax. "Now that the blockade is back, we can't count on the *Defiant* deflecting any comets away from the planet."

"But the Klingons holding the hostages—"

"Can't get any help from us if we've broken cloak and been attacked by Klingons. We'll have to assume that the comets are going to keep coming. As it gets darker, we might be able to see them hit the atmosphere, maybe get a better feel for the volume and frequency."

"Unfortunately," the science officer sighed, "that won't help us pinpoint the impact zones." Dax lifted her eyes only a fraction, but Kira knew she'd made eye contact with the Klingon matriarch still hovering behind Kira's right shoulder. "We'd be safer if we moved farther inland. Right now, a major impact in the ocean could flood this camp."

Kira couldn't help blurting a disbelieving laugh. "We're fifty kilometers from the ocean!"

"Someday, when we have time," Dax said sweetly, "I'll tell you all about how tsunamis on twelfth century Caladaan created coast-to-coast flood plains on most of their lesser continents."

Kira didn't really care to hear the whole explanation—the fact that the example existed was point enough. "What about initiating a physical search for the survivors? Have we found out *anything* of use in your interviews?"

Dax shook her head, sighing. "Even if we knew exactly where to look, we can't get through the undergrowth unless we use phasers. And that would take longer than we have."

"What about using the *banchory?*"

Kira had meant the question to stimulate discussion, not to slap shock through the gathering like a hand across the face. The Klingons fell into knife-sharp silence, every one, and Dax asked, "The 'war wagons?' Kira, what are you talking about?"

"They're a native animal, four or five meters tall and built like a runabout. I saw one outside." She pointed behind her, out the door and vaguely in the direction of her encounter. "Dax, you've never seen something plow through brush the way these things can. We could cover literally kilometers every hour."

Dax turned a questioning look on the matriarch. *"Epetai* Vrag . . . ?" she prompted.

Rekan spoke without looking up from her hands, apparently fascinated with their cords of muscle and patterns of veins. "Was anyone with this beast you saw?"

"A girl." Kira tried to decipher the strange flux of emotion across the old Klingon's face, only to find herself wondering if every deep Klingon emotion looked to a Bajoran like anger. "She said her name was K'Taran."

A Klingon so old that his brow ridge had begun to gnarl huffed with sour laughter. "Another intractable daughter of Vrag."

Rekan snarled what might have been a Klingon threat, or perhaps just an animal noise of anger. It came overlaid with a memory of a young girl's voice saying, *Grandmother thinks we can do whatever we want,* and a sudden awareness of how similar two individual faces could be. *"Epetai* Vrag," Kira heard herself saying, almost gently, "is K'Taran your grand-daughter?"

Rekan answered almost before the question was finished. "I do not have a granddaughter."

"They do not cease to exist simply because you

might wish it so." The older male Klingon who'd spoken before shook off one elder's grasping hand, and aimed a backhanded swing at another.

The *epetai* composed her face into a haughty mask that might almost have been convincing if not for the anguish in her eyes. "The young ones who have left us live and die by their own choosings now. They have chosen a path that holds no honor and are no longer a concern to this House."

"They're a concern to *us*, if they are the ones who found our comrades." For about the fiftieth time since beaming down to Armageddon, Kira wondered how Dax could maintain such a show of nonjudgmental courtesy when all Kira wanted to do was tear stubborn Klingon heads off. "If you know where they are, tell us, so we can talk to them and perhaps help them all survive."

Rekan met Dax's gaze with a glare of challenge, but otherwise gave no sign that she'd heard much less intended to answer. "Honor dictated that this House be destroyed," she said instead. "That could not be avoided, but it was never *my* decision. We stand where we are because honor gave us no choice."

"And because you've agreed to die, everyone else has to die here with you?" Even Dax's voice had begun to sharpen with annoyance.

"She does not know where they are." The older male sniffed at the air as though displeased with the smell. "None of us knows. They have made themselves native. They wander the *tuq'mor* like animals. Except for the trails from their *banchory*, we see nothing of them."

Dax glanced at Kira. "But you said K'Taran was just here?"

Kira nodded. "She thanked us for bringing in a doctor and said—" The words were barely out of her mouth before their implication kicked her in the stomach. Turning slightly away from Dax, away from the others, she slapped at her comm badge so hard she was sure it would bruise her palm. "Kira to Bashir."

Furious at her own stupidity, more furious still at her embarrassment when nothing but silence echoed back across subspace.

"Kira to Bashir!"

Nothing. No doctor, no wayward Klingon, not even an open channel to hint that Bashir's communicator still existed. The doctor was gone.

Rekan Vrag was the first to break the silence, and although there was triumph in her voice, its icy chill told Kira it wasn't a triumph she was proud of. "You have given up another hostage," she said accusingly. "Now do you begin to see what an abomination is a Klingon without honor?"

CHAPTER
5

BASHIR WASN'T SURE which irritated him more—being bound and blindfolded like some sort of political prisoner, or knocking his head against the floor of his captors' lumbering vehicle every time it jolted over uneven terrain or crashed its way through a new stand of underbrush. He *did* know that the coil of fear gaining strength at the pit of his belly only exacerbated the more facile emotions that lurched to the surface. Fear for the *Victoria Adams*'s still-missing crew; fear for his two assistants, who shouldn't be abandoned to deal with so many Klingon casualties on their own; and, yes, fear for himself at the thought of being separated from his landing party with a star system full of potential disaster hanging over all their heads. Being all alone in an alien scrub forest when a comet sterilized the ecosystem was not one of his more romantic visions of a heroic death.

He felt the little flutter of his comm badge's chirp from where his body weight pinned it against the rocking floor. Above him, the Klingon whose knee had been in contact with his back since the beginning of their trip stirred uneasily, grunting.

"Look, this is ridiculous." Bashir paused, waiting with muscles tensed for a blow or a shove or a wad of gag in his mouth to silence him. When none came, he swallowed hard and disciplined his voice into something resembling composure. "That's my away team. If you don't let me talk to them, they'll just trace my badge signal and find me."

A strong hand snaked beneath him, prying him away from the floor less roughly than Bashir expected and plucking the badge from his uniform breast with the same casual dexterity an entomologist might use to capture a roving beetle. He thought he felt his captor shift and spin the way a person did when flinging a small object, but couldn't very well listen for the whisper of the badge's flight over the crash and rumble of their transportation. Fear finally cut its moorings in his stomach and diffused throughout his system.

"All right. The badge is gone. Fine." Pushing up with one knee and one elbow, he managed to roll himself clumsily. If hopelessness had one good trait, it was that it wasted little time converting fear into the anger more useful for survival. "Can you please untie me now?"

A grab at the front of his uniform caught him when he struggled to his knees. "Sit!"

It was the first time anyone had spoken to him since the girl who'd served as bait lured him into the underbrush in search of casualties. This voice sounded suspiciously the same. "Just tell me where—"

"Sit!"

She didn't wait for his compliance this time. Tugging firmly downward on the front of his tunic, she clearly meant to muscle him back to the floor, where he'd spent the first part of this liaison. He didn't consciously resist—rearing back away from her grip was no more than an instinctive reaction against being forcibly placed anywhere when he couldn't see the world around him. But he knew it was a mistake the moment his center of gravity slipped past thirty degrees. Hands clutched first at his shoulders, then at his waistband as he tumbled backward, then disappeared entirely when he hit free-fall.

The ground he landed on was softer than he'd thought, not to mention much closer to the start of his fall than it had seemed when he'd first been hauled up several meters and dumped into the transport's open bed. It poked and prodded him like a bundle of sticks, but gave just enough not to puncture anything. Springy vibrations sketched frantic movement all around him, but it was the young girl's voice—"Get aside! Humans are fragile—let him breathe!"—that surprised him the most. Perhaps he wasn't such an insignificant prisoner after all.

Thin, rough fingers picked at the bindings on his wrists, the knot at the base of his skull cinching his blindfold into place. He squinted hard against the light—

Oh, God, it's only barely morning back home!

—and blinked focus into the ring of faces crouched around him.

For one instant, the term "going native" meant a little more to him than it ever had before.

Then he realized that none of the muzzled, grayish faces bending over him were Klingons, and it relieved his confusion at least a little. Their eyes seemed big only in comparison to the smallness of their other features, muddy green and curious above a button rodent-nose and a mouth so tiny that it announced "insectivore" even before the first of them rolled out a long, prehensile tongue to swipe at its corneas. Bashir thought he might be able to scoop one up under either arm—they couldn't have massed more than fifteen kilos apiece—but they probably didn't need his help to move about their native environment. They ran on all fours like lemurs, their slim question-mark tails lifted playfully over their backs. The grace with which they navigated the upper storys of dense foliage put a zero-g dancer to shame.

They didn't even scatter or squawk when the young female Klingon jumped down into their midst. "Are you damaged?" she demanded of Bashir, somewhat testily.

"I . . . uh . . ." He managed to tear his eyes away from the plushly furred primates, only to fixate all over again on the huge, armor-plated monster calmly picking at whatever brush and limbs it could reach. It had smashed an impressive trail through the knotted undergrowth without even breaking a sweat; Bashir was suddenly glad he'd been caught by the foliage canopy and hadn't toppled all the way to the ground, another two or three meters down. "Uh . . . no . . ." he finally stammered. A Klingon—that's right, there was a Klingon, and he should probably look at her when he answered instead of staring at her strange menagerie. "No, I'm fine, thank you . . ."

"Good." She clapped both hands to the front of his uniform, then hauled him very carefully to his feet, as though afraid he might break if she dropped him again. "Then will you behave?"

Bashir hazarded a glance to left and right. Except for the winding trail torn like a scar through the brush cover, there was nothing to see except kilometer upon kilometer of undulating, scrubby plain. As though the plants had clawed their way a half-dozen meters above the ground and re-created their own surface beyond the touch of mud and burrowing creatures. Even though a loose, light foliage above them shielded most of the humid undergrowth from the sun, Bashir couldn't glimpse so much as a hint of the massive trees that had marked the perimeter of the Klingon's camp.

"Will you behave?" the girl asked again, more loudly.

How many days would it take people on foot to cross the same terrain this creature had traveled in an hour? "Yes," he admitted faintly. "Yes . . . I guess I will."

The big herbivore was more comfortable to ride than Bashir expected. More comfortable than when he'd thought its broad back was the floor of a land-going truck, at least, and he'd been forced to endure every bump and thump and rattle. He knelt just aft of the great beast's shoulders the way the girl showed him, tucking his heels beneath him and being careful to keep all body parts clear of where its bony skull ridge scissored against the plates on its back when it moved its head. The rocking of its big, slow steps proved almost soothing now that he could see where he was going and move his body to compensate.

It pushed through the snarl of plant life with such unhurried power that Bashir smiled slightly in awe. One ponderous step at a time, chin lifted above the froth of greenery, casually splintering thickets and trampling bracken like a ship smashing through Arctic ice. It didn't even seem to notice the schools of primates capering alongside it, dolphins in the wake of a great whale.

Bashir twisted to look at the silent girl behind him. "This . . . animal—"

"They're called *banchory*."

This was the first word she'd spoken that wasn't in Standard. The unconscious data collector at the back of his brain noted this as an interesting detail, even though nothing about it really seemed to mean anything. "These *banchory*, then. I saw some of their carcasses when we first beamed down, back on the beach near Gordek's camp." Feeling the life and majesty in the animal under him only made that memory all the more horrific. "They're clearly not Klingon in origin. I hadn't realized you'd had time to domesticate anything on Armageddon."

The girl still didn't look at him, her eyes trained forward as though guiding the *banchory* with her own sight. "The Klingons have domesticated nothing here. The *banchory* belong to the *xirri*."

"The . . . ?" He broke off the question when she swept a gesture toward the rear of their mount. No point trying to turn any further without standing— he'd only tip himself off the *banchory* again. Besides, he had a feeling he knew what she'd meant to indicate. They surrounded the *banchory* like monkey-tailed butterflies.

The slender, silent primates snatched handfuls and tonguefuls of bugs from the air as the *banchory* shook the undergrowth with its passage. Once or twice, a bevy of what appeared to be adolescents bounced eagerly up from below with forelimbs full of broken nuts and shattered seed pods. Bashir couldn't tell if it was insects their agile tongues probed for among those broken pieces, or pulverized bits of plant meat to complement the rest of their diet. Whichever it was, they hardly looked the role of master *banchory* trainers as they chased after swarms of disturbed lizards and jumped for escaping flies. More like ramoras, taking advantage of some greater creature's impact on the world.

It didn't seem an observation worth sharing, considering his situation.

Looking behind him, he offered his hand over his left shoulder and tried on one of his more charming smiles. "By the way, I'm Dr. Julian Bashir. I thought you might like to know who you were kidnaping."

"I know." But, to his surprise, she still took his hand and shook it with solemn gusto. "K'Taran."

"Of the House of Vrag?"

A flush of warm magenta darkened her face, and she gnashed her teeth quietly. "Of the House of me."

"I see . . ." That seemed as good an end to that round of discussion as any. Shifting himself to look forward again, Bashir watched the world dip and sway in time with the *banchory*'s ground-eating strides. "Might I ask where we're going?"

"You're a doctor," K'Taran said bluntly in his ear. "We have wounded."

His first thought was to question who exactly "we" might be. Then he caught a flash of velvet khaki out of the corner of his eye, as three playful *xirri* raced past in some kind of game, and he thought perhaps he already knew. "K'Taran . . ." He glanced away from the bobbing horizon, wanting to look back at her but unsure if she'd appreciate his scrutiny. "You realize there's a very good chance everything on this planet—*xirri* and *banchory* included—will be dead in just another few days?"

He almost thought he felt the chill of her denial sweep its way up his spine. But perhaps it was just the threat of imminent rain that seemed to hang on every dew-damp leaf they passed. "Klingons don't cease to fight just because the odds are hopeless."

"I'm sure that's true. But the crash victims you've been holding hostage aren't a part of your fight. If you let us evacuate them, I'm sure we can make arrangements to take anyone else who—"

"My grandmother will never let anyone go." For just that moment, she sounded like a little girl—petulant, angry, despairing for something she'd hoped for from her adults but never gotten. "Besides," she continued in a more defiant tone, "my shield-mates and I would never leave without the *xirri*. They're our friends. Like your scientists, they took no honor promise to die."

Neither did I, Bashir wanted to tell her. But a roll of distant thunder distracted him, and a vision of tragedy swirled up from the forest floor to swallow his thinking before he could recapture his train of thought.

Despite the unchanging nature of the planet's overgrown surface, the site of the devastation somehow snuck up on them when Bashir wasn't ready to see it. Naked, burn-scarred limbs jutted out over a wasteland of mud, charcoal, and blackened bone The brush was singed well beyond this terminal edge; it hadn't been easy to see amid the normal mix of woody scrub and needlelike leaves, but now Bashir recognized the sere of heat so intense it had razed a vast patch of forest down to stubble. The local plants had already begun to fight their way back— faster-growing and more tenacious even than Britain's notorious heather. A furry blush of green laid an inch-high carpet over stubble, stones, and half-dead brush. Rather than renewing the desolation, though, it served instead to highlight the great emptiness. As though someone had thrown a hasty blanket over the corpses in the hopes no one would recognize the outlined forms.

The *banchory* brought them some distance into the wasteland. Its heavy steps hushed to a negligible crunching over the baby growth, but it filled the void with a low groaning that sounded almost like sobs. Anthropomorphizing, Bashir realized. It only greeted the pod of other *banchory* milling near a confusion of upthrust stones; they answered in equally loquacious murmurs, waggling their flexible upper lips and swishing the stubs of their hairless tails. It was a hard image to shake, though, when he glimpsed what looked like a half-filled inland sea another kilometer or two toward the horizon. Peaty brown water gushed into it from all sides, waterfalls of runoff from the mud underlying a continent of canopy. Bashir doubted there could ever be enough to fill the void.

"Have you been living here?" he asked K'Taran as she climbed past him to slide down the *banchory*'s nose.

"No." She waved him down, holding out her arms the way a parent might when preparing to catch a child at the end of a slide. "But we came when they needed us."

The *banchory*'s nose was as solid as the rest of it, and it hardly seemed to notice his weight as he shuffled down it. Mud, slick and swimming with ash, belched up around his ankles when he landed, and he added another couple of days to a search party's travel time. Assuming, of course, anyone had a chance to come looking for him at all.

They slogged toward a long row of shelters at the edges of the destruction. Long, stiff fans of greenery had been stacked across what remained of the undergrowth's canopy, pitiful protection from both sun and rain. The cadre of Klingons milling among the injured *xirri* tested and reinforced the structure almost unconsciously as they went about their duties. A deeper mat of branches had been piled directly on top of the mud to form a crude bedding for the wounded. Bashir reassured himself that they'd at least tried to keep their patients above the mire, if not strictly out of the elements. This was a great show of consideration for Klingons, if what he'd seen at Gordek's camp was any indication.

"How did you know they needed you?" He dropped to his knees on the edge of the branch carpet, not wanting to actually walk on the mat and spread muck among the wounded. "Did the *xirri* send for you?"

A pair of Klingon men—neither much older than K'Taran—glanced up from a few feet away, but it was K'Taran who finally answered. "We knew they had a home near here. Once Kreveth realized what had happened, we knew the *xirri* would be needing help. So we came." She remained standing behind him, out of both his light and way. Even so, Bashir could feel defiance rolling off her like heat. "I told you before— they're our friends."

Indeed she had. He decided not to press the question further.

A *xirri* appeared with his medkit, dropping out of the brush's fringes like a bird hopping off a branch. Bashir thanked the little primate absently, and didn't even think about blushing until after he'd cracked the case and dug out his tricorder and one of the smaller tissue regenerators. It wasn't as though K'Taran would laugh at him for such a display of automatic courtesy. In fact, she was probably delighted to see him apparently taking her pronouncements so seriously. Still, he didn't want to lie to her, not even by implication. What he saw in front of him was a thin, sick lemur with no more evidence of sentience in its expressionless face than there was in its prehensile tail. It didn't change his willingness to help it in any way he could, but it also didn't distract him from the awareness that there were perfectly sapient creatures hidden somewhere in this jungle who also desperately needed saving.

He was almost halfway through the medical tricorder's primary scan when he realized that nothing about the readings made any sense. Frowning, he reinitialized the sequence and passed it over the *xirri*'s unmoving body again. K'Taran waited until he aborted that scan altogether before demanding, "What's wrong?"

Something about being so close to an impact site, probably. Interference on a level Dax could no doubt explain, but which left him only with a kit full of half-useless equipment and not even a suspicion of how to fix it. All the same, he punched up the tricorder's recalibration command. "Something's the matter with my equipment," he explained, not looking up from the growing scroll of gibberish on the small device's screen. "I'm not getting intelligible readings."

"Fine." She suddenly bent close over one shoulder and plucked the tricorder from his hand. "Then you can stop playing with your toys and start helping them."

Bashir stopped himself from attempting to snatch back the device, scowling up at her instead. "It's not that simple. I don't know anything about *xirri* physiology. Unless I can collect data on how their bodies function, I can't determine what drugs they can tolerate, or what treatments they might require. I don't even know how to calibrate a tissue regenerator!"

"The *xirri* will tell you if what you're doing is right."

Frustration throbbed dully at the back of his forehead. He hunched over and rubbed at his eyes, suddenly wanting to be home and safe and sleeping in his own Cardassian bed with no Klingons or alien lemurs to worry about. "K'Taran," he sighed. "Can the *xirri* even speak?" He hadn't heard a sound from them. Not even so much as a grunt.

K'Taran verified this observation with a simple, "They make no noise at all."

Of course they didn't—speech, language, true communication . . . It would all make things too easy, too straightforward for this mission. "They're monkeys," Bashir heard himself saying. The sound of his voice wrapped around those words almost shocked him. "However close you've grown to them, whatever feelings they might have for you, it's not the same as language. You can't run on your own instincts and call it communication." He looked up, expecting to see fury on her face, and added sincerely, "I'm sorry."

She stared back at him, a surprising amount of weary frustration in her own young features. Waving brusquely at the *xirri* who'd first approached with the medkit, she fished into her pocket without saying so much as a word. The skinny primate flashed over to her, green eyes intent, and K'Taran flipped a small polygonal token toward it with a flick of her thumb.

The *xirri* caught it with its tongue, then spat the chip into one naked palm. It looked like something broken off a seal of pressed wax, or chipped from a larger stone. Popping the token back into its mouth, the *xirri* leapt into the burned-out brush and disappeared.

Curiosity burned sleepily in his eyes, but Bashir had learned better than to ask for what K'Taran hadn't volunteered. He sat with the remnants of his medkit, and waited.

By the time the *xirri* returned, sitting still had combined with the abysmal lateness of the hour shipboard to sink Bashir almost over the brink into dozing. He thought at first that he'd imagined the *xirri*'s multicolored companion, a nonsense dream caricature brought to life. But when it approached to within touching distance, he could smell the musky plant life odor of the pollen scrubbed into its fur, and see the sheen of drying wetness among the crust of colored muds striped over its skull and face and shoulders. The painted *xirri* squatted into a tall sit that placed it almost on a height with Bashir, and peered intently first at the doctor's hands, then the insensate patient on the grassy mat before them.

K'Taran slapped a tissue regenerator into Bashir's lap. "Go on, healer. Heal."

It was pointless. Bashir knew it was pointless—he was too tired, the *xirri* was too badly injured, and he just didn't have time to learn everything he needed to know to be an adequate physician to these animals. But even if he could find it in his heart to deny treatment while there was some small chance he could give relief, he had a feeling K'Taran and the other Klingons now gathering around her wouldn't have much patience with his ethical standards. Hadn't he said everything on the planet would be dead in a matter of days, no matter what they did here? So what real difference did it make if even his best efforts couldn't save a single *xirri*? His best efforts couldn't save any of them. He had to depend on Dax and the captain for that.

He examined the little *xirri* in front of him as best he could by touch and sight, making assumptions about its body chemistry based on such slight evidence as the condition of its mucal membranes, the color of its blood. Where muscle showed beneath folds of torn dermal layer, he probed the elasticity with gentle fingers, pretended its ropes and striations told him anything really useful. Then he set the regenerator with a few tentative taps at the controls.

He'd barely turned the head of the device toward his patient before the painted *xirri* next to him reached out and wound cool fingers about his wrist. Bashir hesitated, switched off the regenerator by reflex, and blinked down at the little primate.

Licking its eyes in what might have been agitation, the painted *xirri* abruptly ducked one long finger into the pucker of its mouth and brought it out smeared with the same colored pollen that tinted its hair. It drew slowly, lightly around the edges of the wound. Brilliant red on the innermost edges, followed by rings of saffron and umber shot through with smears of green. Apparently happy with whatever it had meant to convey, it settled back on its haunches with a final flick of its long tongue, and cocked an unreadable look up at Bashir.

He didn't know what else to do—the pounding of his heart against his breastbone seemed to drown out rational thought, leaving him to flounder in emotion. He reset the device almost at random, moved toward the patient again.

This time when the *xirri* stopped him, it was already busy accentuating the ugly green, blotting out the saner colors with bold, hectic strokes. Bashir adjusted the regenerator in the other direction; the *xirri* didn't interfere again.

As he watched bundles of muscle gradually repair, and skin begin its slow crawl across the open wound, it occurred to Bashir that it was probably best that his main diagnostic equipment had failed him for the moment, limiting what treatment he could supply. The way his hands were shaking, he wouldn't have been safe doing surgery, anyway. And even the most newly recognized sentient species—no matter how silent and unassuming—deserved better than the jitterings of a shell-shocked Human doctor.

Sisko's luck held for four of the five hours he'd allotted himself for sleep. His dreams roiled uneasily with cloaked Klingon vessels that turned out to be Cardassian warships hurling comets at the *Defiant*. When Odo's gravelly voice condensed out of one thunderous collision, Sisko at first burrowed deeper into his pillow and tried to ignore it.

"Captain Sisko, report to the bridge," Odo repeated impatiently. "There's a Cardassian vessel entering this system."

"Damn!" Sisko rolled out of his bunk, still feeling

trapped in the remnants of his nightmare. He yanked on his uniform and boots. "Have the Klingons done anything to it yet?"

"No, but they may just be biding their time. The Cardassian ship is still out of weapons range."

"I'm on my way." He headed for the door without waiting for an acknowledgment. Worf met him in the narrow corridor bisecting the crew's quarters, looking much more alert than Sisko felt. They strode into the turbolift and told it, "Bridge!" in curt unison. The lift hummed upward.

"Any news from the away team?" he asked his tactical officer.

Worf slanted him a curious glance. "You were aware that I had the away team's secure channel routed to my cabin?"

"Just a lucky guess. What have you heard?"

"Little of promise," the Klingon said somberly. "Dr. Bashir was discovered missing after Commander Dax last spoke with us. They have a fix on his comm badge and are looking for him now, but Dax estimates it could take several hours to reach his presumed location."

"How did he get lost?"

"Unclear, sir. Major Kira believes he might have been kidnapped by the same group holding the *Victoria Adams*'s crew."

"Lovely." Sisko scrubbed a hand across his face, wondering what else could possibly go wrong on this mission. The turbolift doors hissed open before he could ask further questions.

Odo turned to face them from his watchful stance

beside the command chair. As far as Sisko knew, the Changeling never did sit there, even when he was left in command of the *Defiant's* bridge.

"The Cardassian ship is preparing to enter the far end of the cometary belt," Odo said, passing information along with Starfleet succinctness. Sisko glanced up at the viewscreen, but Farabaugh's computer model had been replaced by a real-time image of Armageddon against a comet-hazed starfield. A blinking red cursor now marked the position of the cloaked Klingon vessel, in what looked like a geostationary orbit above the comet-scarred main continent. "Mr. Thornton is constructing an approximate sensor image of the Cardassian vessel, using preliminary data from our long-range scans."

"Good." Sisko sat and gave an approving nod to the dark-haired engineering tech who'd replaced Farabaugh at the science console. "Put it on screen when ready."

"Aye, sir. Convergent resolution coming up now."

The viewscreen abruptly distorted, shrinking Armageddon to a distant dust-stained globe in the upper corner, while a steady twinkle in the background enlarged into a massive battle-armored ship, many times larger than the *Defiant*. Sisko whistled when he saw its familiar military markings. "Looks like we have some very official Cardassian visitors," he remarked.

"My data banks identify this ship as the Cardassian battle cruiser *Olxinder,*" Odo said from his console. "Commanded by our friend *Gul* Hidret."

"Why am I not surprised?" Sisko leaned back in his chair, frowning as he watched the Cardassian ship enter the comet field. Unlike the Klingons, they took no evasive action, nor did they appear to slow and angle their shields to deflect the comets they encountered. Sisko wondered if Hidret understood the danger he was in—unlike the small *Defiant* and equally small *Jfolokh*-class Klingon vessel, the *Olxinder* was practically guaranteed to get itself slammed with comets at the speed it was traveling. A moment later, the blue-white flare of phasers across the viewscreen answered his question. *Gul* Hidret was dealing with the comets with characteristic Cardassian arrogance, by summarily shattering to pieces every large fragment in his battle cruiser's path. Sisko supposed the ship's heavy armor could take care of the rest.

"For someone who was worried about Klingon aggression, he's not exactly trying to sneak in, is he?" Odo commented.

"No," Worf agreed. "I thought *Gul* Hidret did not believe us when we said there were no Klingons here."

Sisko shook his head. "Commander, I've found that what Cardassians say they believe and what they truly believe have about as much in common as Ferengi prices do with the true value of an object." He watched the *Olxinder* execute a gracelessly efficient turn, its corona of phaser fire leaving an afterglow of superheated gases in its wake.

"But then why come? He must know he cannot locate either of us while we are cloaked," Worf pointed out. "Why would Hidret make himself such a tempting target for attack?"

"Perhaps to provoke us into it," Sisko said.

Odo snorted. "More likely to provoke the Klingons into it."

"Thus giving the Cardassians all the excuse they need to start a war," Sisko finished grimly.

"The Klingons have just opened a hailing frequency to the Cardassian battleship, Captain," Thornton said, glancing over his shoulder. "It's on an open channel."

Sisko exchanged puzzled looks with Worf and Odo. The last thing he'd expected the Klingons to do was talk first and shoot later. "Put it on the main screen, split channel."

"Aye, sir." The phaser-wreathed glow of the *Olxinder* vanished, turning instead into *Gul* Hidret's furrowed visage on one side and an even more familiar Klingon face on the other. It wasn't the magnificent mane of gray hair or the broad brow that jogged Sisko's memory so much as the surprising glint of humor in those crinkled eyes. He snapped his teeth closed on a surprised curse. What in God's name was Curzon Dax's old drinking buddy doing out in the middle of the Cardassian demilitarized zone?

"Ah, Hidret," Kor purred in the same tone of pleasant reminiscence he might have used to greet an old lover. "What a joy it is to see your face and recall once more the delightful memory of how I demolished your last battle cruiser. How nice of the Cardassian High Command to give you another."

"It pleases me, too, Dahar Master Kor, to see that your legendary drunken stupors have not cost you *all* of your titles and privileges in the Klingon Empire," Hidret shot back with equally venomous politeness. The old *gul*'s lined face was rigid with some fierce emotion, but Sisko couldn't tell whether it was fury or satisfaction. "Although they have obviously condemned you to manning an obscure post in an unimportant system."

"How unimportant can it be, when a Cardassian ship as magnificent as yours drops by to pay a visit?" Kor retorted. "Although it is a Klingon tradition to welcome visitors, I'm afraid you might not like my particular brand of hospitality."

Hidret raised his brows in mock incredulity. "Are you telling me I have to leave? And here I thought you would welcome my help in evacuating the planet."

"What?" All traces of humor evaporated from Kor's eyes, giving Sisko a glimpse of the formidable warrior Jadzia Dax had once been willing to risk her life for. "What are you talking about?"

A little more satisfaction leaked out around the edges of Hidret's inscrutable expression. "Aren't there Klingons stranded down on that planet, being bombarded by comets? I came to help you rescue them."

Sisko exchanged startled glances with O'Brien and Worf. "I thought Hidret suspected those exiles of being planted, to give the Klingons an excuse to claim the planet."

Worf snorted. "More Cardassian lies."

"More Cardassian lies!" Kor echoed, his voice a bubbling growl. "I don't know where you got that information, but it's wrong. No one here needs to be rescued."

"You're telling me there are no Klingons on that planet?"

The Dahar Master bared his stained and shattered teeth. "I'm telling you that *no one needs to be rescued.* The Klingons on this planet have chosen their fate, and it is my duty as a Dahar Master to make sure that no one interferes with it. It is a matter of honor."

Hidret pointed an accusing finger at the viewscreen. "And you can make no allowances for the Cardassians who are dying of *ptarvo* fever, and need the drug that only this planet can provide?"

Kor snorted. "Bring me a Cardassian dying of *ptarvo* fever, and I'll be glad to let him beam down to Cha'Xirrac to be cured. In the meantime, old enemy, the only allowance I will make is to let you turn tail and run before I start firing."

"But—"

"But *nothing!*" The Klingon's sudden eruption into a roar made even Sisko start. "And if you ask one more question, your answer is going to be a photon torpedo!"

Gul Hidret snorted in apparent disgust, but the triumphant glint in his eyes made Sisko's stomach roil in apprehension. He was starting to suspect why the old Cardassian had engineered this unlikely confrontation. "From you or from your ally?"

"Ally?" Kor demanded.

"The cloaked Starfleet vessel we spoke to several hours ago. Her transmission originated from within this system."

"You spoke to a cloaked Starfleet vessel?" Kor's eyes narrowed. "That means the *Defiant* is here."

"And they didn't even bother to inform you?" *Gul* Hidret showed his own teeth in a maliciously triumphant smile. "How rude of them—" A photon torpedo explosion slammed across the open channel, and the Cardassian's smile vanished. "All right, I'm leaving, damn you! Stop shooting!"

Hidret's side of the connection sizzled and went black, but Kor's scowling face didn't vanish with it. "I know you're listening in on this, Benjamin Sisko. If not, then Dax probably is. Take my advice, both of you, and follow that old Cardassian fool out of this system. If you don't, I'm afraid I will be honor-bound to hunt you down and kill you."

CHAPTER
6

"Now I know why they call this stuff *tuq'mor*."

From several feet above Dax's head—which was currently at the same elevation as her feet, although none of her was actually on the ground—Kira peered down through the tangled vegetation at her. Even higher up, an eerily silent troop of lemur-like primates leaped and skittered through the swaying twigs of the scrub forest, spattering them with dislodged rain drops and pollen.

"What does *tuq'mor* mean, anyway?" Kira asked, her tone so carefully measured that Dax knew she was trying hard not to laugh.

"It's the name of an ancient Klingon goddess. Also known as the mother of curses." Her rump-first fall into a pocket of weaker branches had left Dax suspended in a position too jackknifed to scramble out of. Even though she was surrounded by thickly grown shrubs and intertwining ivy, their rain-slick branches gave her nothing to grab onto. She wriggled a hand down beneath her to see if she was close enough to the ground to push off. Cool muck promptly closed around her fingers, soft and clinging as liquid silk. She cursed in Klingon and wiped her hand across her damp trousers. "See what I mean?"

"I'm starting to." Kira reached a hand down to her through the greenery. "You better let me help you up."

"Brace yourself," Dax warned as they locked hands. "My skeleton alone probably weighs more than you do."

"Never fear. I won't drop you." Kira dug her boot heels into the braided mat of branches on which she stood, making it bounce a little beneath her. She used her smaller weight to advantage, Dax noticed, leaning back to leverage it into her motion without overbalancing. With one smooth pull, she hauled Dax out of her jackknifed spill up to stand beside her, then lifted a smug eyebrow. "Easy as a zero-gee somersault."

"Don't rub it in." Dax snagged an overhead vine to steady herself, feeling the branches creak and sag beneath her weight. Now that she was upright and free, she had time to notice the welt of smarting skin on her cheek where a branch had slapped her during her fall. "I'm already jealous that you can walk across branches I break."

"Sorry." Kira took a backward step to ease the load on the swaying *tuq'mor*. "Maybe you better go first from now on, to make sure the branches can hold you."

"I probably should." Ever since they had entered the maze of vegetation, they had been forced to walk anywhere from one to three meters above the densely forested ground level, with another meter or two of shrubbery making an interlaced canopy overhead. The air inside the *tuq'mor* was shadowed and cool, mist-filled in places, and always soundless. No vagrant breeze could stir the densely knotted branches of this ecosystem. It reminded Dax of a coral reef, braced to withstand the crashing of unseen waves. "Although that means we'll be going even slower."

Kira glanced up at the place where the leaves glowed brightest, backlit by unseen sunlight. "We're only making about half a kilometer an hour through this stuff as it is. Another hour or two shouldn't matter. At this rate, we're not going to catch up with Dr. Bashir until sometime next week."

Dax tapped a familiar command into her tricorder, then frowned as she compared the response it gave her with previous readouts. "No, we're getting much closer. According to Julian's comm badge, he's located just a few hundred meters northeast of us."

Kira must have heard the worry beneath her words. "His readings haven't changed at all?"

"No." Dax pushed onward through the tangled branches, trying not to think of all the ominous reasons for that consistency. More to herself than to Kira, she said, "If these Klingon children really are trying to protect the whole planet, they have no reason to hurt Julian. They could have taken him to tend to some wounded survivors—"

"But Boughamer said he was the only one badly hurt," Kira reminded her.

More rain drops dappled down from the forest canopy, stirring up shreds of mist from the swamp below. Tiny, silent lizards leaped through the leaves to escape Dax's progress, jeweled flashes in the shadowy light. "Didn't you say, though, that K'Taran herself was hurt?"

"No, I said she *looked* hurt," Kira said, gloomily. "She had a bloody bandage wrapped around one leg. But that might have been as much a lie as the rest of what she said."

Dax slanted a curious look back through the greenery at her. "Did she really lie to you, Nerys? I thought you said she admitted to being *epetai* Vrag's granddaughter."

"She did," the Bajoran admitted with grudging fairness. "And mostly what she talked about was how she didn't think there was any honor in killing the *banchory*. Or in waiting around for the comets to hit. I suppose she was telling the truth about that, too." Kira snorted. "She's at least fighting to survive *sylshessa*, instead of just folding her hands and getting sanctimonious about it. I might not like how she's doing it, but I have to give her credit for trying."

Dax shook her head at her friend's exasperated comment. She should have known that Kira, former freedom fighter and military officer, would find more to admire in K'Taran's active resistance to death than in Rekan Vrag's honorable acquiescence to it. "There are as many codes of honor among the Klingons as there are interpretations of Prophecies among the *vedeks*," she informed the Bajoran. "By not lying to you when she kidnaped Bashir, K'Taran may have been obeying her own code. But, in a larger sense, by struggling to evade the justice meted out by the High Council, in her *epetai*'s eyes she has dishonored their house."

"And was Chancellor Gowron being honorable when he exiled the House of Varg to certain death on this planet?" Kira demanded.

"Possibly." Dax felt the branches below her thin out over a more watery stretch of swamp, and angled to the left to find more secure footing. Another troop of primates skittered out of a flowering hedge as she skirted it, their velvet-plush shoulders freckled with colorful blossoms and pollen dust in an unconscious imitation of Trill freckling. "What a Klingon considers honorable depends as much on context as on precedent. Depending on what infraction the House of Vrag committed, this sentence of exile might have been vindictive, or it might have been an act of mercy."

Kira heaved a sigh. "I'll never understand Klingons."

"And they'll never understand us," Dax smiled. "They find our Vulcan and Human and Trill codes of law almost totally incomprehensible, because they're meant to apply no matter what the motive or result." She paused to map a path across an almost-open stretch of running water before she trusted her weight to the arching branches. "I can understand *epetai* Vrag and I can even understand her granddaughter. The only Klingon here I find hard to decipher is Gordek."

"Really?" Kira leaped through the screen of delicate branches to land on the other side, if her wildly swaying perch on a flexing limb could really have been called a landing. Her athletic ease was all the more enviable because it was totally unconscious. "What's so hard to figure out about him? He's a petty tyrant who wants to start his own little empire, even if it's only going to last until the next tsunami levels the coast."

"True." Dax ventured out at last on the largest bridging limb. "But the fact that he was willing to bargain with us to get the equipment he wanted—"

The wood cracked ominously beneath her weight as she reached the end. Dax cursed and took a long, not entirely directed step across the cooler breeze of the stream chasm with its murmur of hovering insects, then found herself sinking through bracken like a turbolift descending. A small hand reached out and caught her, this time by the indestructible nape of her Starfleet tunic, and hauled her back to safe footing for a second time.

"Thanks," she said, regaining her breath. "Damn *tuq'mor.*"

"Mother of curses," Kira reminded her. "Maybe we should have made a sacrifice to her before we started chasing after Bashir."

"Or maybe we should have followed that *banchory* trail, even though it didn't seem to lead in the right—"

Dax broke off abruptly. She'd found an open crevice through the hedge wall and thrust her head and shoulders through it, only to emerge into an unexpected chasm in the *tuq'mor.* It looked as if someone had taken a phaser and carved a canyon through the dense vegetation: one meter wide, four meters high and stretching out of sight along its sinuous length. Coppery gold sunlight slanted down into it, warm and inviting. She cursed again, long and hard this time.

"What is it?" Kira demanded, wriggling through the dense hedge to pop out just to Dax's left. "Blood of the Prophets!"

"Mother of curses," Dax said again, wryly, then hauled herself free of the hedge and clambered down to the open path. It was floored by the same silk-soft mud as the rest of the *tuq'mor,* but her boots sank only a few centimeters in before they hit firmer soil. The *banchory* had compacted this forest highway as well as blazed it. She cocked her head, listening to the distant, deep hooting that echoed up the path. "If we follow this now, we might have to make a real quick exit."

Kira landed beside her with a squishy thump, oblivious to the spatters of mud that threw across both her and Dax. "Will it take us to Bashir's comm signal?"

Dax consulted her tricorder and nodded. "Yes, it's the perfect heading from here. Almost too perfect . . ."

Kira glanced over her shoulder, squinting against the sun. "You think it's a trap?"

"I don't know." Dax kept her tricorder on as they walked, watching their mapped coordinates get closer and closer to the ones she was receiving from Bashir's comm badge. "But it's definitely not a coincidence." She skirted a large pile of olive brown *banchory* droppings. Their half-sweet, half-fetid alien smell was so strong in the still air that she knew they had to be recent. "Wait." She grabbed at Kira's shoulder to stop her, then swung around with the tricorder chirping a proximity alert at her, louder and louder. "According to this, Julian should be within a meter of us. It looks like the signal's coming from the wall of *tuq'mor* over there."

Kira scowled and began yanking apart the thick stems of succulents, ivy, and shrubs, trying to find a place wide enough to step through. The *tuq'mor* seemed thicker along the edges of the *banchory* trail, almost as if it was defending itself against further inroads by the massive animals. When the Bajoran finally found a gap wide enough to squeeze through, however, the shadowy interior looked just as pristine as the rest of the scrub forest. There was absolutely no sign of Bashir, alive or dead.

Dax fought her way into the dense vegetation, then glanced down at her tricorder and frowned. The two sets of map coordinates were now dead-on, but her proximity display still insisted she was a meter away from where the comm signal was originating.

"I'm reading a vertical discrepancy," she said, puzzled. "Julian's comm badge must be at least a meter up from here."

"Or down." Kira slanted a grim look at the wet muck of the *tuq'mor,* now only a few centimeters beneath their feet. The interwoven mat of shrubbery above it looked undisturbed. "Although it doesn't look like anything's been buried here."

"No." Dax tilted her head back, peering up at the maze of branches above their heads. "Here, you hold the tricorder."

Kira took it reluctantly. "I can climb up there more easily than you can—"

"I'm not climbing." Dax flexed her knees, then leaped upward, catching hold of the two largest branches within reach and shaking them with all her considerable weight. The entire forest canopy creaked and flexed under her assault, sending a scurry of tiny gleaming lizards out in all directions. One of the jeweled glitters didn't leap, however. It fell straight down from the branches, half a meter too far away for Dax to catch.

Fortunately, quick Bajoran reflexes sent Kira diving after it before Dax could even open her mouth to shout. A mat of intertwined ivy strands bounced beneath the major's impact, trampolining her back again just as Dax dropped from her precarious overhead hold. They collided hard enough to elicit mutual grunts, but Kira's fingers never unclenched from around her catch.

"Is it—?" Dax demanded, steadying her companion.

"Yes." Kira rebalanced herself in the tangled *tuq'mor,* then uncurled her fingers to show Dax the gleam of gold and silver from the Starfleet communicator pin. The frantic chirping of the tricorder confirmed that it was Bashir's. "And it looks like it was at just the right height to have been tossed off a *banchory.*"

From the first moment he'd seen the *Defiant,* Sisko had loved it for its surprising combination of cheetah speed and leonine power, purebred sleekness and alley cat durability. However, the one thing he had to admit his ship didn't have was space. Where a larger starship like the *Saratoga* boasted a wardroom for conferences and planning sessions, he had to make do with a bridge where veteran command officers mixed with untested young ensigns and technicians. And when a renowned Klingon warrior has just announced his intention to hunt you down and kill you, the last thing a commander needed was panic among his crew.

"Mr. Thornton," he said, more by way of test than because he really needed to know, "do we still have a fix on the cloaked Klingon ship's position?"

"Aye, sir." The junior engineer glanced over his shoulder, not looking particularly panicked. "I have the long-range sensors cranked to maximum sensitivity. Even though the Klingon ship has reduced its ion emissions to zero and is modulating its waste heat to match the planetary infrared spectrum, just like us, we're still picking up a minute gravitational anomaly along its extrapolated orbit."

"Enough of an anomaly to link to our weapons targeting systems, so we can track and fire on the Klingons?" Odo inquired.

"Yes, sir." Thornton tapped a command sequence into his science panel. "I can also export my tracking data to the viewscreen display, if you want."

"Do it." Sisko watched a fuzzy, computer-generated halo bloom on the distant curve of Armageddon's oxide-stained atmosphere, then glanced over his shoulder as the turbolift doors hissed open to admit his chief engineer. "We've got a Klingon Dahar Master on the lookout for us, Chief. How invisible are we?"

"We've battened every electromagnetic hatch we've got, from ions to infrared." O'Brien detoured long

146

enough to cast a critical look at Thornton's sensor settings, then gave his young technician an approving clap on the shoulder before continuing to his own seat at the empty engineering console. "Providing you don't want to leap into warp any time soon, the Klingons shouldn't even be able to prove we're here."

"How close can we get to their ship without getting caught?"

"Seventy kilometers, give or take a few." O'Brien grinned at Sisko's surprised look. "I did a little retuning on the shield voltage controls. We're still putting out some magnetic discharge, but now the polarity is tuned to look just like the planet's magnetosphere."

"What about our gravitational field?" Odo asked. "Can't the Klingons track us the same way we're tracking them?"

"No," Worf said, before the chief engineer could reply. "Not unless they already know where we are. A cloaked vessel cannot be detected by gravitational signature alone."

"Especially in a system as orbitally complicated as this one," Thornton added. "The gravity well's way too bumpy to resolve individual events unless you already know roughly where you're looking."

"Good." Sisko leaned back in his command console, as pleased with the coordinated response of his bridge team as with the information they'd given him. He thumbed the communicator controls. "Ensign Farabaugh, how soon do you have us scheduled to intercept an incoming comet?"

"In a little over ten minutes, sir. I was just about to alert you." The junior science officer sounded as tired as O'Brien looked, his voice scratchy but confident. "Sorry for the short notice, but we had to redo half our calculations after that Cardassian battleship banged its way through the debris field."

"Understood. Are we still scheduled to nudge that comet off course on the opposite side of the planet from the Klingons?"

"Aye, sir." Farabaugh hesitated, and Sisko heard the murmur of a second voice in the computer room. "But to get to our intercept point, we're going to have to pass pretty close to the Klingon ship on at least one orbit."

"How close?"

"About one hundred kilometers."

Sisko winced. "My old piloting instructor at the Academy used to call that kissing distance." He looked over at O'Brien again. "You're *sure* the Klingons won't be able to pick us up?"

"Not unless they have their scanners focused directly on our position when we pulse the impulse engines," O'Brien assured him. "Otherwise, we'll be running on gravitational forces and momentum. We should slip by like a Ferengi going through a customs check."

"Then let's do it." Sisko sat back in his command chair, listening to the distant whisper of cometary dust vaporizing off the shields. It occurred to him that the sound couldn't actually be coming from the ice itself as it smoked and vanished into empty space. It must be the internal echo of the shield compensators, constantly readjusting to keep the voltage gap steady and the external forces balanced across the ship's hull.

"Course plotted and laid in for minimum impulse

thrust," Worf announced, his deep voice anomalously loud in the thrumming silence. Sisko wasn't sure if that was the result of his tactical officer's tension or his own. "Ten seconds to engine pulse."

"Mark." O'Brien sounded much calmer, but, then, he was the only one who really knew how well their waste-heat output blended with the ambient infrared. "Five, four, three, two . . . pulse detected."

Sisko could have told him that. Despite the parsimonious engine firing, designed to put the cloaked *Defiant* into the correct orbit with minimal expenditure of energy, his years as her commander had attuned him to the little warship's slightest movements. He felt the shiver of redirected momentum, subtle as the shifting weight of a baby asleep in its mother's arms. "New heading?"

"Orbital plane forty-three degrees to spin axis, rotation thirty degrees from planetary prime," Worf said with satisfaction. "We are on the correct heading for comet intercept at the lip of the gravity well."

Sisko glanced over at Thornton, whose gaze never seemed to waver from his sensor output. "What about our Klingon intercept?"

"Still one hundred kilometers, assuming the Klingons maintain their orbit. Estimated time of closest passage: two-point-five minutes."

"Commander Worf, please lay in potential course changes to prepare for possible Klingon detection. Straight attack, evasive attack, evasive retreat."

"Aye, sir."

Sisko swung his chair back toward O'Brien. "How's the magnetic signature of our shields holding out?"

"Still matched to planetary polarity, plus or minus

ten percent. I'm slowly modulating as we cross the magnetosphere."

"Good." Sisko brushed his gaze across the viewscreen, eying the familiar face of Armageddon with its halo of cometary debris only long enough to be sure that nothing had changed. He tapped his communications control panel. "Farabaugh, any changes in comet trajectories caused by our new orbit?"

"No, sir. We're traveling far enough inside the gravity well to be out of range."

"Good," Sisko said again, but he was frowning as he lifted his hand. That unexceptional answer had left him with nothing left to do, no occupation to soak up his surging tension for the final minute of countdown. He contented himself with drumming his fingers softly on the arm of his command chair and running through all the possible battle-plans, should the Klingons somehow detect their presence. It wasn't that he didn't trust his chief engineer's camouflage or his chief tactical officer's piloting skills. But to a Starfleet officer who'd had ingrained a thousand kilometers as the minimum undetectability limit throughout most of his career, the idea of sliding invisibly past a Klingon bird-of-prey at one hundred klicks or less fell just short of requiring divine intervention.

"Klingons off the aft side," said Thornton. His voice was so quiet and emotionless that it took Sisko a moment to realize the announcement meant they'd slipped past. "No sign of ship activity detected from passive scanning."

The *Defiant*'s bridge murmured with the exhaled breath of her five vastly relieved officers. No, make that four, Sisko thought wryly. Odo looked just as relieved as the rest of them, but the Changeling didn't have the lungs needed to produce a thankful sigh.

"Estimated time of encounter with comet?" he asked briskly. After a tense encounter like that, a good commander knew how to focus his crew's attention on the next challenge. Otherwise, relief had a way of turning to distraction.

"I am not sure," Worf said unexpectedly. "I have the orbital course, but I do not have the exact coordinates of the comet copied to my piloting console."

Sisko frowned. "Thornton?"

The dark-haired engineering tech shook his head. "Sorry, sir. I can get sensor readings on all the comets, but I'm not sure which one Farabaugh's aiming us at."

A frustrated breath trickled out between Sisko's teeth. Trying to deflect a comet without getting caught by the Klingons was like trying to leave Quark's bar without leaving a tip . . . it seemed easy to do at first, until you kept getting tangled in one layer of obstacles after another. Unfortunately, in this case you couldn't flip a coin to a Ferengi barman and have the obstacles magically vanish. "Odo, open an on-line channel to Farabaugh so he can hear us down in that science lab. O'Brien, I want you and Osgood to start working on transferring the comet impact model up to a spare station on the bridge. And someone find out where that damned comet is!"

The words had no sooner left his mouth than the *Defiant* shuddered under a scraping impact. A moment later, a massive, smoking, black hulk of cometary ice floated into the main screen's view. One whole side was sheared freshly white from its contact with the *Defiant*'s angled shields.

"I hope," said Sisko ominously, "that was the comet we were supposed to be deflecting. Because if not . . ."

"Comet deflection one hundred percent successful, sir!" The excitement in Farabaugh's voice echoed brightly across the open communications channel. "With the momentum added from sublimation, its new trajectory will take it out of the debris field entirely."

"Well, there you go." O'Brien looked up from his shield modulator controls with a mischievous smile. "All we need is to do that another hundred-thousand times, and Armageddon will be safe."

Even Sisko felt his lips stretch into a smile at that image. "By then, most of the Klingons should have died of old age," he agreed. "Allowing us to leave the system just in time to collect our pensions." The stifled spurt of laughter that trickled out of his communicator panel told him Odo had added a permanent channel between the bridge and the science lab. He didn't bother reaching for his panel controls. "When's our next deflection scheduled for, Ensign?"

"Not for another forty-five minutes, sir." There was a pause while two young voices conferred in a murmur at the other end of the channel. "With your permission, sir, Osgood and I would like to grab some breakfast before then."

"Breakfast?" O'Brien said blankly. "Don't you mean lunch?"

Worf rumbled disagreement from his piloting station. "According to the ship's chronometer, it is currently fifteen-twenty hours. Any meal served now would be classified as supper."

Sisko felt his own stomach growl uncomfortably. "I don't care what you call it, anyone who wants some can get it. Just be sure to be back on station by sixteen-hundred." He sat back in his chair and steepled his fingers. "We have an appointment with a comet, and it won't wait for us if we're late."

By the time they met up with their fourth comet, Sisko's bridge crew had subversive interception down to a fine art.

"Critical point coming up at coordinates two-sixty and four-forty-three mark twenty-nine." Farabaugh looked up from the makeshift tracking console O'Brien had rigged from one of the life-support stations at the back of the *Defiant*'s bridge. They'd spent the slow hours between comet deadlines moving both junior science officers back onto the bridge, streamlining their data transfer procedures, and perfecting their deflection maneuvers. Osgood had settled in at the main computer access panel, where she could concentrate on the constant adjustments they needed to make in their cometary impact model, while the *Defiant* jockeyed back and forth through the cloud of cometary debris. Thornton and Odo had adjusted the main viewscreen's detection parameters, autoprogramming it to focus on their cometary targets both before and after impact.

So far, their peripatetic path and jarring encounters with comets hadn't drawn any unwelcome attention from the Klingons, although with Kor's ship settled in a stable equatorial orbit, Sisko feared it was only a matter of time until one of their intercept points fell recklessly close to their enemies. In the meantime, the constant short-range passes they had to endure on their unpowered gravitational orbits made the muscles between Sisko's shoulders harden with accumulated tension. Worf claimed the additional challenge of evading detection while deflecting comets made them better warriors, and even O'Brien admitted that the adrenaline rush of those close passes kept him awake and gave him new motivation as the hours dragged on. Personally, Sisko thought he could have limped along on the old motivation—saving Armageddon and all its inhabitants from mass destruction—for quite a while yet.

"Time to gravity-well intercept?" he asked, knowing the routine now by heart.

"Twelve minutes and counting." Osgood swung around at her computer station, blue eyes somber in her fine-boned face. "Captain, this comet fragment masses three kilotons, four times as big as the others we've intercepted. We're going to have to give it a much stronger nudge with the shields to deflect it."

"It's also heading straight-line into the gravity well," Farabaugh warned. "There's no curve-back capture loop at all. We're not going to get a second chance to bump it if we miss."

"Understood." Worf punched the new data into his navigational computer, then transferred the resulting course changes onto the orbital model of Armageddon Thornton had inserted in a corner of the main viewscreen. The new loops added additional frills to the fading lacework of their past orbits. Sisko narrowed his eyes, watching the golden target spot that beaded their path on the third orbit.

"Mr. Farabaugh, correct me if I'm wrong, but it

looks like we're deflecting this comet on the same side of the planet the Klingons are orbiting."

"We are, sir," the young man admitted. "Due to this comet's straight trajectory, it was the only intercept point we could find. But at least we'll be in the terminus when we do it. The dusk might help disguise the comet's change in direction."

"Let's hope so." Sisko glanced across at Worf. "What will our closest pass to the Klingons be this time?"

"One-hundred-and-twenty-five kilometers," the tactical officer replied.

"Piece of cake," said O'Brien.

Sisko grunted. "Begin preparation for course change—"

The blinding shock of a phaser blast across the viewscreen sliced across his words like a *bat'leth*. Sisko cursed and leaped to lean over Odo's shoulder, scanning the *Defiant*'s shield and systems outputs for damage. All the indicators were bafflingly normal. "What the hell did Kor just shoot at?" he demanded.

"As far as I can tell, absolutely nothing." Odo swept an impatient hand across his displays. "It looks like the shot went wide of us by several hundred kilometers. There's no evidence of impact with any comet fragments, either."

"Don't tell me they're just shooting in the dark, hoping to hit us?" O'Brien demanded incredulously.

Worf let out a scornful snort. "The odds against that are far too high to justify the waste of power. I would have expected better from a Dahar Master. Unless he was very, very drunk."

"The odds will get a lot better at a hundred-and-twenty-five kilometers distance," Sisko said grimly. More phaser fire shattered across the screen. "And Kor only needs one hit to extrapolate our location and zero in." He stood and began pacing, even though he knew the motion couldn't ease the frustrated ache of inactivity between his shoulders. He needed to be out doing something, going somewhere—not trapped in this clandestine, cloaked orbit, unable to move a muscle for fear of Klingon detection. "All right, gentlemen, time for a quick command conference. Do we try for deflection and risk getting shot at by Kor?"

Odo gave him a somber look. "What other options do we have? That comet isn't going to wait for us to find a safer orbit."

"We could allow the impact to occur." Worf's scowl looked as if it had embedded itself permanently in his massive forehead, but his voice remained carefully neutral. "That would allow us to remain at maximum distance from the Klingon ship."

O'Brien threw the Klingon an astounded look. "But it would break the deal the hostage-takers offered us—who knows what they would do to the *Victoria Adams* crew then? Not to mention that Julian and Dax and Major Kira will be left at the mercy of that comet!"

Worf's face darkened. "True. But if we chase this comet to our death, many others will fall on Armageddon after it. Should we sacrifice our ability to deflect them all just to deflect this one?"

Odo cleared his throat, a humanoid habit he'd learned in his years among solids. "You're assuming the first one we deflect will be our last? Why? Is Kor so invincible in battle?"

"The last time I saw Dahar Master Kor," said Worf succinctly, "he was a drunken, reckless, nonsense-spouting old fool. But he was at one time one of the mightiest warriors of the Empire. I would not under-rate him, even now."

A last flicker of phaser fire stabbed across the nightside of Armageddon, then the Klingon ship slid around the planet's curvature, still firing randomly into space. Farabaugh glanced over his shoulder. "Captain, if we're going to deflect that comet, we've got to move soon. Otherwise, we won't be able to maneuver into an intercept orbit at all."

Sisko rubbed a hand across his slim beard, giving in to the frustrated longing for action that had been building in him since they'd first arrived. "Command-er Worf, lay in course change for comet intercept. Chief, get our warp engines on-line and our shields back as close to battle-ready as you can without losing all magnetic polarization. Odo, punch a high-security contact through to the away team. We need to let them know what's going on."

"Aye, sir," said O'Brien and Worf in unison. Odo merely punched the order into his screen, moving so rapidly that Sisko suspected he'd been practicing the sequence in advance. "I've got Major Kira now, sir."

"Major," Sisko said without preliminaries. "Any luck locating Dr. Bashir?"

"No, sir." Sisko could hear the heavy rattle of rain on leaves all around her, with a background thrum from some nocturnal creature chirping despite the downpour. "We followed the trail of whoever took him as far as we could, but we never even caught sight of them. If they really are using the native pachyderms for transport, they can probably cover nine times the distance we can in a day."

"Understood." Sisko drummed his fingers on the arms of his console, wrestling with the decision he had to make. "Major, I want you to return to the main Klingon camp," he said at last. "If the hostage-takers decide to contact you or to release any of the survivors, that's where they'll expect you to be."

He heard the breath Kira drew in, even through the sound of distant thunder. "You're expecting a comet to fall?" she guessed. "But the hostage-takers—"

"—can't keep Kor from finding us sooner or later, so long as we keep bouncing comets away right under his nose," Sisko finished.

For a moment, all he heard in response was rain and chirping. "What about the survivors from the *Victoria Adams?*" Kira asked at last. "And Dr. Bashir?"

Sisko grimaced. "We'll have to gamble that the comets won't hit near them. Once the battle's over—with luck—we'll be able to resume the search for them. And to resume warding off Armageddon."

"Sylshessa." He could hear the wry smile in Kira's voice. "I suspect Kor's not going to give you enough time to drop your shields and transport us now. So I guess I'll see you after you've won."

Sisko allowed himself a smile in return. "And good luck to you, too, Major. Sisko out."

"Captain." Odo turned to catch his glance as soon as the transmission was cut. Sisko turned to face him, barely noticing Armageddon's terminator spinning massively toward them as they crossed the planet's rusty dayside. "We're being hailed on all wide-beam channels by the Klingons. Should we acknowledge?"

"Under no circumstances." Sisko slapped a hand down on his communications console. "All hands to battle stations," he snapped over the ship's intercom, trying not to think of how few souls were actually aboard the *Defiant* to hear him. "I want all phasers charged and all photon torpedoes armed and ready."

"Captain." That was Odo again, glowering down at his panel as if it had betrayed him. "The Klingons didn't wait for our acknowledgment. Kor is broadcasting some kind of message to us on all channels."

"Put it on screen," Sisko said curtly.

Armageddon's rusty image vanished, replaced by a broad Klingon face tipped back in a roar of gusty laughter. Kor looked very cheerful and very drunk, but not a whit less threatening for that.

"Sisko!" he roared, sloshing what looked like blood wine toward the viewscreen. A spray of ink red droplets momentarily blotted the display, then trickled into a few out-of-focus runnels dripping down it. "I know you're out there, Sisko! Come out of hiding and *fight!"*

"Not if I can help it," Sisko said between his teeth. "Odo, get him off the main screen, but monitor his transmission, just in case he says something useful."

"Yes, sir." The ancient Klingon warrior's brazen face and disheveled gray hair vanished, but the image that replaced them wasn't the planet below. It was a crusted, black bulk of ice, fractured in places and on the verge of breaking into multiple, smaller fragments.

O'Brien whistled. "We'll have to be careful how we hit that."

"Yes," Osgood agreed. "Too strong a blow will fragment it and send some pieces falling onto the planet. Too weak a nudge, and we won't deflect it at all. What we should probably try for is—"

An explosion splashed through the cometary haze before she could finish speaking, the familiar searing glare of phaser fire. Sisko cursed and swung toward Thornton. "Where's that coming from?"

"The Klingons." The sensor tech sounded shaken by the data now scrolling across his output screen. "They must have changed orbit while they were rounding the planet—they're coming up fast, heading fourteen-forty mark three—"

More phaser fire, this time near enough to send a ripple of magnetic interference humming through the *Defiant*'s shield controls. "Still firing randomly?" Sisko demanded.

"Yes." That answer was Odo's, confident and calm at his panel. "They should pass us in approximately—"

A closer phaser blast interrupted him, spasming the entire viewscreen to white in a way that only a close-range blast could do. "Damage report!" Sisko ordered over the automatic shrilling of proximity alarms.

"Shields at ninety-eight percent, no direct hit on any sector," O'Brien said promptly. Sisko opened his mouth to acknowledge, but the image condensing into view on the main screen stopped the words in his throat.

The cometary fragment they had intended to hit was glowing like an incendiary had hit it, all of its fractures and breaks standing out like shards of jagged lightning against the black-crusted surface. The light inside grew brighter instead of dimming as phaser fire refracted and reflected its way through the weakest points—until, with an explosion of smoking icy debris, the comet shattered into a spray of high-velocity fragments. Each chunk spun off in a different direction, almost too fast to see except for the plume of white vapor left behind it like a contrail. With a cold ache in his stomach, Sisko abruptly understood why Farabaugh had advised them against trying to destroy the comets with phaser fire.

He spun toward the science officer, holding his voice steady with an effort. "Do we need to stop any of those fragments?"

"Working on that now, sir." Farabaugh's words were clipped, his voice tense enough to make the skin on Sisko's back crawl with foreboding. "Osgood, check intercept on fragment nine, that's the fastest one—"

"Too late." Even muffled across the hum of the computer, Sisko could hear the frustration in the other ensign's voice. "It's already gone atmospheric."

"Can we hit it again with our phasers?" O'Brien demanded. "Maybe blast it smaller, into more harmless pieces."

"I don't have any targeting data," Odo warned. "I need specific coordinates transferred in from the computer, *now!*"

Sisko opened his mouth to confirm that order, but a brilliant explosion across the viewscreen stopped him. That hadn't been the fierce, probing flare of Kor's phasers—it had been the raging red-tinged fireball of a comet, exploding up from Armageddon's dense lower atmosphere. Fragment nine hadn't waited for them to intercept it.

"Damage report," he said grimly. "On the planet."

"Long-range sensors show that fragment nine exploded over the open ocean, Captain," Thornton said. "There'll probably be some damage from shock waves and tsunamis along the coast, but the away team shouldn't be affected."

Jaw muscles he hadn't even realized he'd locked unclenched with Sisko's sigh of relief. Before he had even exhaled the last of it, however, Osgood had spun to give him an urgent look.

"Computer models show three more large fragments and a mass of smaller bodies on impact courses, Captain," she warned. "They appear to be headed for the main continent, near the away team." She saw Odo's scowl and swung back to her station. "Transferring data to weapons control—"

"It's too late for us to run an intercept course on them, Captain," Farabaugh added unnecessarily. "We'll have to use photon torpedoes for deflection."

"And we can fire only two at a time," Worf pointed out. "In the meantime, the Klingons will have pinpointed our location."

Sisko grunted, rapidly weighing up his options and finding them all unpleasant. "Farabaugh, mark the two largest fragments for Worf to aim at," he snapped. "Commander, fire when ready." He took a deep breath, seeing the distant flare of phasers that told him Kor's ship had passed them and was rolling merrily along their course, oblivious to their cloaked presence. That wouldn't last much longer. "Odo, prepare for evasive course maneuvers on my mark. Prepare to engage upon firing, at my mark."

"Firing torpedos, *now.*" Worf tapped at his controls with fierce restraint, making the distant hiss of torpedo launch echo through the ship. An instant later, two blossoms of rose-stained light sprouted within the dust brown curve of Armageddon's upper atmosphere.

"Both comet fragments were deflected into high-angle trajectories, and are on course to exit the atmosphere without exploding," Farabaugh reported without being asked.

Sisko grunted acknowledgment. "As soon as torpedoes are rearmed, I want to target the third large fragment—"

"Klingons approaching, seventeen-ninety mark six," Thornton said abruptly. The rusty curve of Armageddon vanished from the screen, replaced by a thousand smeared-out streaks of gauzy light as the cloaked Klingon ship flashed through the comet debris field at close range. "Firing phasers—"

Sisko opened his mouth to order return fire, but the shattering impact of a direct phaser rocked him sideways before he could speak. Instinct more than thought spat the next words out of his mouth. "Red alert! Evasive maneuver alpha!" Worf threw the ship into a skidding turn, hard enough to slam half the bridge crew into their consoles and tear the other half away. "Damage reports."

Odo answered first, as calmly as if they hadn't just been attacked without provocation. "Shields are holding at seventy-eight percent. No structural damage."

"All ship's systems on line and functioning," O'Brien reported. "But it looks like we might have lost one of our comet-trackers."

Sisko spared a quick glance over his shoulder in time to see Osgood prop Farabaugh up from where he'd been flung by the shock of impact. Blood trickled down the young science officer's forehead, but his eyes were already fluttering open. He groaned a protest as Osgood used her own weight to wedge him into the corner between his console and hers, but she sensibly ignored him.

"Klingons are firing again," Odo warned. A moment later, the *Defiant* shuddered under a second direct impact, this time knocking Thornton away from his science station. "Shields holding at sixty-three percent."

"Evasive maneuver delta!" Sisko snapped, then braced himself as the *Defiant*'s spinning course reversal again tugged at them harder than the inertial dampeners could compensate for. "Increase speed to warp five. Where are the Klingons?"

Thornton had to scramble to regain his seat, but his response was still fast and confident. "Klingon ship is four-hundred-and fifty-kilometers away and dropping fast. We'll be out of phaser range in fifteen seconds."

"Maintain evasive maneuvers until then." Sisko turned to check on the status of his comet-tracking team and found Farabaugh on his feet again, squinting painfully at his display screen. "Mr. Thornton, please call someone up from the medical bay to treat Mr. Farabaugh."

"I have, sir. Medic Walroth's on her way."

"It's too late, Captain," Farabaugh murmured.

Sisko frowned, but the young science officer looked so unaware of his own bloodstained condition that he couldn't mean himself. "Too late to stop the last comet fragment, Ensign?"

"Too late to warn the away team, sir." Farabaugh gave him an anguished look. "I can't be a hundred percent sure, but it looks like that fragment is headed for the area of the Klingon's main encampment. It will hit in just a few seconds."

Sisko's gut clenched in dismay. "Notify them anyway," he snapped at Thornton, then vaulted up to scowl at the latest computer model results. "How large an impact are we looking at?"

The sidelong glance Osgood gave Sisko held a wealth of regret. "The fragment was the smallest of the three, but it was still larger than a shuttlecraft. And its velocity was low enough to allow it to penetrate deep into the troposphere. The best estimate is that it will probably be about as powerful as a hundred quantum torpedoes. And there are a dozen smaller fragments right behind it."

A somber echo of silence filled the bridge, until the first bloom of light burst through the blue-black shadow of planetary night. "God help the away team," O'Brien said, watching the light spread like a stain across the atmosphere. His voice was so fervent it was hard to tell if the words were a curse or a prayer. "God help Armageddon."

CHAPTER
7

SHALLOW, RESTLESS SLEEP. Hours after Bashir's body had collapsed in exhaustion, his mind remained feverishly kinetic—aware that he slept, yet frustratingly unable to order his thoughts beyond a miasma of dreams. The bark and cough of Klingon voices melded with the skritch of *xirri* feet on *tuq'mor*, an eerie symphony of worry and unidentifiable sounds.

Even the sharp, here-again-gone-again thunder that had preceded each spastic downpour throughout the long evening had soaked into his unconscious until it twisted into a rolling, swollen snake, filling the world, licking the edges of the sky. It coiled into a knot that filled his empty stomach; his sleeping body rearranged on its stiff bower of limbs, hands clenching into fists in front of his eyes to block the actinic glare of the thunder's menace. *I can't even run from you,* he admitted wearily. *There are wounded here I can't leave, and I'm too tired to be afraid anymore. Whatever you're going to do, you might as well get it over with.*

The serpent struck with explosive speed, and Bashir jerked violently awake.

What could only have been thunder's contrail still echoed off toward infinity. Its deep, almost physical waves pounded hotly inside Bashir's skull. The warm, plush bodies that had nestled on all sides of him during sleep popped up with equal alarm, all of them slapped from dreams by a giant's hand. He reached instinctively to smooth the fur on the closest *xirri*'s skull. Light stung his eyes—daylight, except . . . not daylight. Bashir rose slowly, his breath squeezed into a fist in his chest, and raised his eyes to a roaring, flame-colored sky.

Overlapping shadows swung in wild arcs across the ground, across the faces and bodies of Klingons and *xirri*. Burning ribbons crisscrossed the night sky like flares. Beyond the farthest stretch of horizon, a fat cylinder of fire rocketed straight downward, dragging a brilliant scar of light behind it. Gas and dust and fire mushroomed suddenly skyward, exploding light across the *tuq'mor* canopy, bathing the world in a scarlet-and-gold brilliance that somehow leached all life from it. Bashir stared into the roiling inferno in an agony of silence. It seemed hours later that the coarse cannonade of thunder finally cracked through their tiny camp.

"Is that the direction we came from?" For some reason, he expected someone other than the painted *xirri* doctor when he looked down at whoever clenched his hand. Panic, struggling awake through his confusion, lifted his voice to a near shout. "Was that anywhere near the main camp?" he asked, looking all around him for someone who could understand the question.

Xirri scampered past, some of them already carrying wounded on their backs, others randomly snatching up blankets, foodstuffs, tools in their flight. The crash and rumble of *banchory* plowing their way into the *tuq'mor*'s leading edge almost drowned the Klingons' alarmed shouting, but not the brave battle-chants some of the young men had begun as they swept up gear and passed it off to others. Bashir wondered if they intended to stay and fight. Against what? He spun about, searching the swarm of bodies for a familiar face, and found K'Taran herding her own small flock of *xirri* into step with the rest of the exodus. He ran to her, grabbing at her arm. "Where did that come down?"

"Over the ocean." She took hold of his hand, gripping it possessively instead of pushing it away as he expected. "There's nothing that direction but the poacher's camp."

The poacher's camp . . . and Heiser. Bashir watched the blackening cloud slowly turn itself inside out. It was a terrible thought, but he found himself hoping dismally that the comet's destruction had been horrifying—that a lone Human physician's assistant would have barely had time to notice the approach of the light. That no one had felt any pain.

The rank stink of burning wood feathered into their clearing like fleeing ghosts.

"Come." K'Taran pulled insistently at his hand. "We can't stay out here."

Bashir tried to tug himself free, resorting to peeling her fingers loose one at a time. "I've got to get back to my friends."

"You'll never make it."

"Then take me on a *banchory!*"

"No."

He pried his hand from hers with a last angry yank. "If there's another comet strike—"

"Then you will all die together." She made an abortive swipe to catch him again, but took the hint and clenched her fists at her side when he jerked back out of her reach. "It will serve no purpose!"

What purpose did it have to serve? Die apart or die together, they would still all die in the end. And Bashir had no honor issues to prevent him from being with his friends when that happened. Whirling away from her, he pushed through the jostling crowd, squeezing his way against the flow of bodies until he reached the makeshift bed he'd shared with his *xirri* helpers.

He didn't need any extra light to riffle through his small clutter of belongings—the sky was still bright as dawn, crisscrossed with contrails and filled with a rumbling like a million launching shuttles. His tricorder lay where it had fallen when he passed into sleep, open and on its side atop the pile of branches. The regenerator he found a few layers farther down, where it had slipped between gaps in the foliage. Its power cell still glowed reassuringly, charged and ready to work.

Only his main medkit was gone.

He dragged aside handfuls of branch, searching with both sight and feel for the metal satchel. Mud, bits of broken *tuq'mor,* the remnants of what might have once been some thick-skinned fruit, but no medkit. Twisting in place, he caught a glimpse of movement through the dancing shadows, and watched three *xirri* heft one of the unconscious patients between them by each grabbing an outflung limb. A fourth *xirri* trailed them, its arms filled with supplies and the strap of a square metal container slung over one narrow shoulder. The medkit bounced noisily along the burned ground behind it as it ran.

"Hey!" Bashir scrambled to his feet. A growing layer of smoke met him when he stood, catching at his breath and making him cough. "Hey, wait! You have my gear!"

As though the *xirri* might understand. They disappeared into the confusion and smoke, scaling the charred edges of *tuq'mor* and joining the general mass of activity between the fires in the underbrush and the fires in the sky. When K'Taran appeared at his side again—this time minus any *xirri*—he asked breathlessly, "Where are they going?" as he fitted his tricorder back into its pouch.

She moved him a few steps to one side, out of the path of a *banchory* half-loaded with supplies. "I don't know."

Bashir watched two *xirri* pet a fidgeting *banchory* into stillness so four waiting Klingons could clamber aboard. "But you're going with them," he said, more to indicate that he realized it than because he expected any sort of explanation.

"Wherever it is"—she stepped up close behind him to avoid another approaching *banchory*—"it has to be safer than here."

And then her arms were around him, iron-hard and tight. Bashir barely had the chance to gasp a protest before she yanked him off balance with enough force to shock the wind out of him.

His feet skittered in the mud; a clink of boot-on-metal kicked his dropped regenerator out of sight beneath a skirt of branches and burned leaves. K'Taran dragged him backward as inexorably as a tractor beam. When the pungent smell of wet *banchory* wrapped around them like a wool blanket, panic swelled in Bashir's stomach. He surged against her hold, tried to tangle his feet in the burned detritus all around, kicked back against K'Taran in a desperate attempt to wrench himself free. New hands—bigger, stronger—pinned his arms, lifting him against an armor-plated side.

"Let me go!"

Then he was flat atop a *banchory's* wide shoulders, pushed face downward by the weight of two Klingons, his tricorder grinding into his hip. "Stop it!" he pleaded. "You can't do this!" He managed to work one arm under himself, but couldn't gain the leverage to lift himself before the force of the *banchory* lurching up from its kneel knocked him flat. *"Let me go!"*

He felt K'Taran's hand flex slightly between his shoulders, but she said nothing.

The trail they used stretched wider than their *banchory,* smashed open by everyone who had fled ahead of them, then gnawed at by the streamers of flame that still trailed randomly from the sky. Smoke curdled at *banchory*-height, snaking through the *tuq'mor* canopy; Bashir heard the shattering crash of a tree cleaving its own path toward the ground disturbingly nearby. Coughing, he struggled upright, away from the worst of the heat pouring off the burning *tuq'mor.* This time K'Taran let him.

I hate you, he wanted to growl at her. Except he didn't, not really. He hated this grief, and the leaden, aching despair, but K'Taran hadn't been the one to bring the comets raining. She'd just forced him into what a Klingon no doubt considered honorable inaction. And he hated that. Hated having no way to save himself, and no one else to save.

Xirri raced along the crumbling canopy, some slower than the laboring *banchory,* some faster. Everything scorched by the impact that had first exploded the clearing—everything two kilometers on all sides—crackled and puffed into flame in uneven spurts. The burn front seemed barely moving, just irregular platters of fire scattered throughout a nightmare landscape. When he first glimpsed shadow figures jerking and turning behind the tongues of light, he unconsciously identified them as refugees like themselves, heading into whatever insanity waited at the end of this pointless flight. Then something in the parallax between *banchory* and *tuq'mor* penetrated his stunned numbness, and he realized that the trio of *xirri* were simply struggling behind the path of the flame, not actually moving; K'Taran and her *banchory* were passing them by.

He didn't consciously decide to rescue them. One moment, he knelt on all fours on the back of a running *banchory;* the next, he was grabbing at ash-blackened *tuq'mor* limbs and hauling himself off his mount and into the inferno.

"Human, *no!*"

But he was free of her, still moving, outrunning her in truth even as his thoughts raced precious seconds into the future.

He gained the weave of charred canopy easily enough. It gave gently under his weight, springy and firm, like a trampoline. But the narrow fingers of vine and wood felt more like a tightrope beneath his feet as he picked his way across the surface. Thank God and his parents' vanity for the coordination needed to navigate the deadly course. Little worms of fire twice darted unexpectedly upward from below. The understories were burning, he realized. Suddenly, the image of creeping along a tightrope was replaced with a burning mine field, and Bashir felt a sting of sweat trickle into his eyes.

The painted *xirri* looked up when Bashir bent over it. A tiny, bloodstained figure that could only be a child clung to the older native's back, and the adult *xirri* dragged imploringly at the arm of another, unconscious, adult. Bashir recognized her from his earlier round of triage on the *xirri* wounded—a young female suffering from what had seemed like smoke inhalation and dehydration. Lucky, compared to the others. He'd assigned a geriatric male to keep her upright and feed her water, but hadn't had the ability to do much more for her at the time. Now, only the faint twitching of her eyelids betrayed that she was still alive. Too much smoke, too much excitement. Tug as it might, the painted *xirri* wouldn't get her even five steps closer to wherever they headed.

"Go." Stooping, Bashir set his feet as widely as he

dared and scooped the panting female up with one arm. "Go!" he shouted again, pushing at the painted *xirri*. "I've got her."

For a terrible instant, he thought the message wouldn't pass between them. Then the painted *xirri* touched his hand, light as a butterfly's kiss, and bounded away with startling speed, the youngster still clinging to its back.

Cradling the unconscious female against his shoulder to shield her from the smoke, Bashir straightened and turned back for the trail. He could hear K'Taran shouting, even though he couldn't make out the words, and thought he glimpsed her a ridiculous distance away. Flames cracked and snapped in a wandering line between them; she'd moved farther down the trail, away from the unburned path he'd clambered across to reach here. The thought of circling around turned his stomach to lead. All he would do was lose himself and never find his way back to the others before the fires overran him. Taking a deep, smoke-tainted breath, he hugged his patient protectively and ran at the line of fire before his common sense could suggest otherwise.

Heat washed across him like a blast of desert air. A brief, searing sting across the exposed backs of his hands, then he was clear of it. Not even burned, he realized as the trampoline canopy caught him and staggered him with its chaotic gives and bounces. Then his foot crashed through to nothingness, and he fell to one knee so heavily that his jaw cracked against the top of the little *xirri*'s head.

"K'Taran!"

Instinct, that was all—he'd shouted because some

foolish primate instinct said that any other ape close enough to hear you might be recruited to help. He could see her already leaping onto the *tuq'mor,* so very far away, too very far away to do anything about the predatory fire or the unravelling footing beneath him. Still, when the next layer caved in with a roar, and K'Taran abruptly slipped above his line of sight, she was the one who called out. Bashir was too busy jamming his foot into a knot of *tuq'mor* vines to answer.

He had to lift the little *xirri* over his head to roll her onto the top of the canopy. He couldn't take her with him—*refused* to let her fall and burn simply because he'd been too stupid to find a path through the *tuq'mor* that would hold his Human weight. When K'Taran's ash-stained face appeared above the lip of the ever-growing hole, Bashir thrust the *xirri* toward her. "Take her! Take her!"

But he couldn't tell if K'Taran understood. Before her hands even found a grip in the little creature's fur, the world fell out from under him, and he went plunging into the abyss.

The sky ignited two seconds after Kira's hoarse shout of warning echoed down the *banchory* trail. Dax knew what it was immediately—her third Trill host, Emony, had seen an asteroid impact in her youth from the outskirts of Ymoc City. The memory had burned indelibly into her symbiont's neural circuits: the explosion of light in the sky and the long rumbling roar that followed, the iron-scented wind smashing down from fire-colored clouds, the thunder of flames in the distance as the central city burned. And, for hours afterward, the slow downward drift of silent, black flakes of ash.

The light this time was different—bright and sharp as a photon torpedo blast, consuming the entire sky with its flare. "Get under cover!" Dax shouted back at Kira, then turned and dove for the most open spot she could see in the wall of *tuq'mor* rimming the trail. The thick tangle of leaves and branches resisted her entry, snagging in her hair and gouging deep scratches across the exposed skin of face and hands. Dax cursed and dragged herself deeper, worming her way down through the underbrush to the muddy wetlands below. The drenching rains had covered the mud with a running glitter of water, making all of it look exactly the same.

Dax paused, unsure where to burrow in. With the clumsy noise of her passage through the *tuq'mor* silenced, she could hear the ominous stillness that had enveloped the scrub forest, as if every living creature held its breath in fear. Jadzia's blood jolted with a distracting surge of adrenaline, but the symbiont's shielded inner brain was less subject to such animal instincts. It calmly sent her eyes sweeping across the wet glimmer, seeking out the place where the *tuq'mor* sent the least roots snaking into the mud. That was where the water would be deepest—

Dax took a deep breath and dove headfirst for the hidden pool, feeling water and mud splash up around her even as her ears cracked with a sound so loud it registered as pain, not noise. An enormous boulder smashed down on her from above, slamming her breath out of her lungs and hammering her so deep into the muddy bottom that she felt the silken hug of sediment close over her entire body. Panic spiked through symbiont and host alike, and Dax struggled to stop her downward momentum, thrashing her arms and legs through the thickening sediment in a vain attempt to escape the rock pushing her down.

An instant later, the enormous weight was unaccountably gone. Dax twisted and speared her arms upward, fireworks exploding across her vision from lack of breath. She felt a last, sick surge of energy kick through her muscles—the release of her symbiont's inner reserves of oxygen and glucose in a desperate attempt to save its host's life and its own. With an effort that strained every muscle in her body, Dax hauled herself upward, swimming and climbing simultaneously through the mud to unseen light and air.

Two convulsive jerks broke her head free of mud—and slapped her face with scalding hot water instead. Instinctive panic launched Dax further upward, her face lifting with a gasp to meet the hot, dry kiss of air. There wasn't time to worry if the comet's fiery breath would burn her lungs—air rushed into her starved chest without her even willing it, oxygen and smoke and heat all mixed together in treacherous blessing.

Dax gasped twice, then smoke burned her throat like acid and she lost all her breath again in helpless coughing. She sank back down into hot water and cooler mud, submerging up to her chin before her frantically outstretched fingers caught hold of an exposed root and steadied her. Her next breath, however, was surprisingly free of smoke. She opened mud-crusted eyes and saw a swirl of steam and exhaled gases rising from the wetland's scalded surface, creating a layer of clear, warm mist that buoyed up the sinking smoke from above.

For a long time, Dax did nothing but lie there, gasping like a beached fish and allowing her symbiont's internal reserves to build up to tolerable levels again. The blinding light of the comet's first impact was gone, but Armageddon's night sky still glowed with the pale radiance of explosive afterglow. The top of the *tuq'mor* glowed, too, sullen charcoal red where the topmost branches and leaves had withstood the worst of the fireball's passage. A flaming brand fell into the water beside her, its ruby embers turning cold and black after it hit. Something about that wasn't right. It took a minute of muzzy thought for Dax to realize she hadn't heard the sizzle the burning wood must have made as it quenched. In fact, now that she had time to think about it, she realized she couldn't hear anything at all—no crackling of fire from the forest canopy burning overhead, not even a splash of water when she moved. The only noise her brain registered was a sort of soundless shrilling that she guessed came from her own deafened ears.

Another burnt branch dropped into the water from above, this time close enough to splash Dax with *raktajino*-hot water. She cursed—silently—and scrambled to free herself from her muddy sanctuary. The burning canopy wouldn't stay alight much longer, she guessed; the smoke was already starting to clear as the fires were extinguished by water-sodden wood. But deaf as she was, she had no way to find Kira if she stayed inside the tangled scrub forest. She would have to return to the *banchory* trail—and hope her companion was ambulatory enough to do the same.

With a scientist's unquenchable curiosity, Dax noticed that the lower levels of the *tuq'mor* had survived the comet explosion amazingly intact, protected from the fireball by their own dense, damp foliage. Many of the softer ivy leaves had curled and crisped from the heat, but the thicker succulents looked undamaged. Even some of the ivy-brambles had survived where they dipped long tendrils into the wetlands. This odd ecosystem may have been damaged by the comet's blow, Dax thought, but it had by no means been destroyed.

The same thing couldn't be said of the *banchory* trail, however. Huge swathes of its *tuq'mor* rim had been smashed across the once-clear path and now lay smoldering on the seared ground. The lack of interlaced support at the scrub forest's edge must have allowed the comet's shock wave to penetrate more deeply there, while the open air of the slashed trail had let the fireball blacken the vegetation all the way down to the ground. Dax's hopes of locating Kira sank as she realized her line of sight wasn't much better here than it had been back in the forest interior. For a long moment, she hesitated on the edge of the destruction, watching the silent flakes of black ash drift slowly downward. Uneasy memory stirred inside her, sparking the same morbid fear in Jadzia that Emony had felt at Ymoc City . . . were any of those ashes the remains of someone she had known?

Under her drying crust of mud, something fluttered against her shoulder. Dax cursed again and slapped at her uniform tunic, convinced she must have inadvertently hauled some inhabitant of the wetland out with her when she emerged. All she felt beneath her fingers, however, was the cool lump of her Starfleet communicator, clinging stubbornly to her despite her head to toe immersion in mud. It wasn't until the small metal pin quivered again that she realized she was being hailed by someone, and just couldn't hear the chirp.

She tapped down the communicator's response button and held it to override whoever was hailing. "Dax here," she said, feeling the vibration of her words in her mouth and jaw even though she couldn't hear them. "If this is the *Defiant* calling, I can't hear you. You'll have to buzz the communicator off and on in universal signal code."

She got a reply as soon as she lifted her fingers, but it wasn't the staccato coded message she'd expected. Instead, it was a long, chirping pulse, almost exactly the same length as hers had been.

Eyes narrowing in suspicion, Dax held down the communicator response button again, but didn't speak into it. This time, she was careful to keep her transmission much shorter. She was rewarded with an equally short quiver in response, despite the silence that was all anyone on the other end of that connection would have heard. Assuming they could hear at all.

"Kira!" It was joyful instinct that made Dax say it into the communicator, even though she knew her companion had to be just as deaf as she was. Then she slowly buzzed the same message through the pin in short on-off bursts, spelling out each letter of the Bajoran major's name in universal signal code.

There was a long pause after she finished, during which Dax began to worry that Kira's lack of Starfleet training meant she might not know how to translate that coded message. Then her own pin began to vibrate, long and short bursts beneath her cupping fingers. "Dax," it spelled out first. Then, more slowly, "Tricorder position."

Dax cursed and yanked her mud-covered tricorder up from her belt, praying it worked. It wasn't the immersion in mud she was worried about—the legendary durability Starfleet built into its equipment could withstand much worse conditions. But air-burst explosions like the one they'd just endured had a tendency to emit an invisible wave of electromagnetic radiation in addition to its atmospheric shock wave. Depending on how strong that EM pulse had been, there was a good chance the tricorder's delicate quantum circuits had been fused by stray electrons.

The instrument's display lit up correctly, but the babble of machine code that streaked across it when she punched in the request for Kira's communicator pin coordinates confirmed Dax's fears. It looked like all the higher-level programming circuits had been scrambled. She scowled down at the display's final result. *Alett gerivok*—Vulcan computer code for the number twenty-seven. But twenty-seven of what units? In what direction? Could she even be sure the tricorder had understood her request to begin with, and wasn't just spitting out random nonsense?

Well, there was only one way to find out. Dax took three experimental steps down the cluttered banchory trail toward the place she'd last seen Kira, then paused to reinput the request for her coordinates. This time the racing lines of codes steadied out on *prern gerivok te prern*—the code for twenty-five-point-five. She glanced back at her initial position, gauging the distance she had traveled. A meter and a half seemed just about right.

Encouraged, she continued walking in that direction, pausing to recheck the tricorder's output every time she had to clamber through another tangle of downed trees. At her sixth checkpoint, the Vulcan number on the tricorder was higher than before. Painstakingly, Dax retraced her steps and checked both sides of the trail until the readout would go no lower, then shoved herself into the charred embrace of the *tuq'mor*. According to the tricorder, Kira was only six meters away from her now, and the sky still held enough luminous violet light to see through the tangled vegetation. Dax rechecked the readout once more to make sure she was heading in the right direction, then clipped the tricorder back on her belt and started searching through the smoky shadows.

After a moment, her communicator pin quivered again. Dax paused, translating the vibrating dashes and dots in mounting impatience. "Turn right under," they spelled out enigmatically. Dax turned right as ordered but saw nothing to go under, just more tangled *tuq'mor* wetland. "Log," added her communicator pin in slow, tired quivers. "In water."

Dax cursed, loud enough this time for her recovering ears to give her a faint, tinny backwash of the sound, and knelt down to scan the water line, looking for a charred log big enough to trap a Bajoran female. She found it not half a meter away, protruding from a wetland pond like a tilted obelisk. Its burnt wood was still ruby-warm on the upper surface where it hadn't been quenched. The dying firelight sparked glowing reflections in two dark eyes, peering up at her caustically from beneath the log's heavy shadow. Kira tilted her chin up just enough to lift her mouth above the waterline and, faint as a cricket's chirp, Dax heard her say, "About time."

Dax didn't bother replying, instead plunging down into the still-warm muck beside her friend, fearful that her position meant crushed limbs or battered organs. To her relief, she found the log split into a twisted fork half a meter below the water line, trapping Kira's half-turned torso in a vise of chokingly thick thorned branches. At least half a dozen of them had snagged on the tough fabric of her Bajoran uniform.

Kira said something else, too faint for Dax's shrilling ears to hear, then demonstrated by reaching both hands up over her head and wrapping them around the still-smoldering log. Her wet uniform sleeves began to steam before she could even lock her hands for one good tug against the tangled thorns. She pulled them away a moment later just as smoke began to rise. Dax winced, seeing the places where the cloth had seared through on the major's more stubborn attempts to extricate herself.

Lifting a finger at Kira to make her wait, Dax pulled out her phaser and set it to its narrowest, knife-thin firing spray. Taking a deep breath, she let herself sink down into the muddy water. She couldn't see much through the murk, but by patting her way along the edge of Kira's torso with one hand, she managed to sweep a careful line of phaser fire at a ten-centimeter distance, severing thorny twigs from their parent branch without trying to disentangle Kira from them. She bobbed up to take a second deep breath, then submerged again and sliced through the tangled vegetation on the other side of the fork. By the time she'd surfaced again and swiped the muddy water out of her eyes, Kira was already reaching up to grasp the smoldering log again.

"Wait." Dax tugged her friend's arms apart, then began scooping water onto the glowing wood with both cupped hands. It sizzled and steamed and exploded in little hissing pops, making the log slowly darken. Dax kept splashing until most of the surface was completely sodden, then stepped back and came around the log to stand behind Kira, holding a thumb up where the major could see it. She nodded and lifted her arms to clench tightly around the dampened wood.

"Now!" Kira's voice said faintly, and she hauled herself half out of the water with one strong upward jerk. Dax caught and steadied her when her momentum faded, giving Kira a chance to shake one booted foot free of the thorny tangle. With the flexibility that came with her size, the Bajoran then planted her heel on the log at the same height as her chest and kicked herself clear of the thorns, so powerfully that she staggered both of them back a step in the mud.

Dax caught her balance first, grabbing hold of the nearest unburnt branch to steady them both. "Are you all right?" she shouted at her companion.

Kira grinned at her through a mask of ashen dribbles. Despite the burns on her sleeves and the thorn cuts that had already started dappling her legs with drops of blood, the Bajoran major looked surprisingly unaffected by her ordeal. "I've been through worse tortures in low-security Cardassian prisons!"

she shouted back. What little Dax could hear of her voice sounded cheerful. "At least here the water's nice and warm."

Dax shook her head, remembering the instant of scalding heat just after the fireball's passage. Her face still felt tender from that momentary immersion. "Too warm for me!" she shouted back, then paused to listen. A distant rumble echoed through the fading shrill of her blasted ears. "That sounds like another comet strike, either smaller or further away. This must have been a major debris cluster."

Kira winced. "Don't say that like it's a good thing. Another one could hit right here."

"That's statistically unlikely," Dax informed her.

"So is a stable wormhole." Kira hauled herself out of the muck, swinging up to balance with enviable ease on the low-hanging branch. Dax groaned and forced her aching muscles to scrabble their way to the same perch, feeling weighted down by her wet and mud-sodden uniform. "Our first priority right now is to get back to the Klingon exile camp and see if anyone's still alive there. After that, we'll contact the *Defiant* and see if they're still—I mean, see if the battle with Kor is over."

Dax lifted an eyebrow at her. "Are we going to beam up if it is?"

"No. We're going to stay here and locate Bashir, even if we have to throw away our communicator pins to do it." Kira took a deep, decisive breath. "I never left behind a member of the Shakaar who could have been rescued. And no matter what Captain Sisko says, I'm not going to start now."

"Sounds good to me." Dax led the way back

through the charred *tuq'mor* to the smoke-filled chasm of the *banchory* trail. The late night sky was even more radiant with afterglow than before, spiked near the horizon with a sunrise-bright flame and banded above that with rust-tinged sky and coppery clouds. If she hadn't known better, Dax would have thought it was dawn. "Of course, by the time we make it back to *epetai* Vrag's settlement, Julian may already have been there for hours, waiting for us."

Kira opened her mouth to reply, then caught sight of the destruction wrought in the *banchory* trail by the comet strike and broke into a fit of startled coughing instead. "Not hours," she said sourly, when she finally regained her voice. "Weeks. Because that's how long it's going to take us to get back."

CHAPTER
8

ALL HE KNEW was that he was coughing. So hard and so breathlessly that he thought he'd tear his body apart. No up. No down. He didn't know who he was talking to when he croaked, "Stop! Stop! Put me down!" But they listened to him. And even though the pain followed him and rode up through him in waves so thick he thought he'd vomit, Bashir realized it was true darkness pressing in all around him, not just his own unconsciousness. Strong Klingon hands lowered him into a sitting position against a cool, uneven wall.

Distant thunder—or perhaps the explosions of primitive mortars—trembled through the hard floor, shivered through his stomach. *Shock.* Undoubtedly. Whatever had happened, the pain alone was enough to bottom out his blood pressure, and he harbored a morbid suspicion that the cold wetness he felt collected in his boot was something other than water.

A vague sixth sense of other bodies in the same enclosed space. Bashir stirred only enough to rocket pain up his leg and into his stomach, but felt someone move touchably close in response to his gasp. He wound his fingers in that someone else's sleeve. "Where are we?" he whispered.

Another bone-deep rumble shuddered through the world, just below the level of hearing. Then K'Taran's voice, aberrantly loud, "Underground."

It told him nothing. But told him enough: all the rules had changed. "The *xirri* . . . the one I gave you . . ."

"She's fine. She's with the others."

Better than could be said for him. He closed his eyes and leaned his head back against the wall.

A warm blur of light bloomed against the outside of his eyelids. He blinked, forcing himself alert, watching a handful of Klingon youngsters appear behind the spread of light as though chasing it ahead of them. Singed and filthy, they each brandished some form of fire, most of them carrying burning handfuls of *tuq'mor* in the slings of their wet tunics. The huge cave came alive with firefly motes of light as they scattered to distribute fire all over the chamber. Voices—some Klingon, some not—bloomed in the warming darkness alongside the light.

"The fire outside is dying." One of the boys drew closer, a tree limb almost as thick as his arm wrapped in cloth and sputtering erratically. "But more fire is coming from the sky. We will be here for some time."

He knelt beside K'Taran. The flames strengthened somewhat now that he'd stopped moving, and the sudden flare of their intensity hurt Bashir's eyes. "Will he die?"

K'Taran reached to take the torch from the boy, her own eyes stark and gray in the unreliable light. "He is the Human doctor. He will tell us." And she held the light across his outstretched legs. As though doing him some favor.

Years of practice with trauma patients prevented him from vocalizing any sounds of horror, but Bashir couldn't stop the panicky whirl of his thoughts any more than he could stop his heart from thundering. His uniform was soaked and muddy, tunic and trousers all reduced to the same ash-riddled iron gray. Rents in the fabric exposed minute flashes of scarlet, but none of them accounted for the glossy overlay of blood down the inside of his right leg. He followed the stain upward to a knee already misshapen with swelling. Then realized that it wasn't edema pushing the fabric of his trousers medially out of alignment. It was bone.

His hands trembled as he pried his tricorder out of its pouch. Its normally reassuring warble rang piercingly off the flowstone walls, and at least the scroll of readings made a modicum of sense. BP was better than he expected, although he didn't like his heart rate or the shallowness of his breathing. Just reading the figure on how much blood he'd lost made him dizzy. Still, there was no arterial damage, and at least the hemorrhaging was slowing. Folding the tricorder closed in his lap, he rubbed shakily at his eyes.

"So . . ." K'Taran glanced down at his leg, then up at his face again with painfully adolescent bravery. "Will you die?"

Leave it to Klingons to stick with the most basic of questions. "Not immediately." And for some reason, that struck him as funny. He decided not to laugh, for fear he'd frighten them. "Where's the rest of my equipment?"

Even as he asked, the bump and scrape of a dragging container hurried up on one side. Bashir turned his head and smiled at the painted *xirri* doctor. "Thank you," he said, taking the strap of the medkit when it was offered. As though some signal passed between them, the Klingon boy left abruptly, and the little *xirri* sidled over into his place.

Only two at a time with any given dead man, Bashir found himself thinking as he fumbled with the latches on the kit. It unfolded clumsily, the front panel clattering onto the floor. *Just another of many quaint Klingon traditions.* He found a vial of stimulant and fitted it carefully onto his hypospray. "I'm sorry about this," he said as he calibrated the dosage.

A brittle, unreadable expression flitted across K'Taran's face. "It is not your fault."

"I should have stayed to the trail. The first rule of emergency medicine is to avoid making new victims."

This time she caught his hand, halting him just before he delivered the injection. "It is not your fault!" she declared when he blinked up at her. Then, in a tone of choked embarrassment, "It is my fault. You were caught in the *tuq'mor,* and the fire was coming . . ." She released him and clenched her hands miserably in front of her. "I did not realize you would break so easily."

He wondered what she would think if she knew he was far less fragile than most.

Arguing the finer points of blame was ultimately useless, though. Die from a comet strike, die from starvation, die from an open leg fracture. What difference did it really make? Digging a container of sterile water out of the open medkit, Bashir held the almost-empty bottle out toward the painted *xirri*. He remembered using most of his supply irrigating *xirri* wounds, and remembered his native counterpart following him from patient to patient with keen interest as he performed the procedure. Now, Bashir only had to shake the bottle once before the *xirri* ducked forward to take it from him and scampered away—hopefully in search of water.

K'Taran watched in silence as Bashir sorted through the rest of his limited pharmacy in search of something that might tackle the pain of a comminuted fracture. Nothing powerful that wouldn't also render him useless for both himself and any other wounded. Choosing a more lightweight analgesic, he was still counting vertebrae upward from his sacrum when K'Taran asked quietly, "Is it true?"

Bashir finished counting, then carefully injected as large a dose as he dared into his spine. "Is what true?"

She swallowed hard, but didn't drop her gaze. "That you will die."

Ah—that eternal Klingon pragmatism again. Moving slowly to give the spinal time to do its work, Bashir twisted apart the hypospray and tossed the empty vial back into his kit. "I don't know," he admitted wearily. "I've lost a lot of blood, and with no other Humans around, I can't replace it. And whenever fractured bone is exposed to air . . ." Just mentioning it made his leg shriek with remembered pain, but the spinal already smothered some of the reality. He managed to push the phantom anguish aside. "Well, that's not good even when you've got a whole sickbay to work with. If we're really stuck down here, and this is all the treatment I'll receive . . ." He met her gaze frankly, not wanting her to see just how badly he was afraid. "Yes," he said at last. "I'll very likely die."

The *xirri* returned with the water; Bashir was just as glad to distract himself from K'Taran's disturbing fixation with his impending demise. He flash-sterlized the entire container, then screwed on the irrigation lid with more dexterity than he expected. Bending forward flexed the spur of protruding bone, so he only sliced away the fabric at the point of the actual break, instead of opening his pantleg to the ankle the way he would have with another patient. Blessed numbness let him approach the procedure at a professional distance. A patient's fracture, a patient's blood. It didn't matter who the patient was. He showed the *xirri* how to hold the bottle overhead so gravity could work its magic on the water, and used both his own hands to explore the fracture as he irrigated. Only once did he find himself wishing he had gloves or even sterile drapes. No sense wishing for things that couldn't be had in an emergency, though; he banned the thought from his mind and went back to concentrating on his patient.

They were almost through the third bottle of sterilized water when a reassuring hand closed on his shoulder and a warm voice remarked, "You know, I'm getting less enamored with the native botany by the hour."

It was the humanness of the voice that jerked Bashir's head up; the swiftness of his movement scattered sparks across his vision. He clapped one hand abruptly to the floor, steadying himself, and blinked furiously to keep from losing sight of consciousness. The slim, elderly Asian man squatting beside him rolled smoothly to his knees and closed both hands protectively around the doctor's upper arm. "It's all right—I've got you."

And the Klingons have us both. Still, it eased his dizziness to relax his weight onto someone else's strength. Leaving the *xirri* to finish with the water, Bashir let the older Human ease him back against the stone wall. He almost felt a rush of blood back into his brain as his sense of his surroundings realigned and sharpened. *Well, thank God,* he thought wearily, turning to really look at the man kneeling beside him. *At least we've found the* Victoria Adams's *crew.*

He was fit, trim, and flexible in a way completely at odds with the ancient wisdom in his dark eyes. At least one hundred, Bashir decided, for all that he looked not a day over seventy. He wasn't one of the scientists—the cheerfully commercial jumpsuit on his slim frame was a familiar staple of the Interplanetary Space Foundation, a nonprofit organization that supplied volunteers to research projects in need of enthusiastic, unskilled help. Although their advertisements promised nonspecific "adventure and opportunity," Bashir had a feeling being shot down by

Klingons wasn't the type of adventure the Foundation had intended. Still, there was something about his friendly, high-cheeked face and the cut of his iron gray hair that said "Starfleet Brass," and Bashir found himself wishing he could sit up straighter to convey his respect. "Captain . . ." He wasn't even sure why he said it. It just seemed the proper title for the easy competence surrounding this man.

A little glimmer of something bordering on panic chased itself through the old man's eyes. "Not here, son," he said gently. Just that quickly, his contagious smile resurfaced. "Here, we're just two Humans stuck in the same problem." He shifted position to offer one hand. "Why don't you call me George?"

Something in the keen way the old man watched him after this pronouncement said that this was both a lie and an order. Bashir nodded to show he understood, and lifted his own hand for shaking. "I—" Blood coated him like a torn glove. He pulled back before their palms could make contact. "My name's Julian, Julian Bashir."

"Dr. Bashir." He flicked his eyes across Bashir's medical uniform and dipped an acknowledging nod. "Our hostess tells me you could use a few willing donors."

The blood. On his hand, his pantleg, the floor. Everywhere but where it should be. "B negative," he admitted, "at least two units." Which would buy him time, clear his head a little, but hardly solve his problem. Necrosis was necrosis, no matter how much blood your heart pumped through it.

"Well, I'm A positive," George told him. "But we've got at least seventeen other Humans I think we can count on." He braced one hand on his knee in preparation to stand, and Bashir reached out to catch his wrist. George halted, eyes alert.

"No wounded," Bashir said firmly. He held the other officer's gaze to make sure his commitment to this was clear. "If they aren't completely healthy and uninjured, I won't take their blood." First rule of emergency medicine: avoid creating new victims.

George nodded solemnly. "Understood. You hang tight until I get back." Then he trotted briskly into the deeper cave, leaving Bashir feeling cold and unaccountably alone.

"Honor grants you the right of restitution." K'Taran waited until the doctor flicked a glance at her, then continued formally, "Traditionally, your family would inherit the right should you . . . no longer be able to exercise it yourself. But as you have no family here . . . I will take whatever action you require of me. By my own hand."

Taking the empty water bottle from the *xirri*, Bashir shook his head to stop the little native from running off for another refill. "What are you talking about?" he asked K'Taran.

"If you ask me, I will kill myself." She lifted the bottle from his shaking hands and carefully wrapped it with its own bloody irrigation tubing. "A life for a life."

Bashir snugged the bottle and its tubing back into the kit, shaking again and feeling a little sick. "Don't be ridiculous. I don't want you to kill yourself."

"Then what? Should I maim myself in equal measure?"

"Stop it," he said firmly. There was only one hypo

of system stimulant left, and he wasn't sure he wanted to use it just yet.

K'Taran surprised him by slamming the kit shut almost on his fingers. "No!"

Bashir jerked away from her slightly, pushing himself back against the wall. Some distant awareness knew he'd moved the bones in his leg again, but what the spinal didn't fully quench surprise had already washed away.

"Do not leave me with this dishonor on my name!" K'Taran bent over him fiercely, her breath hot against his face and her eyes bright with a pain rivalling his own. "I have done you a terrible wrong. I know from your face that even Human blood will not erase it. Please . . . allow me to balance the debt."

He tried to imagine offering up his life for anything when he was only fourteen. Then he thought about Dax and Kira, trapped God only knew where as the sky fell down around them, and he wondered if it was really worth raising such impassioned children when they only grew up to be inflexible, impassioned adults.

"There's only one thing I want." He made himself relax, but stopped just short of touching her hand. "Go find my friends. There's room enough for everyone down here, your grandmother's people included. But I can't go to them now. Do that for me."

At first he thought she might refuse him. The mention of her grandmother darkened her brow ridges with anger, and her jaw muscles bunched in frustration. Then her eyes strayed for only an instant to his twisted, bloody leg, and all her adult determination returned with leonine grace. "I will take the duty," she solemnly announced. "Will you accept this as honorable restitution for my crime?"

The last painful knot of fear loosened its grip on Bashir's heart. "I will."

She nodded once, grimly, and sprang to her feet with all the vigor of a warrior marching into honorable combat even though she'd almost certainly lose. Perhaps that was all that was really facing her now. Still, Bashir put out one hand to stop her before she could launch herself toward the outside. "I have one more favor to ask of you."

K'Taran hesitated, eyes dark and flinty with suspicion. "Our honor is in balance," she told him.

The doctor shook his head, suddenly strangely embarrassed at having been misunderstood, as though caught in a grave imposition. "Not an honor debt," he assured her hastily. "A favor." Then, swallowing hard, Bashir sat as straight as he could, and clenched his hands behind his back. "I was wondering if I might impose on you to set a fractured bone. . . ."

According to Dax's autistic tricorder, they were halfway back to the main Klingon encampment when their communicators chirped again. This time, Dax could actually hear as well as feel the signal, although there was still an odd metallic flatness to the high-pitched sound. She waited a moment for Kira to tap her pin and answer, frowning at her when she didn't.

"Aren't you even going to acknowledge the captain's hail?" It was one thing to contemplate disobeying orders when it came to evacuating without Julian, Dax discovered, and quite another to simply ignore the chain of command.

"That's not the *Defiant* hailing us," Kira answered. "It's the wrong frequency."

Dax took a breath, realizing that for once her aching ears hadn't lied to her about a sound. "Why would someone else be hailing us?" she asked, then answered in the same breath. "The Klingons."

"From Kor's ship?" Kira shook her head. "If they knew we were here, they'd either beam us out or phaser us. No, this has to be someone who wants something from us . . ."

Their communicators chirped again, strangely high and urgent. "Should we just ignore them?"

"Probably," Kira said. Her dark eyes met Dax's in a mutually thoughtful look. "But what if it's the group who took Bashir?"

In response, Dax tapped her communicator on. "Jadzia Dax here," she said calmly. "Identify yourself."

"I am sending coordinates." The shock of hearing Gordek's gruff, graceless voice on the other end of that connection was only exceeded by the shock of his next words. "Come and help us, or I will have the Cardassians destroy your ship and all aboard it."

Dax lifted her hand to break the connection. "Cardassians?" she asked Kira in astonishment. "How could a member of *epetai* Vrag's exiles have any control over the Cardassians?"

"The same way he could have a subspace communicator," Kira shot back, her face hardening to reveal the ruthless guerrilla leader she'd once been. "Because he's been dealing with the Cardassians all along."

Dax blinked at her for a long, disbelieving minute. "Dealing in what? Armageddon isn't exactly brimming with galactic treasures."

"That's what we're going to find out." The Bajoran tapped her communicator pin on. "Send your coordinates, Gordek," she said shortly. "We'll be there."

The Klingon grunted and rattled off a string of planetary coordinates, then cut the connection as rudely as he'd opened it, giving Dax no chance to tell him that those numbers meant nothing to her. "He must be using Cardassian plotting data," she told Kira in frustration. "I have no idea where this location is."

"Could we focus in on his communicator signal, if we could get him to turn it on again?"

Dax gave her tricorder a jaundiced look. "Not unless O'Brien beams down and fixes this first."

"I don't think the captain will let me do that," said a totally unexpected Irish voice from her communicator. "But if you really want to have a heart-to-heart chat with your friend Gordek, I may be able to get you there."

"Chief?" Dax demanded. "Were you listening in on that transmission from the Klingons?"

"We've been scanning every frequency for your signal, old man, ever since the EM surge of the comet impacts cleared." That was Benjamin Sisko's familiar coffee-dark voice, sounding more impatient than relieved. "What took you so long to report in? Didn't you think we'd be worried about you?"

Kira and Dax exchanged slightly guilty looks. "We

wanted to ascertain the condition of the Klingon refugees at the main encampment first, sir," Kira said at last.

"And give Dr. Bashir a little more time to show up before you abandoned him?" It was never easy to fool Sisko, Dax thought wryly, especially when what you were trying to do would have been his first instinct as well. "Are you two all right?"

Kira's answer to that was more confident, if no more accurate. "Just a few bumps and bruises, sir. Request permission to stay on planet and investigate the nature of Gordek's dealings with the Cardassians."

"Granted with pleasure, Major," Sisko said grimly. "We're currently out of Kor's firing range, so we can drop shields long enough to beam you and Dax straight to the origination point of Gordek's signal."

"Any idea how many Klingons are with him, Captain?" Dax asked.

She heard the mutter of an unfamiliar voice on the bridge, then Sisko said, "Long-range sensors indicate at least a dozen life-signs there, although not all of them are strong. Watch yourself, old man."

"Yes, sir." Dax dropped her hand from her pin and braced her aching muscles for the jerk of transport. An instant later, the smoke and downed trees of the *tuq'mor* vanished, replaced by a crackling red-gold inferno. Dax barely had time to squint her eyes shut against the glare before a pair of fierce hands seized her shoulders and dragged her closer to the fire.

"This is *your* fault!" Gordek's dark mane of hair was half-seared on one side, but his blistered face held more fury than pain. "Your shield generator didn't protect us when the comet came! Look what came of it!"

"Look what came of not telling us the truth!" Kira might have been half the Klingon's size, but her determined shove and angry scowl still backed him a step away from Dax. With her vision tempered to the glare, Dax could now see the charcoal ghosts of three pole buildings engulfed in the flames. The sprawled bodies of several dead Klingons rimmed the edge of fire, as if they'd been dragged out only far enough to be checked for life-signs before their rescuers dropped them and went back for more. The injured had been moved to the shelter of the one building left standing, built where the damp wall of *tuq'mor* around this forest clearing had deflected the cometary blast. A handful of Klingon hunters looked up from that sanctuary, then came to ring Gordek, Kira, and Dax in a deadly circle.

Dax took a slow, steadying breath and turned to watch their backs, making sure the phaser on her hip faced Kira rather than the exiles. "Why is this our fault?" she demanded, aiming the question at the hostile watchers rather than Gordek. "We never claimed that shield would save you from a direct impact. And we offered you evacuation to our ship—*you're* the one who insisted on staying here!"

That sparked a mutter of unease around the ring of fierce, furrowed Klingon faces. Dax pressed the advantage, pointing a finger at the Cardassian communicator Gordek still carried in one meaty fist. "If you would rather wait for the Cardassians to evacuate you than have the Federation do it, that's fine. But where are they now that you need them? Are they braving the Klingon blockade? Have they responded to your calls for help?"

It was a shot in the dark, but it went home. Two of the hunters turned scowling faces toward Gordek. "Why aren't the Cardassians here?" one demanded. "We told them we had the last *geset* for them days ago. Didn't they promise to evacuate us?"

"That was before the Starfleet ship was here!" Gordek snapped back at them.

"So? If our homeworld was dying, as they claim theirs is, would we not invade Hell for the cure?" growled an older, battle-scarred Klingon. He pulled out a vial of golden brown fluid from one tattered pocket and held it up to catch the firelight. Its high-tech polytex surface glittered anomalously bright in this primitive setting. "What is the character of their honor, these Cardassians you have bound us to, Gordek? They will not brave a single Klingon ship for the drug they say saves their children's lives! I say we let their children die!"

He dropped the vial contemptuously to the ground, then wrung a shout of protest out of Gordek by smashing it with one heavy, booted foot. "That is our passage out of here!" the Klingon house leader growled as the frothy yellow liquid ran and puddled underfoot. An unpleasantly caustic smell rose up from it—not familiar, but evocative of something else Dax knew. She frowned and juggled out her mud-encrusted tricorder, then ran a discreet analysis of the fluid running between her boots. The display panel flickered, then coughed up a response in enigmatic Vulcan machine-code.

The older hunter spat into the spilled *geset,* making his opinion of it offensively clear. "I see no Cardassian ships here to rescue us," he said brusquely. "All I see here is an outcast from a once-noble Klingon House—a small creature who cannot salute the sky."

Gordek snarled in wordless anger at that insult, his shoulders rolling for a roundhouse punch that Kira's lifted phaser stopped in midswing. The big Klingon took a step back, glaring down at her and breathing hard between bared teeth. "Our wounded die while we dither here! You should be transporting them up to stasis on your ship, as your doctor did before."

"No." Dax's harsh voice jerked the Klingon's furious glare over to her instead. "I may not know the character of the Cardassians' honor, Gordek, but I know the character of Benjamin Sisko's. He'll defy the blockade to evacuate innocent Klingon refugees, but he won't give shelter to a single Klingon traitor."

Her accusation ignited the roar of response she'd expected from all the hunters. "Who calls us traitors?" demanded a younger, dark-skinned male. "We have done nothing to betray the Empire!"

"Except sell this to the Cardassians." Dax lifted her tricorder to show the frowning Klingons the Vulcan chemical symbols it displayed. "According to my instrument, this is the active ingredient in that *geset* you just spilled on the ground. And if any of us were Human, we would be dead now."

Kira scowled down at the yellow rivulets trickling toward her boots, stepping back to make sure none of them came into contact. "What is it?"

"Drevlocet," Dax said simply.

Even the Klingons hissed in response to that statement. "The neurotoxin that the *Jem'Hadar* used to murder hundreds of Humans at the Hjaraur colony?" Kira growled.

"Yes. One of the native animals—I'm guessing the *banchory,* considering the number of them you've killed—must synthesize it naturally, as a defense against the biting insects here. It's been outlawed in every military convention signed in the Alpha Quadrant since Hjaraur." Dax fixed Gordek with her coldest look. "But you've been purifying it and stocking it up for the Cardassians. What did they promise you to get you to make this drug for them? It must have been something worth turning down our offer of evacuation."

"A return to the Klingon homeworld?" Kira asked shrewdly.

Gordek snarled and spit toward their feet. "As if I would gratify that fool Gowron by giving him a chance to exile me again. No, they said they would give us our own ship and escort us through the wormhole, so we could disappear into the Gamma Quadrant. It was a high price, but they said they were desperate to cure their home planet of *ptarvo* fever."

"Ptarvo fever?" That made Kira snort. "That's about as lethal as a foot cramp!"

Another wash of discontent rumbled through the surviving Klingon hunters. "Then why would they pay so much for this drug?" a younger one demanded, brow ridges clenched with suspicion.

"Because it can be chemically modified to attack almost any humanoid race—Romulans, Vulcans, Trill, and Klingons as well as Humans," Dax said flatly. "In fact, the only species whose neural matter we know it can't affect are the Cardassians." She aimed another ice-cold gaze at Gordek. "Did you know, when you agreed to purify this drug for them, that it could be turned against your own people?"

"No!" The exile's roar was loud, but the undertone of guilt in it rang clear to Dax's ears. "How could I? We didn't have the equipment to know they were lying!"

"No," said the older, scarred hunter. "But we knew they insulted our honor by the way they forced us to bargain our lives for this drug. We should have refused to deal with them from the beginning." He turned toward Dax, dark eyes narrowed in suspicion. "We have been in exile many months. Are the Cardassians at war with the Humans now?"

"Not yet," Dax said. "But they are certainly at war with the Klingons."

"Then they will use this drug against the Klingon Empire?"

"Quite possibly," Kira agreed, her voice caustic. "When it comes to war, Cardassians don't pay much attention to ethical conventions."

The older Klingon took a deep breath, eyes closing for a long, bitter moment. *"Epetai* Vrag was right. We should have resigned ourselves to this new life, and relinquished any hope of honorable redemption. Now we have endangered our entire race through our dishonorable striving."

"And what if we have?" Gordek snarled savagely. "Did the Klingon High Council care that they had endangered us when they abandoned us on this death-trap planet? Our crime was misplaced loyalty, nothing more! Should that condemn us to bear the brunt of heaven's wrath and die beneath this Armageddon sky, just for the sake of our honor?"

Silence followed his words, a silence filled with the sullen crackle of dying flames. Then the scarred older hunter spat again, this time aiming his contempt directly at the leader of his house. *"Batlh potlh law' yIn potlh puS."* Then he raised his long hunter's knife and stabbed it deep into his own throat.

Kira gasped and stepped back from the sudden rush of bright Klingon blood, but Dax had been steeled for it. She knew this proud warrior race almost as well as she knew her own. From the moment she had discovered what *geset* really was, she had known no honorable Klingon could survive learning he had doomed his own people with it.

The ring of hunters watched their eldest fall to his knees in indomitable silence, then slowly collapse face down in the frothy yellow toxin. Then, with a wordless glance of agreement, all beside Gordek drew their own knives. "Before I die, I will hold the knife for those wounded who are still conscious," said the dark-skinned youngest, and the others nodded. He turned slitted obsidian eyes toward Dax. "You can transport the others up to your ship to heal, but you must promise afterwards to give them the truth. And a knife."

"I promise," she said in somber Klingon. "And I promise also to sing the honor of your actions in every great house in the Empire."

"Then it is a good day to die." The young man nodded a silent farewell to his companions, then turned on his heel and headed for the survivors in the unburnt hut. Kira frowned after him, then turned an urgent gaze on Dax.

"Do we have to—"

"Yes." Without flinching or protest, Dax watched the last two hunters of Gordek's house end their lives in equally dignified silence. Hers was now the task of *cha'DIch,* the honor witness, even if the battle here was only one of internal principles. She let her cold gaze settle afterwards on Gordek, still standing with clenched fists and scowling down at his fallen hunters as if their deaths had been an insult he could fight them over. "Gordek," she said softly. "You also have a knife."

His fire-lit gaze lifted to meet hers, swirling with resentment and frustrated fury. "Yes," he said thickly. "And I will use it on you!"

Dax took a quick step back when he launched himself, reaching desperately for her phaser even as her eyes judged the distance and her heartbeat drummed out *too late, too late, too late!* She heard the familiar shrill sound, but it wasn't until the big Klingon actually thudded down across the seared ground, sprawling limply over his own dead warriors, that she realized Kira had pulled her own weapon even earlier.

"Is he dead?" Dax demanded.

"Of course not." Kira rolled her victim off to one side, careful not to let any of his clothing come in contact with the *geset.* "He's coming back to the *Defiant* with us."

Dax frowned, her stomach roiling with the injustice of four honorable Klingons dead and this self-centered traitor saved. "You're really going to evacuate him from Armageddon?"

"That's right." Kira gave her a hard-edged Bajoran smile. "I'm going to wake him up just long enough for Odo to extract a confession that names the Cardassians as his buyers. Then we're going to extradite him—straight to Dahar Master Kor's ship."

CHAPTER
9

"GET ME KOR. NOW."

Sisko never particularly noticed how his voice sounded, especially in the middle of a tense situation. The only reason he suspected something about it changed was the way his bridge officers and ensigns dove into their work at times like these, as if Furies stood behind them breathing fire down their necks. Even Worf wasn't immune to the effect, although his stiff posture made it clear he could have resisted that aura of command if his officer's instincts ever told him to. Sisko suspected he himself had looked much the same way when he'd been on the receiving end of Admiral Nechayev's steely voice only a few hours before.

"Excellent work, Captain," the admiral had said, her ice-pale eyes gleaming despite the cometary interference that danced through her high-security transmission. "The loss of the *Victoria Adams*—perhaps even the loss of her passengers—may very well be worth finding out that the Cardassians planned to smuggle drevlocet off this Armageddon planet of yours. You may have just saved millions of lives."

"Thank you, Admiral," Sisko said shortly. "But don't start filing any obituaries. I haven't given up on the crash survivors yet, or on my away team."

Nechayev arched her eyebrows. "But I thought you said you had to drop back into a depowered and cloaked orbit to evade the Klingon blockade. How are you going to protect the planet from comet impacts now?"

Sisko grimaced. "I don't know." Dropping abruptly out of warp with his exhaust camouflaged and his shields repolarized to blend in with the magnetosphere had seemed like the best way to evade Kor's drunken, wild chase. It wasn't until after the fact that he'd realized he'd once again trapped himself into doing nothing. "I'll think of something."

"Perhaps," Nechayev suggested, "you could negotiate with Dahar Master Kor."

Sisko eyed his sector commander in deep suspicion. He'd never known the admiral to make a joke, especially not in a situation as tense as this one, but surely she couldn't be serious now. "What makes you think the Klingons are going to be any more amenable to negotiation now than when they fired on the *Victoria Adams?*"

"Because now," she pointed out gently, "you can inform them that this planet is a natural source of drevlocet."

That brought Worf's head up from his intent scrutiny of his piloting screens. "The Klingon High Council swore to uphold the military convention banning drevlocet!" he growled. "On the Honor of the Emperor Kahless! They would never use it."

"I am aware of that, Commander," the admiral retorted. "In fact, it's all that's keeping me from ordering five starships to take control of that system immediately. I trust the Klingons will protect Armageddon adequately, once they know how dangerous the planet really is."

"That's why you want me to talk to Kor," Sisko realized. "So he knows the real reason why the Cardassians have been trying to goad us into a fight."

"Precisely." The admiral transferred her steely gaze back to Sisko. "The stakes in this game are now very high, Captain. Whatever you and Kor decide to do, make sure it doesn't leave the system open to Cardassian intervention again. And that," she added, tapping her Starfleet Academy ring on the table in front of her for emphasis, "is an *order.*"

Sisko gritted his teeth and agreed, recognizing the unwritten code that meant Nechayev really meant it this time. And as soon as her transmission had flickered out, he'd ordered the confessed traitor Gordek transferred over to Kor's ship. It had been his best stab at getting the Dahar Master to turn a sympathetic eye on Armageddon's evacuation. If Kor didn't respond to a warning that could save millions of Klingons from dying in a Cardassian chemical attack, he wasn't going to respond to anything.

Unfortunately, after an hour of silence, that looked to be exactly the case.

"Kor refuses to acknowledge our hail, Captain." Thornton looked frustrated, as if the Klingon's stubborn silence were his own personal failure. "I've coded it as a priority request, but the Klingons still won't answer."

"Are they jamming our transmission?"

"No, sir. Just refusing to reply."

"Maybe Kor's still interrogating Gordek," O'Brien said doubtfully. "Just because he told Odo all the gory details of his dealings with the Cardassians doesn't mean he's going to be as cooperative with Kor."

"Unlikely," Worf said. "We transported the exile collaborator over three hours ago. By now, Kor has either debriefed him or killed him."

"Or both," Odo said dryly.

Sisko rubbed a hand across his beard, his gaze never leaving the dangerous haze of cometary debris haloing Armageddon's horizon. "Ensign Osgood, how much time do we have before the next fragment is scheduled to impact the planet?"

The science officer glanced up from her computer model, looking worried. "Almost forty-five minutes, sir—but the next impact isn't a single fragment, it's a cluster that stretches over two degrees of arc. Unless we start soon, I'm not sure we'll have time to deflect them all."

"Then we can't afford to wait on Kor's convenience." Sisko launched himself out of his chair, a flare of anger burning off the stiffness that came from too long a period of inactivity. "After seeing us fire on the comet fragments that he blew apart, he must know what we've been doing to protect the planet. He might even know what maneuvers we've been using to do it. The only thing he doesn't know right now is exactly which comet fragments we need to deflect."

"I wouldn't be too sure of that, Captain," Thornton said. "I've been seeing a lot of diffuse scanner activity from the Klingon ship in the past three hours. It looks like they're tracking the whole cometary debris cloud now, just like we are."

"Kor is making sure he knows our next move in advance." Sisko smacked a hand against his useless weapons panel as he passed it, making both Thornton and Osgood start. Odo merely gave him an inquiring, upward look. "So when we go to deflect those comets—"

"—Kor will obliterate us," Worf finished grimly.

Sisko scowled and paced off another circuit of his bridge. "What we need is a way to distract the Klingon blockade long enough for us to deflect that cluster of comets. The trouble is, if I were Kor, I wouldn't be taking my eyes off those comets for a second. What could possibly distract me and my whole crew?"

"An act of God?" asked O'Brien. "Like an ion storm or a solar flare?"

Sisko shook his head. "Hard to duplicate in under an hour, Chief. What else?"

"A summons from the Emperor, or from Chancellor Gowron?" Odo suggested.

"Constable, if a summons came in from Starfleet calling us away from Armageddon right now, would you believe it?"

"No," Odo admitted.

"Me, either. What else?"

A long silence followed his question this time. It was broken at last not by words, but by one of the rarest sounds Sisko had ever heard on the bridge of the *Defiant*.

Worf was laughing.

It was a full-throated roar of Klingon amusement, barely distinguishable from a warrior's fighting bellow. It made Odo jump and O'Brien curse, while Sisko swung around to stare at his tactical officer in disbelief and dawning hope. *"What?"* he demanded. "What have you thought of?"

"The *Batlh Jaj!*" Worf's eyes gleamed with the dancing red sparks that either danger or delight could ignite. He saw Sisko's baffled look and shook his head, so hard his braid whipped against his shoulders. "The *Batlh Jaj,* Captain. The Klingon Day of Honor. It is today!"

"What?" Two long strides took Sisko over to the nearest panel, which happened to be Osgood's. She gave him a quizzical look when he leaned over her shoulder, but it wasn't the arcane model of cometary orbits he was interested in—it was the standard date-time readout in the corner of her display screen. "Stardate 3692 is the Day of Honor?"

"It varies from year to year, since the Klingon calendar does not correspond to Federation standard," Worf informed him. "But the day we left Deep Space Nine was *wa'ChorghDIch*—first day of the ninth month. The Day of Honor falls three days after that."

"I don't know about the *wa'ChorghDIch,*" said O'Brien. "But it has been almost exactly three Standard days since we left the station."

Adrenaline began to fizz through Sisko's blood, born of both excitement and foreboding. "Let me see if I can remember my Klingon history," he said slowly. " 'On the Day of Honor, the Klingons treat even their fiercest enemies as blooded Klingon warriors, with all the privileges and rights and ceremonial duties that entails.' " He threw a challenging look at his tactical officer. "Are you thinking what I'm thinking?"

Worf's savage, glinting smile told him the answer without any need for words.

"Oh, no." Odo's deep voice was heavy with foreboding. "Commander, you're not going to make us fight one of those hand-to-hand ritual battles again, are you?"

"In reality, the *Suv'batlh* is not a ritual," Worf replied. "It is a battle to the death to resolve a challenge to one's honor."

"And on the Day of Honor, the combatants don't need to be blooded Klingon warriors. They can even," Sisko said in deep satisfaction, "be Starfleet officers."

"Correct," said Worf.

Sisko swung to face Thornton again. "I want you to ram a connection through to the Klingons—don't wait for them to acknowledge it, just patch it straight into their display. Can you do that?"

The young sensor tech grinned back at him, as if his reckless energy were contagious. "I can feed it right through their viewing sensor circuits, sir, so it replaces their external scan. The only problem is, they can probably jam it within a few minutes if they want to."

"They won't want to. Just give me a minute's warning before we're on-line." Sisko turned back toward Worf. "We'll need to hold the *Suv'batlh* on the Klingons' ship, to distract them while the *Defiant* deflects comets."

"Agreed. But allow me to point out, sir, that if we win, we will not only have defended our honor." Red battle sparks were dancing in Worf's eyes again. "We will also have forced Kor to grant any request we ask on that day."

"Any request?" Sisko demanded. "Even cooperating with us to keep the Cardassians away from Armageddon?"

"Yes, sir."

Sisko's breath hissed between clenched teeth as he weighed the odds and juggled probabilities. "It's a gamble," he said at last. "But I think we have a chance of success. And if we fail, we'll still have managed to distract the Klingons without making any overt acts of war against them."

"Somehow, that wasn't what I had in mind for my official Starfleet obituary," O'Brien commented.

"Don't worry, Chief," Sisko told him. "You're not going. You've got a family at home to worry about—"

"—and you'd like a chance to actually win this fight," O'Brien finished, sounding resigned. "Thank you, sir. So who are you taking?"

"Worf," Sisko said, then glanced over his shoulder inquiringly. He got a reluctant Changeling nod in return, but the metal-hard gleam in his constable's eyes told him his instincts were correct. "And Odo. That way—"

"I've punched into the Klingon sensors, Captain," Thornton interrupted, voice calm despite the frantic way his fingers flew across his controls. "Communications signal will be on their viewscreen in ten seconds. Nine . . . eight . . . seven . . ."

Sisko took a deep breath and prepared himself to glare straight at the unoffending curve of Armageddon's rusty atmosphere. He'd get no return signal from this unauthorized transmission, at least at first.

". . . three . . . two . . . on-line."

"Kor, this day is *Batlh Jaj,*" Sisko said, cutting straight to the heart of the matter with Klingon-like brusqueness. "You cannot refuse a challenge, even from a Starfleet officer who has interfered in your blockade. I challenge you on behalf of my insulted honor to engage in *Suv'batlh,* three on three." He saw Worf nod at him approvingly, although he wasn't sure if it was his phrasing or his Klingon pronunciation that was being evaluated. "Right here, Kor. Right now. *Suv'batlh.*"

There was an agonizingly long pause, during which the distant spiked bloom of an upper-atmosphere comet impact flared at him from the curve of Armageddon's smoke-clouded sky, a foretaste of the disaster looming just outside the gravity well. Then the screen rippled and became Kor's broad-shouldered form, seated in his own stark command chair. The older Klingon's furrowed face was alight with surprise, respect, and laughter.

"A noble effort, Sisko!" Kor applauded in the Klingon style, fist thumping on chest, while the warriors around him watched and rumbled with amusement. "Ironic, but still noble!"

Sisko narrowed his eyes, ignoring the queasy ripple of unease that twisted in his gut. "What do you mean, 'ironic'?"

"Ironic because your request comes just a little too late." Kor's grin showed stained and straggling teeth, but its honesty couldn't be doubted. "You may have matched the Klingon calendar to your Federation days correctly, but you forgot about the length of the Klingon day. The day of *Batlh Jaj*—what you call our Day of Honor—ended ten minutes ago."

The devastation to Armageddon's surface seemed endless. Kira had given up hoping to find any sign of life among the burned and buried wreckage. Ash carpeted what remained of the *tuq'mor* like a silky gray shroud, and the mud no longer steamed or simmered. A featureless black cloud of ejecta had crept inland from over the ocean, dimming the sky to dull amber. Only the hiss and creak of cooling embers accompanied them as they trudged along the dark tunnel that used to be a *banchory* trail. That, and the distant, hollow *boom* of comet fragments bursting not nearly far enough away.

Kira couldn't remember the last time her body had hurt so much. Her ankles ached from supporting her full weight on toes and arches while climbing the jungle-gym roadblocks of *tuq'mor* thrown down in their way; every other muscle all the way up to her ass burned with a fatigue so deep she almost couldn't imagine it fading. Dax had made her last humorous comment uncounted hours ago. Now, all Kira heard from the Trill was the squelch and slap of her feet in the sticking mud, and hoarse panting that sounded suspiciously like Kira's own.

If I ever get home, Kira thought, *I will never walk anywhere without pavement again.*

Dax's grab at her sleeve stung the burns on her arm and made her gasp. "Do you hear that?" the Trill whispered, hauling her to a stop.

Hissing through her teeth, Kira pried the Trill's fingers from around her scorched forearm. *No,* she wanted to grumble. *I don't hear anything but us hiking into oblivion!* But something in the dark wasteland silenced her—something about the metronomic quality of the thunder she'd first taken for exploding bolides. Something about the way it shivered in her stomach and made the *tuq'mor* rattle.

She pushed Dax toward one singed-but-still-living hedge. "Come on!"

Finding cover within the blackened *tuq'mor* was probably the easiest thing Kira had done in the last seven hours. Wriggling between knotted limbs like a fish darting among river reeds, she hauled herself into what now served as the topmost story. What parts of her weren't already blackened by ash, burns, and mud readily picked up a grimy coating of soot from the limbs and brush that had taken the brunt of the last big air strike. She crouched as low to the burned-out canopy as exhausted muscles would allow, then hoped she looked like any other clump of burned foliage as she peered back down the trail.

The *banchory*'s huge shadow preceded it. Dark as

the bordered path seemed to Kira's night-adjusted eyes, it washed darker still, smothering even the vestiges of detail. A figure, slim and wild-haired, perched astride the moving mountain; Kira doubted the rider would have stood out more clearly on the brightest day. She didn't even have to worry about missing the *banchory*'s back when she leapt from the *tuq'mor*.

Her phaser jabbed the startled Klingon in the spine before he could do more than jerk a startled look over his shoulder. Kira used the flat of her hand to push his chin forward, then looped her arm around his throat for good measure. "Yes," she announced, very close to his ear, "this is a real weapon. No, I have no reservations about using it. You'd better hope you can tell me something I want to hear."

The Klingon spread both hands with fingers splayed—the age-old symbol of unarmed threat. It was a youthful female's voice that told her, "A Human doctor named Bashir has sent me to find his companions so they can wait out the comets in a place of safety." K'Taran tipped just the slightest glance back at Kira's startled face. "Will that do?"

Nighttime cloaked the worst of the destruction, but a few Klingon-tended fires and a renewed blast of light in the southern sky let Kira pick out enough details to know that honor hadn't spared Rekan Vrag's encampment from Armageddon's wrath. She clung uneasily to K'Taran's middle as the *banchory* minced with surprising delicacy around lumps in the carpet of ash. Kira only recognized them as charred corpses with considerable use of her imagination. It wasn't worth the effort. As the beast finally slowed to a shuffling standstill in what might have once been the camp's center, Kira realized she didn't even know for sure which part of the camp they were facing. Nothing about the place looked the same; only the bottommost rootballs of the trees were left standing.

Oh, Prophets, I want to go home!

"Major! Commander!"

LeDonne's slim, dark figure peeled away from one of the still smoldering tree hovels. Kira saw the eager relief in the young Human's movements, knew what the nurse must be thinking when she slowed abruptly and looked carefully from front to rear on the *banchory* again.

Still, it was Dax who announced, almost cheerfully, "We found him," as the *banchory* labored meticulously to its knees.

"Sort of." Kira slid to the ground, suppressing a grimace at the packed-dirt fullness in her knees and the overall anguish in the soles of her feet. "K'Taran says Dr. Bashir sent her to get us." She caught at the *banchory's* small, conical ear for support in the hopes none of the approaching Klingons would sense her weakness. "There are caves several kilometers west of here. They'll be protected from the explosions—safe from anything but a direct ground strike. There's room enough there for everyone." Everyone who was left, at least. Kira could count the gathered faces on both hands. She looked around for *epetai* Vrag, and found her standing stiffly near the middle of the tiny crowd.

"She's lying." Rekan didn't even move her eyes toward Kira.

221

K'Taran, proudly matching her grandmother's glare, hopped to the ground beside Kira and lifted her chin. "An honorable Klingon does not lie."

"And I say again"—Rekan bared teeth still sharp despite her age—"you are lying."

Kira felt K'Taran flash with anger hot enough to reignite the foliage. Stepping quickly away from the *banchory*, Kira threw up one elbow to halt the girl's forward surge, and thanked the Prophets when K'Taran stopped without a protest. Kira was in no shape to reinforce the suggestion. "What possible motive does she have to lie to us?" she asked Rekan.

The old matriarch looked as though she wanted to spit. "Dishonor needs no motive."

"You have no right to question my honor!" This time, K'Taran shrugged off Kira's restraining arm and lunged forward to shove aside the two adults standing between her and Rekan. "I stand here, do I not?" she snarled. "I have tied my life to this cursed planet. I held my head proudly while our ancestors' keep was burned and our family name shattered and thrown to the dust. What more would you have of me?"

"Honor does not abandon its House!" Rekan's eyes gleamed with a passion brighter than all the stars Armageddon had thrown down on them. "Honor does not bend law to whatever meaning suits it."

"Law said only that we should remain exiled on this planet," K'Taran reminded her. "Law never stated that we must necessarily die."

"The intent of a command is as important as the words."

Kira blurted a disbelieving laugh without having meant to. "That's what this is all about?" she asked,

222

limping away from the *banchory* to stand shoulder-to-shoulder with K'Taran. "Because Gowron expected you to be killed here, you're not allowed to take action to prevent it?"

Rekan lifted her eyes to a place just above Kira's head, not even deigning to meet her gaze. "I will not have this House judged as being without honor," she stated grimly. "I will not have this family go to Sto-Vo-Kor and recite to Kahless how we tried to trick honor—how we held hostages unrelated to our battle and tried to run from our duty like Ferengi picking holes in a contract of their own making."

K'Taran moved in front of her grandmother's stare. The electricity when their eyes met made Kira's stomach twist. "You do not believe I am lying." The girl's voice sounded only hurt, and not as angry as Kira had expected. "You fear I'm telling the truth—that there actually *is* some chance for life."

For the first time, Kira glimpsed what might have been the love fueling this angry war between them. "I fear that you are *wrong,*" Rekan almost whispered. "I fear we will die while fleeing, irrevocably disgraced."

"Shouldn't everyone be allowed to choose their own path?" That was a question that had gnawed at Kira since Rekan's first refusal to evacuate her clan. "Is it honorable to force your own fears on the rest of them?"

Rekan hissed at her through the darkness. "Swallow your bile. You know nothing of honor."

"I know that my people can feel right and wrong inside their own hearts," Kira shot back. Fear, anger, and fatigue stripped her of all social graces. It was all she could do not to shake the older Klingon. "We

223

don't need a High Chancellor or anyone else to tell us how to be honorable. Are Klingons so simple that they can't decide that for themselves?"

Rekan's backhanded blow didn't surprise Kira so much as the raw force in the old woman's swing. She was on the ground, stunned and blinded with pain, before her conscious mind even identified what had smashed her down. "Be glad you are not a Klingon," the *epetai*'s scorn rained like comet-fire from above her. "I would feed your own heart to you where I stand."

And Kira heard her own voice say groggily, "I accept."

Her vision cleared with painful slowness, seeming somehow brighter and less focused that it ought to be. But the shock and suspicion on Rekan Vrag's face was unmistakable, even through a haze of pain and rattled thinking. "Your challenge to combat," Kira continued, more carefully. "I accept."

The *epetai* frowned. "I did not challenge you!"

"You struck me." It was one of those moments Odo would have scoffed at as being more creative than was good for her. Some disconnected part of her kept spinning out the words, with no particular concern for the battered body still splayed out on the ground. "When one Klingon strikes another, it means you want to do combat."

"You are not a Klingon!" Rekan countered.

And at last Kira's instincts let the rest of her in on what they were doing. *"Batlh Jaj."*

The silence that crashed down among them was almost hard enough to hurt. Certainly heavy enough to crush most of the breath from Rekan's lungs; her voice was thin when she said, "You cannot conduct *Suv'batlh*. There are only two of you."

"Three."

Even Kira felt the hurt that must have throbbed in Rekan when K'Taran stepped forward. The older Klingon growled and swiped at the air; Kira forced herself to crawl to all fours, then slowly to her feet.

"If we win," Kira said, moving to form a bridge between K'Taran in front of her grandmother and Dax still waiting by their *banchory,* "then that will mean our honor is more true. We can lead anyone who wants to follow us to K'Taran's refuge, and you won't do anything to stop us."

Rekan didn't nod. "And if I win?"

"Then we all die." It was the answer that had been true since before the challenge was even leveled. Kira pulled herself as tall as her aching muscles would let her. "I believe the choice of battlefield is mine."

CHAPTER 10

"Ten minutes!"

It was a simultaneous exclamation from at least three of the *Defiant*'s officers. Odo said the words in frustration, O'Brien in disgust, but their voices were almost completely overridden by Worf's furious roar of indignation. Sisko was the only one who remained silent, keeping his gaze locked on Kor's until the uproar on both ships subsided into uneasy silence.

"I never thought to see a day when *Klingons* hid like cowards behind the letter of the law," he said at last, and had the satisfaction of seeing Kor's laughter wiped abruptly from his eyes. "What does the Day of Honor really mean? That it is the only day on which Klingons will behave honorably?"

A snarl whistled between Kor's clenched teeth. "Take care what you say, Benjamin Sisko. If you were

226

a Klingon, that would be an insult worthy of *Suv'batlh* on any day."

"Would it?" Worf growled, before Sisko could reply. "Then allow me to say that I, Worf, son of Mogh, never thought to see a day when Klingons hid like cowards behind the law, acting as if *Batlh Jaj* were the only day on which they needed to behave honorably!"

Kor crashed the mug he was holding against the arm of his chair, splashing dusky blood wine out in a violent spray. Anger had darkened his broad face to almost the same shade. "You insult my honor, Worf son of Mogh!"

"Good," said the Klingon tactical officer between his teeth. "That was my intention."

Kor fell abruptly silent, staring at them with a flicker of wariness breaking through the wine-soaked fury in his face. After a moment's pause, however, he acknowledged Worf's challenge with a stiff, ceremonial nod. "As the one whose honor has been challenged, we hold the *Suv'batlh* on my territory. Your party will beam over in fifteen minutes, Worf, son of Mogh, armed and ready to fight. *Qapla'!*"

The connection sliced off, leaving the bridge of the *Defiant* suspended in disbelieving silence. "You did it, Worf," O'Brien said at last, sounding dumbfounded. "You actually got Kor to accept the challenge."

Sisko let his breath trickle out, feeling his jaw muscles quiver with the release of accumulated tension. "Now all we need to do is win it. Or at least entertain Kor long enough for the *Defiant* to finish sweeping up that comet cluster." He vaulted out of his command chair, fiercely eager to be off the bridge and accomplishing something. "Worf, Odo, you're with me. Osgood, Thornton, plot the fastest deflection course you can through that cluster, and don't worry about keeping out of sight of the Klingons. Just try not to use photon torpedoes unless you have to. O'Brien, you've got the conn. Call Clark and Nensi up to man navigations and weapons while we're gone."

His chief engineer winced, uncomfortable as always with the assumption of command, even though he was technically the highest-ranking member left of Sisko's decimated crew. He swung around at his station to watch as they headed for the turbolift. "Captain, don't you want a subcutaneous transmitter? How else will you know when we're done chasing comets?"

"It will not matter," Worf said sternly. *"Suv'batlh* cannot be conceded. It can only be fought to the finish."

"Oh." O'Brien looked as glum as if he'd just been condemned to a long prison sentence, Sisko noted in amusement. "Well, in that case, good luck and—er— *Qapla.'"*

Odo snorted his scorn at that send-off, but followed Sisko and Worf into the turbolift with no visible reluctance. The doors hissed shut, locking the three of them in tense, prebattle silence. Odo broke it at last, his voice gruff.

"I assume that, since this is a ritual combat, I won't be permitted to use my shape-shifting abilities to win it."

"No." Worf's voice was equally brusque and businesslike. "A Klingon warrior does not attack by subterfuge. Any change in shape would be considered

228

a deceit and would disqualify you from the *Suv'batlh.*"

"Too bad," Odo said. "I might be able to look just like a Klingon warrior, but that doesn't mean I can fight like one." Especially true, Sisko knew, because the Constable would refuse to wield any weapons.

Worf frowned across at the Changeling, but it was a thoughtful rather than an angry look. "Klingons measure their worth as warriors by the strength and valor of their enemies. The honor that accrues in ritual combat increases as the task becomes more difficult. I think it would be acceptable to ignore any blows that do not actually decapitate or dismember you."

"Good. Then I won't have to actually wear armor." Odo followed the others onto C Deck, heading not for the main transporter room but for the equipment bay next to it where they had a closet-sized clothing replicator capable of creating authentic Klingon outfits. As he went, his dun-colored Bajoran uniform swelled and shifted, turning to polished lacquer plates in gleaming shades of ebony and maroon.

Fortunately, Klingon weapons and armor were stock items in the replicator's data banks, along with most clothing items from known space. Worf was humming as he waited for his weapons to be made, a song so deep and tuneless that it had to be a Klingon battle-chant.

"Klingon armor and *bat'leth,* suitable for ritual combat," Sisko told the replicator when it was his turn. A moment later he was settling chest-armor over his shoulders, making sure all the side-latches were snugged tight. He'd lost count of how many times he'd done this over the last few years, sparring Dax in various holo-suite recreations. This time was different, however. This time his life really would depend upon what he was wearing.

He became acutely aware, as he hefted the shallow helmet whose curving cheek-plates had been designed more for intimidation than protection, that this was armor meant for warriors whose arteries ran deep under leather-tough ligaments and whose skeletons already made bony protective plates around their vital organs. The warm pulse of blood beneath the skin of his throat, a mammalian evolutionary quirk he'd never had cause to regret before, suddenly seemed like an invitation to disaster.

"Second thoughts, Captain?" Odo asked, when he stepped out.

Sisko glanced up at his security chief, startled, then realized he'd put on and taken off his spiked gauntlet three times, searching for a comfortable fit that just didn't exist. Worf paused on the threshold of the clothing replicator, looking dismayed.

"Only about the armor." Sisko motioned Worf into the machine, managing an almost-real smile. It was ironic that the two warriors in their party with the least mortal weaknesses were depending on him for their morale. He rubbed a hand across his exposed abdomen and sighed. "I'll just have to hope Kor went to school before the Klingons were teaching Human anatomy."

"I shall endeavor," Worf said from inside the replicator, "to make sure you do not have to face the Dahar Master personally, Captain. You are as good with a *bat'leth* as any Human I've seen, but Kor would have you disarmed and at his mercy within . . . minutes."

Sisko raised an eyebrow at him as he stepped out. "Why do I get the feeling you were about to say 'seconds,' Mr. Worf?"

The Klingon's chagrined look told him he was right. "It is not that I doubt your skill, Captain. But to become a Dahar Master, you must have fought a hundred battles, survived a hundred *Suv'batlh*, and trained a hundred blooded warriors. No amount of blood wine can dull the fighting instincts of such a warrior."

"Are you sure *you* can survive for more than a few minutes in a fight with him, Commander?" Odo demanded, never shy about asking embarrassing questions.

"No," Worf said frankly. "But in *Suv'batlh*, it is the overall outcome that counts, not the individual winners and losers. If you and the captain can surprise your opponents and win your matches, then it does not matter that Kor defeats me."

"Unfortunately," Sisko said, "that is a rather big 'if.'" He slid on his helmet, then hardened his face to the expressionless mask that served him so well during space battles. "Gentlemen, let's go defend our honor."

He'd stopped being physically conscious of the pain what seemed a whole lifetime ago. K'Taran, following his instructions with stern determination, reduced the fracture with an ease Bashir almost envied; the advantages of physical strength. Then, after she left with one of the sluggish *banchory* trailing behind, Bashir had taken further advantage of Klingon prowess by coaxing one of the boys to carry him around the massive caverns to check on the *Victoria Adams*'s crew and his *xirri* patients. Bad enough that he didn't have the proper equipment to do any of them any good—the traumatic relocation to this damp, cool chamber wasn't helping the wounded, either. He almost felt guilty accepting blood from two hale and youthful volunteers, considering he had no such panacea to offer the *xirri*.

He didn't specifically remember returning to his own little bloodstained corner, and hoped fervently he hadn't lost consciousness before tending the last of the patients. It all seemed so unfair. If he was going to break a leg during a planetary mission, why the hell couldn't he have done it when no one else needed his services? Or, at the very least, have done it so that he didn't hemorrhage a liter of blood in the process?

He wrestled his thoughts back to the moment, and concentrated instead on the small, neat movements of the painted *xirri* near his feet.

The little native doctor—a male, Bashir had finally determined when he'd been able to catch a glimpse of hemipenile bulges while they made their rounds—had found a piece of what looked like broken chert, and now used it to nick carefully, gently at the fabric of Bashir's trouser leg. He'd already extended the doctor's original cut clear to the groin, and was almost finished in the other direction, slicing patiently down toward the ankle and the terminal hem. *I've had nurses who weren't so thoughtful.* He certainly couldn't argue with the *xirri*'s diagnosis—even with the fracture reduced, his knee had swollen dramatically. Another few centimeters, and the clothing would have compromised his circulation.

"Thank you."

The *xirri* blinked huge eyes at him, with no expression Bashir could readily discern. Then it bent again to its work, tongue flicking rhythmically.

Small, unglazed dishes filled with a foul-smelling mash littered the cave floor around them, the contents burning with an almost invisible flame. Bashir patted around him in the thin, watery light, wondering what trick of nature made all the illumination seem to pool in his lap and run no further. By the time his hand thumped against the open medkit, his thoughts had already staggered so far in search of that explanation that he couldn't quite remember what he'd been looking for.

A cool, gray-green hand slipped past his own, pulling his attention toward the instruments laid out in their tray. The scalpels. Of course—he'd wanted something a bit better suited to cutting. But when he tried to lever himself away from the wall to lean forward toward his ankle, a great spasm of pain ripped up his leg and knocked him back again. God, this was so embarrassing. He was supposed to know enough to foresee what kind of movements would send him crawling out of his skin. Opening his eyes, he found the *xirri* watching him with its tongue coiled curiously just outside its tiny mouth. It turned the piece of chert over and over in nimble fingers, then scooted slightly closer to taste the laser scalpel with its tongue.

It tugged at the scalpel very gently. The piece of chert ended up in Bashir's lap almost as an afterthought.

"Here . . ." He tightened his grip just enough to make the native pause and look up at him. "You activate it like this." He turned the instrument until the power switch faced the *xirri* doctor, then turned the scalpel carefully away from them both and depressed the switch with his thumb. A thin, glowing blade of light hissed into being from the end. "Use it like a normal knife, but for God's sake be careful— it'll cut through bone and fingers just as easily as it will my pants!"

Deactivating the scalpel with almost ritualistic care, the *xirri* held it at a respectful arm's length as it repositioned itself beside Bashir's leg.

"It's a shame they can't talk."

Bashir's thoughts seemed to be ringing, his head full of broken glass as he looked meticulously left and right in search of the voice he only half-remembered. He found George just inside the touch of the tiny lights, his head resting back against the same wall that supported Bashir, his hands neatly folded atop his knees. "The Federation may be lenient when it comes to determining sentience, but I have a feeling K'Taran's elders are going to want some more quantifiable evidence than kindness and a good bedside manner."

For some reason, it didn't even seem odd to be sitting in the blood-smelling dark debating sentience ethics with a Starfleet demigod while he felt beside him for the tricorder he couldn't remember last using. "So you believe they're sentient?" he asked George. But quietly, as though their discussion might embarrass the *xirri*.

George turned a wry look toward Bashir across the darkness. "Don't you?"

He finally found the tricorder close against his left hip. He wondered if he'd snugged it there for safekeeping, or simply dropped it the last time he'd slipped away from consciousness. Not that it mattered. The device had reverted to whatever dementia had addled its brain hours ago. A frightfully low blood pressure played hide-and-seek behind a skirl of signal so strong it almost washed his screen to white. By the time the *xirri* tapped the tricorder's casing to gain his attention, Bashir could barely tell he was a Human through the confusion of contradictory readings. Dropping the useless tricorder into his lap, he forced a wan smile when the *xirri* politely offered the butt end of the deactivated scalpel.

"Thank you again." His fingers felt cold when he reached for the instrument, and his thoughts ricocheted briefly off the idea that all his heat had collected into a burning coil by his knee. But whatever rationality he'd half-seen in that thought evaporated as he watched the *xirri* pick up the empty water bottle and toddle off toward the cavern's water supply.

Even the exertion necessary to follow the *xirri*'s movement with his eyes proved too much to sustain. Leaning his head back against the wall again, he listened to the shiver of his bones as the planet rumbled with distant damage.

"When I was young," George offered, his voice warm and soothing, "I served under a man who had a very flexible view of the Prime Directive." He laughed softly. "He didn't have much patience for politics and rhetoric. If he knew that innocent lives were being threatened, he'd move heaven and earth to save them, and the Prime Directive be damned."

Behind the darkness of his closed eyes, Bashir half-remembered, half-dreamed an image of Starfleet as it must have been on the frontier. "He sounds like a great man."

"He was. The best." George was quiet again, and when he finally spoke, his deep voice smiled. "He would have had a field day with Armageddon."

Bashir would have gladly given it to him. The planet, the comets, the killing, impenetrable foliage, the spiraling, threatening slash of fiery rain. Ice as hard as boulders, boulders the size of houses, shattering the mantle and spewing megatons of ash and rock and gas back into an atmosphere growing wintery cold for lack of sun. Feverish dozing offered a nightmarish flash of Kira and Dax swept up in a vortex of fire. He jerked himself awake, leaping away from that image, and his hand seized convulsively on the tricorder still open in his lap.

It chirped politely, scrolling out a neat queue of test results.

Bashir stared at the device for nearly thirty seconds, trying to remember why seeing the tricorder hum through its paces surprised him. It certainly wasn't the dismal readings and predictions it produced—his white-cell count was no higher than he'd already suspected, and it wasn't like he'd expected any better from his serum O_2. Cupping the tricorder between both hands, he lifted it and passed it across his torso. "Why am I not getting interference?" he asked aloud.

"What?"

"My tricorder . . ." He tipped it to face George as the older man scooted closer. "It hasn't worked since I left the Vrag main encampment. But now . . ." As though the tricorder heard him, a long scrawl of pointless code sketched itself through the middle of the readings, swelling like an amplified virus until it had taken over the small device's brain.

Cool water splashed across his exposed leg, startling him. Bashir looked up, catching the painted *xirri*'s indifferent gaze, and the tricorder hissed with renewed interference.

George's thoughtful, "I wonder what's happened now," barely penetrated the pulselike hammer of Bashir's thoughts.

It had been the *xirri* patients the tricorder first refused to scan. And when he'd first been carried into this cavern, before any *xirri* had come close to him down here—hadn't the tricorder produced perfectly coherent scans in those first few minutes? He made himself really *look* at the bands of distortion while the *xirri* neatly irrigated his leg precisely as he'd done himself a few hours before. What did this look like? What could this be that assumption simply hadn't let him see?

Medical school. A long, painfully boring lecture on

reducing tricorder interference patterns that might crop up during extravehicular triage missions. Oh, God, he'd barely listened because he'd been so worried about an upcoming xenosurgery rotation, and this had struck him as something better left to the engineers. But now his memory—which misplaced so little, even when it was only half-overheard behind a bout of narcissistic fretting seven years ago—exploded the answer across the front of his brain like a supernova.

"Radio waves . . ."

High frequency radio waves, intersecting the tricorder's fragile sensory circuits.

George dutifully held the small device while Bashir popped open the casing over the brains of his tricorder. "A doctor and an engineer," the older officer commented playfully after watching Bashir work for several minutes. "You're a man of many talents."

"You have no idea." By the time he mated the interference signal through the tricorder's translator and back, the result through the tricorder's speaker was no more than squeaky, scratchy nonsense. The *xirri* recoiled slightly, as if from fingernails on a blackboard.

Bashir reached out to catch its hand before it could scurry away. "I know this is just a matter of sampling," he said, keeping his eyes and smile on the *xirri* in the hopes it might realize he was speaking to it. It licked once, twice at its huge corneas, but didn't move away. "Once enough language goes into the translator, something I can understand comes out. So I hope it works the same way for you. Is there something I can do to keep you talking? To make you feed enough data—"

"—wish <wistfully, regretfully> for more true communication—"

The voice seemed almost too small to be real. No emotion, no inflection, just words spelled out as mechanically as type on a bare computer screen. But *words!* Bashir's heart raced against his breastbone. George hissed a little sound of surprise.

"—Noises <loudly, vocally> made become a language? Such kindness comes—"

George couldn't hold himself silent any longer. "Hello?"

The voice snapped silent. The tricorder blinked, but said nothing.

"Can you hear us?" Bashir fought the urge to say the words too loudly, but found it a hard impulse to ignore. "Can you understand what I'm saying?"

The *xirri* licked its eyes again, rapidly, in nervous stutters. "Can you <plainly, clearly> hear me?"

Bashir exchanged a triumphant glance with George, smiling so wide it hurt his cheeks. "Yes."

"These <inanimate, unliving> things—" The *xirri* whisked its tail around in front to hover the tip above the tricorder arrangement. "These give you my words?"

"Yes. I . . ." For the briefest instant, he thought of explaining the differences between sound waves and electromagnetism, and instead said only, "I can't hear your words with my ears without the help of these things."

The *xirri* nodded as though that only made sense.

"Before this, I was only aware of <vocal, random> noises from your kind. We did not know this was <intelligent, rational> speaking."

No more than the Klingons—or Bashir—had expected to discover *xirri* radio language in their silences. "You led us to these caves," he said, gesturing around them. "Do you understand what's happening outside?"

"We have not <personally, recently> seen fire falling from the sky." Its tail swept into a neat bracelet around its ankles as it settled back on its haunches. "But we have <old, remembered> stories of such fires from the past. These caves are where the *xirri* are told to go."

"Then why didn't you? When the first comets fell, there were *xirri* outside who were injured." He thought about the smoke-poisoned female, and the child this very *xirri* had carried all the way from the blast crater. "Why didn't you all come to the caves then?"

"Many <elderly, young> did. Others went in search of our <alien, childlike> friends. They have no <old, remembered> stories to protect them. Some were not among us, and we feared they would burn."

He remembered K'Taran's voice saying, *We knew the* xirri *would be needing help. So we came.* But it was George who finally said, very gently, "The *xirri* have been good friends to the Klingons."

The painted *xirri* cocked its head, reminding Bashir of nothing so much as a serious child considering the weightiness of its reply. "The sky has welcomed them with <fierce, renewing> fire," it said after a very long time. "If that does not forge them into oneness with the *xirri*, what will?"

Bat'leths met and locked with a clash of steel that thundered through the cold, dry air of the Klingon ship. "You fight well," said the stocky warrior scowling across that expanse of blood-splattered metal at Sisko. The thick tendons of his neck had made Sisko's slashing cut a minor annoyance rather than a telling blow, but it had still wiped the smug arrogance from his face. "For a Human."

"Thanks." Blood dripped down Sisko's face and seeped its salt taste between his gritted teeth, but it didn't impair his vision. The spiraling cheek-plate he'd thought was ornamental had stopped a wicked thrust of the pronged *bat'leth* point just short of his eye. His shoulder muscles burned with exhaustion and trembled with the effort of holding off his attacker, but his grin was still exultant. Five minutes into the *Sul'batlh* was longer than he'd ever expected to last.

Much of the credit for his survival had to go to the space in which they fought. He'd known that *Jfolokh*-class Klingon ships were small, but he'd never seen the inside of one before. It was a single cramped and cluttered deck, inhabited by a minimal crew of five in addition to its captain. As a result, Sisko and his opponent—a middle-aged Klingon engineer even more beer-bellied than Kor himself—had ducked and chopped their way through the various ship's stations in a chaos of swinging *bat'leths* and ducking Klingon ensigns.

With the steely clash of their weapons silenced, Sisko could hear the disrupted sounds of Odo's hand-to-hand battle with the young Klingon tactical officer and Worf's more titanic clash with Kor. The Dahar Master had refused to pursue his challenger, forcing Worf to come forward and attack him or risk forfeiting the *Suv'batlh* for cowardice. Despite Kor's stolid stance, however, there was nothing indolent or inebriated about his flying *bat'leth*. The constant, shattering crash of his blade against Worf's at times blended into continuous metallic thunder.

"Captain!" The young Klingon manning the sensor desk swung around, dark braids flying in alarm. "The Starfleet vessel is moving away at full impulse speed!"

Kor grunted, dropping to one knee to avoid a desperation roundhouse swing by Worf, then lunged up from below with the point of his blade. Worf flung himself backward, tripping over the empty chair of the weapon's console. He brought his *bat'leth* up just in time to avoid a wicked downward stab at his supine body, deflecting Kor's blade just enough to skate off his ribcage. Another bloody slash was added to the magenta lacework he already wore.

"Ignore the ship." Kor took a step back, catching his breath and incidentally giving Worf a chance to scramble back to his feet. "If we win, they leave no matter where they are. If we lose, they go wherever they like. Watch them for signs of attack, that is all."

They'd played this same scenario out several times now, the gasping old Dahar Master and the less accomplished but far more fit Starfleet officer. Each break in their furious fencing grew longer and each interval of blade-work shorter, giving Sisko a shred of hope that Worf might yet win, if he could just wear Kor down. Odo, on the other hand, was already teetering on the verge of failure. His long-armed and lithe young opponent had settled on a strategy of lunging and striking, oblivious to Odo's apparently ineffectual attempts to block him. Odo had reformed the rents in his mock-armor so many times that it had lost all its detail now, blurring into a generic solid surface, randomly swirled with black and red. The constant platinum flashes of protoplasmic matter beneath it, revealed every time a blow sliced through him, seemed to egg his Klingon opponent on to wilder and wilder swings. Sisko doubted the constable could hold his shape much longer.

Not that he was in much better condition, with his straining lungs and the dry rasp in his throat that came from trying to breathe the Klingons' harsher atmosphere. With a painful squeal of gouged metal, Sisko's *bat'leth* slipped across the engineer's blood-wet blade and slid violently off to one side. He cursed and swung toward the Klingon's knees, praying that his opponent's defensive instincts would yank him back rather than aiming his descending blade at Sisko's undefended torso.

He was half-successful—his opponent did jerk away, but not fast enough to keep the flat of his blade from unintentionally slamming into Sisko's solar plexus. All the breath from his lungs exploded out, making his vision darken abruptly. Choking, Sisko tried to stagger backward, away from wherever his opponent now was. Fortunately, the small Klingon ship chose that moment to stagger, too, its hull thundering with a barely shielded explosion.

"What was *that?*" Kor bellowed, giving the sprawled and even bloodier Worf another respite to climb to his feet. Seeing that his own opponent had swung around to scowl at his readouts with single-minded engineering focus, Sisko clung, gasping, to the back of an empty console. The black edges faded from his vision just in time to let him see the violent spray of glittering white fragments that erupted across the sensor's field of view. It looked like a firework made of ice.

"Comet impact," the engineer said unnecessarily.

"OI'yaH! Ghuy'cha' gu'valth!" Kor's curses were as magnificently extravagant as his flowing silver-streaked mane. With absentminded ease, he warded off a slashing attack from Worf, then smacked his *bat'leth* against the back of his pilot's chair to express his displeasure. "You're supposed to be flying us through these things, D'jia, not watching the fight!"

She curled her lip without ever breaking her gaze away from the main viewscreen. *"What* fight? All I've seen is a *bat'leth* practice, and not a very good one at that."

"Answer my question!" Kor snarled, seemingly oblivious to Worf's cat-silent approach right up to the second when he turned and struck at the Starfleet officer, hurling him halfway across the deck with the power of his *bat'leth* blow. Blood trickled from Worf's nostrils. "Why are we suddenly hitting comets?"

"We're not." Another shuddering impact hit the

Klingon ship, making the female pilot curse pretty magnificently herself. "They're hitting us. All of a sudden, none of them are where they're supposed to be!"

"Well, take evasive action!"

"I'm trying!" The Klingon ship looped and danced through the thickening platinum haze of debris that seemed to be closing around them. Sisko's stomach lurched, feeling the drag and kick of uncompensated inertial fields. "But something keeps disturbing them, and it's throwing them right at us!"

"What a coincidence." In one fluid motion, Kor tore his engrossed engineer away from his damage reports and threw him back toward Sisko, then met Worf's next *bat'leth* thrust with a blade-locking twist and jerk. "I don't suppose your ship had anything to do with that, Worf, son of Mogh?" he growled into the younger man's blood-streaked face.

"No," Worf said with exhausted honesty. "They are far from here by now, deflecting other comets away from Cha'Xirrac."

Kor's furious roar drowned out the wet, hollow sound of a *bat'leth* sinking deep into flesh, but it couldn't drown the involuntary scream of pain that followed. Sisko didn't have time to see who was hit— he was too busy bracing himself against the ship's drunken swoops to meet the engineer's next blow. Rather than try to parry this one, he used the same maneuver he'd seen Kor try on Worf—dropping to one knee so that his opponent's blade whistled over his head, then lunging up with the wicked tip of the *bat'leth*.

245

The blade hit the Klingon engineer's rib cage at what seemed like an awkwardly obtuse angle, but to Sisko's immense surprise, it slid over one rib and under another to bite deep within his burly chest. The engineer staggered back, looking more dazed than hurt, and peered down at the *bat'leth* still protruding from his chest. "Good aim," he croaked, then collapsed unconscious at Sisko's feet, a bright trickle of blood oozing from the wound. Grabbing at the nearest bulkhead to steady himself, Sisko stared down at him, still not quite believing he had won.

The female pilot glanced over her shoulder. "Beginner's luck," she said in disgust. "You bruised his *gla'chiH*—the shielded nerve plexus in his chest. He's out for a day at least." She jerked her chin at Sisko, scowling. "Go ahead, pull the *bat'leth* out. Nothing will hurt him now."

Sisko did as she said, watching the trickle of blood slow as the wound closed. Then he jerked his head up, suddenly becoming aware of the silence around him. Not a single clash of *bat'leths*, not a thud of falling bodies disturbed the ragged sound of exhausted and pain-racked breathing.

He looked for Worf first, anxiously, and found him in exactly the position he'd most feared. His tall tactical officer lay sprawled across the empty weapons panel, one arm dangling brokenly and the other locked above his head in Kor's massive fist. The Dahar Master had leaned all his considerable weight on his opponent, keeping him trapped despite weakening struggles. When the point of Kor's *bat'leth* dug into his throat, deep enough to spring a bright pulse of blood out with each beat of his strong heart, Worf stopped struggling and just scowled up at him.

"Qapla'." Despite his swollen and blood-wet face, Worf sounded as stubbornly indomitable as ever. It was hard to believe he had really lost. "The *Suv'batlh* belongs to you, Dahar Master. Now kill me."

CHAPTER
11

"Is the *Suv'batlh* mine? On all counts?" Kor glanced over his shoulder, frowning when he saw his engineer recumbent at Sisko's feet. It wasn't until his gaze skated past them toward the third pair of fighters, though, that his face darkened to the consistency of a thundercloud. "Kitold! How in the name of the dead Klingon gods did that happen?"

His weapons officer stepped forward, swaying as another comet thundered off the aft shield. One hand was locked around his battle-gloved forearm to hold his dislocated arm in place. The greenish pallor of his face told Sisko he wouldn't stay on his feet much longer.

"It was subterfuge," he said hoarsely. "The Changeling pretended to be more weary than he actually was, in order to lure me into position for his strike."

Sisko's gaze went past the wounded Klingon to Odo, whose mock-Klingon armor flowed back into the constable's usual pristine uniform even as he watched. "Is that true?" he demanded.

Odo gave him a stiff nod of acknowledgment. "It seemed like a legitimate maneuver. I admit, I did alter my appearance to a certain extent to achieve the deception, but it is not as if I *can* turn pale or sweat with fear. Nothing about my shape-shifting ever endangered my opponent."

"It was trickery!" insisted the young Klingon.

"More like strategy." Kor yanked his *bat'leth* abruptly from Worf's throat, releasing him to stagger back and clutch at his own wounded arm. "You were taken in by the oldest warrior's trick in the book, Kitold! You deserve to lose that arm, but I don't want to smell your corpse all the way back to the homeworld. Go put yourself into a medical stasis chamber—*now!*"

The wounded Klingon growled in ungrateful acknowledgment before he pushed past Sisko, heading toward the bank of stasis lockers at the back of the main deck. Worf watched him go, then turned a puzzled gaze on Kor. *"Wej Heghehugh vay', SuvtaH SuvwI'?* If someone has not yet died, how can a Klingon warrior stop fighting?"

Kor snorted, richly scornful. "Only a fool takes a death that means nothing. I didn't get to be a Dahar Master by being a fool." He reached out to steady Worf as the younger male staggered, either thrown off-balance by the ship's evasive swerves or perhaps just noticing the pain of his many wounds. The only thing splashed on Kor's robe, Sisko noticed wryly, was blood wine. *"Dujeychugh jagh nIv yItuHQo'*. There is nothing shameful in falling before a superior enemy. Through the luck of your captain and the wiles of your Changeling, you have won the *Suv'batlh* you challenged me to, Worf, son of Mogh. What is your will of me?"

Worf opened his mouth, but before he could say a word, the female pilot swung around at her console, pale eyes blazing. "Captain! Security alert! Those comets that keep hitting us—I think they're being deflected by a vessel entering the system!"

"What?" Kor cursed and shoved Worf aside, diving for his command chair. "Identity of vessel?"

"I can't tell!" The young Klingon sensor technician pounded on his unresponsive panels. "My instruments can't even penetrate the mass of comets gathered in front of it! The debris is a hundred times more dense than it should be. Whoever it is, they must have followed the ice-giant's orbital track all the way into the system, collecting debris with their tractor beams the whole way."

"Cardassians!" Kor said with disgusted certainty. "Who else would apply themselves so diligently to such a coward's strategy?" He threw an ironic look at Sisko. *"Gul* Hidret is probably scanning the system as we speak, hoping to find the charred remains of *both* our ships."

"Possibly." Sisko took a step closer to the viewscreen, as if that could somehow make the unknown vessel appear out of the icy haze. It didn't, but the silent, dusty curve of Armageddon's horizon swung into view as the female pilot looped around a particularly thick comet cluster. He felt his gut twist with foreboding. "How many comets is that unknown ship pushing in front of them?"

"Ten thousand, maybe more," the sensor technician said grimly. "All gathered into a space of only nineteen cubic kilometers and accelerated to a quarter impulse speed."

That made Kor's breath whistle out in shock. "In what direction?" he demanded. "Toward us?"

"No." The female pilot glanced up at the blood-colored image of Armageddon on the viewscreen, pity flickering in her cold Klingon eyes. "Toward the planet."

Sisko and Odo exchanged appalled looks. "The away team," Worf said hoarsely. "We must notify them."

"To let them prepare for their deaths with honor." Kor nodded gravely. "It is a reasonable request. Boost their comm badge signals through our transmitter, Bhirq."

Sisko slapped a hand to his chest without even waiting for the Klingon technician to reply. "Sisko to Kira, Sisko to Dax."

"Dax here." Her calm Trill voice brought a reminiscent smile to Kor's face, one that faded into regret an instant later. "Go ahead, Benjamin."

"A Cardassian battleship has just swept up ten thousand comet fragments and launched them toward Armageddon," Sisko said, with brutal curtness. "You've got to beam out, *now!*"

"Understood." The advantage of having a subordinate with three hundred cumulative years of experience was that she knew when to ask for details and explanations, and when not to. "Time to impact?"

"Forty minutes," said the Klingon pilot. "Max."

"Then we might have a shot at getting everyone on the planet into shelter. Julian and the crash survivors have taken refuge in a deep cave system. If we can get there, we should be immune even to the impact of ten thousand comets." Dax's voice had taken on the steely determination that meant she wasn't going to take "no" for an answer. "Permission to stay on planet, Captain?"

"Granted," Sisko said, scowling. "Just be damned sure you're inside that cave in thirty minutes, old man, not out gathering up some last DNA samples from an endangered plant."

The Trill science officer made a wordless noise of amusement. "Don't worry, Benjamin. The plants down here can take care of their own DNA without any help from me. Dax out."

Kor glanced at Worf, who was quietly dripping blood across the empty weapons panel that propped him up. "You could make your *Suv'batlh* request the phasering of these Cardassian comets," the Dahar Master said suggestively. "Every one we shoot—"

"—becomes a cluster of smaller ones and spreads the destruction even further," Sisko said flatly. "And there are far too many to deflect with our shields, even using both our ships."

Odo gave the older Klingon an ironic look. "In any case, wouldn't those actions violate the honorable exile of your countrymen?"

Kor spat toward the comet-clouded viewscreen. "The Cardassians have already done that, Changeling."

The viewscreen flared with wild static for a moment, then resolved into a forced transmission from the *Defiant*. O'Brien's bleak gaze scanned across them, unable to focus on Sisko since the Klingons weren't transmitting back. "Captain, sensors have picked up the arrival of the *Olxinder* on your side of the planet, pushing a forced impact wave of twelve thousand comet fragments in front of them. The away team says you know about it. I'll wait ten minutes for your orders, then start flying through the field, trying to target the largest and most destructive fragments. O'Brien out."

Worf groaned, not entirely in pain. "The *Defiant's* shields cannot survive the onslaught of twelve thousand comets!"

"Ten thousand," the Klingon sensor tech interrupted peevishly.

"So what is your *Suv'batlh* request, Worf, son of Mogh?" Kor repeated impatiently. "To save your shipmates by making us sacrifice our own ship to the comets?"

"No," Sisko said, before his wounded tactical officer could reply. "Our request is to consider this system from now on as a joint Klingon-Federation protectorate. Correct, Mr. Worf?"

His tactical officer nodded, with the utter trust in his commander that had won Sisko's appreciation from the first. "And to cede to Captain Sisko any rights won by me in the *Suv'batlh* combat." Worf fell to his knees with a massive thud that Sisko felt across the deck. "I fear I will not remain conscious long enough to exercise them."

Kor scowled. "The second of those requests is reasonable and I agree to it. But what sense does the first make?"

"It gives us the joint ability to defend this system from the Cardassians," Sisko retorted. "And prove to the entire galaxy that they are not only smuggling banned neurochemical weapons, they are also destroying an ecosystem they don't own to obtain it."

Kor's scowl grew more thoughtful. "You think they didn't just bring those comets in to hide behind? You think they actually planned to wipe out everything alive on that planet, just to get their hands on the last dregs of drevlocet?"

"That sounds like a rhetorical question to me," Odo said caustically.

Sisko took a step forward, ignoring the angry ache of strained shoulder muscles. "Your ship is cloaked, just like the *Defiant,* and we know the Cardassians aren't very good at detecting ion trails. They won't know we're here until we fire our weapons, either at the comets or at them. If we let them think what they want to think—that we destroyed each other battling over this planet, and left the coast clear for them to move in, I have a hunch they'll incriminate themselves exactly forty minutes from now."

"So we play dead, while the planet beneath us dies?"

Sisko grimaced. "I don't like that either—but all our people should be safe and I trust my science officer when she says the planet will recover. What we do have time to save is the rest of the Alpha Quadrant. Now, are you going to cooperate with us, or does our *Suv'batlh* request have to be the self-destruction of this ship?"

Kor gave that ultimatum the fierce snort of disdain it deserved, since Sisko never had any intention of enforcing it. "What about the House of Vrag? If any live after the comet deluge, are they going to be rescued against their will?"

"Federation policy only allows us to evacuate planet residents who wish to leave." Sisko never thought he would live to be grateful for diplomatic equivocation. "The House of Vrag will get to decide their own fate, and preserve their own honor."

The Dahar Master mulled that over, then jerked his head in a satisfied Klingon nod. "That will satisfy the High Council, provided there are no more traitors like that *garg*-carcass you sent here for disposal. When we get back to the homeworld, I'm going to have to decontaminate my stasis chambers just to get the stink of him out of them."

At that moment, Worf slumped into unconsciousness with a violent crash of armor. Sisko cursed and sprang to catch him before he rolled across the deck.

"We need to beam him back to the *Defiant* for medical attention," he said to Kor. "And I need to tell O'Brien not to fly into that comet storm. Have you accepted our *Suv'batlh* conditions? Is Armageddon now a joint Klingon-Federation protectorate?"

"No." Kor grinned wickedly at Odo's startled frown. "But Cha'Xirrac is."

Sisko threw the elderly Klingon an exasperated glare. He was starting to see why Kor and Curzon Dax had gotten along so well. "Then my first request as coprotector of Cha'Xirrac is for you to beam me back aboard the *Defiant*. We'll patrol opposite sides of the planet—whoever first detects the Cardassians beaming down to the planet after the comet impacts gets to confront them, but it has to be on a wide-open channel. Agreed?"

"Agreed." Kor glanced up at the viewscreen, no longer hazed with icy glitter now that they had escaped the Cardassian-gathered swarm. Distant light bloomed in the planet's dust-stained atmosphere, the harmless high-level explosion of a natural comet collision. Sisko's gut still jerked with dismay, anticipating the inferno to come. "Provided there is a planet left for them to beam down to."

"I can't believe you thought this was a good idea."

Kira bent as low as she dared, ignoring the twinge in her lower back, pretending her thighs and knees and ankles weren't screaming complaints loud enough to wake all of Armageddon's past extinctions. "You've got to admit," she grunted, grabbing Dax's arms and hauling back with all her might, "it does give us some advantages."

They toppled to the burn-scarred *tuq'mor* canopy one on top the other. Eyebrow arched, Dax tossed a look at the Klingons still struggling to climb the tangled brush as she extricated herself from Kira and rolled clumsily onto her back. "Let's hope it's advantage enough."

If it wasn't, then they were no worse off than they'd been on the ground. *Give or take a few fall-related injuries.* At least she and Dax weren't pinwheeling their arms or lurching about with one hand always in contact with the *tuq'mor*. She watched Rekan's two honor companions crack the scorched surface of the canopy more than once as they stumbled into the formal *Suv'batlh* wedge. If Dax and K'Taran could lead their opponents over some of the more fire-weakened surfaces, they might be able to keep their footing even when the heftier Klingons broke through. Kira, on the other hand, had a feeling *epetai* Vrag would be harder to displace than her less-dedicated counterparts. She would hang onto Kira's throat with her teeth before she fell.

For some reason, the Klingon matriarch looked taller on top the *tuq'mor,* standing proudly—if not comfortably—with her chin held high. She'd dragged loose the rhodium comb pinning her hair in place the moment the challenge was official. The mass of silver white hair that cascaded down her back gleamed unexpectedly bright in their ash-faded surroundings. A wild mane of icy fire. When she fitted the comb back into her hair, Kira thought it looked like a thin, silver tiara framing the back of her skull, an appropriate addendum to her cool alien beauty.

Kira positioned herself the required three paces in front of the *epetai,* resolutely squaring her tired shoulders. "The *tuq'mor* is the battleground," she announced, loudly enough that the Klingons now crowding the ground level could hear. "Falling from the *tuq'mor* constitutes leaving the combat, and that warrior is forfeit. Agreed?"

Rekan nodded once, fiercely. "Agreed. *Qapla'!*"

Kira had imagined a slightly more ritualized beginning to the combat, although it struck her upon reflection that this was naive. Klingons were nothing if not straightforward. Rekan launched herself at Kira like a leaping rock-cat, slamming the smaller Bajoran with the full weight of her body and driving them both to the *tuq'mor*. Limbs cracked and jabbed at Kira's back like broken ribs, then gave way and dropped her a good foot into the dry underbrush. Rekan pressed down on her from above, her hand clamped under Kira's jaw.

"If this were a true *Suv'batlh*," she growled, "you would be dead and I would already be the victor. Yield!"

Kira sucked a painful breath and locked her arms in the *tuq'mor* beyond her head. "Warriors do not yield!" And she kicked downward with both feet before Rekan could respond.

Limbs splintered in an irregular mass, reclosing around Kira's slim body with springy resilience all out of proportion to their brittleness. Rekan tangled in the upper story, her torso suddenly angled abruptly downward, and Kira willfully snatched double handfuls of white hair to twist among the brambles before dragging herself laterally out of the older Klingon's reach.

It felt like wriggling on her back through a shattered maintenance duct; cables of vine fouled her passage so that spindly fingers of shrubbery could tear at her uniform, prick at her eyes. By the time she found an opening to haul herself back to the upper surface, she bolted into the open like an ice-swimmer reclaiming the surface. The *tuq'mor* canopy no longer seemed such a sturdy playing field. Adrenaline spiked her bloodstream with every placement of her feet, every shift and crackle of failing timber. She floated her arms out to either side in search of a constantly wandering balance, and insisted to her fear that running along the jouncing bushtops was no different than walking scaffolding or climbing trees. The dry sourness at the back of her throat suggested she didn't find herself very convincing.

Kira half-hopped, half-stumbled in a circle to try and place herself in the combat. Rekan had vanished, leaving only snarls of torn silver hair fluttering in the hot breeze. Growls and labored breathing far to her right rear helped Kira locate K'Taran, where the young girl wrestled a tall male almost three times her age near the remnants of one great hut-tree. *She's going to lose,* Kira realized abruptly. It was a wonder she'd held out as long as she had. Wrenching free of the older male's hold, K'Taran jumped nearly as high as his shoulder and scrabbled up the charred stump to leap from its top. Her landing was awkward, but it put distance between her and the big male; he lurched across the canopy like a drunken *mugatu,* huffing and cursing. *That's the way,* Kira thought. *If you can't beat him, wear him out.*

Taking the hint, she trotted a few more long steps away from where she'd left Rekan, scanning the dark battleground for the rest of the *Suv'batlh.* She faced a distressing lack of silhouettes against the flaming sky. "Dax?"

"Down here!" The Trill's voice floated up from below. She sounded distinctly irritated and impossibly far away. "I'm fine! K'Daq fell down with me, so we're both out."

Kira crouched as low as she dared, and peered

between her feet for a closer look at shadow movement within the shadows. "You sure you're all right?"

"Nothing hurt but my pride. Look after yourself!"

Sound advice. If only it had come a moment sooner.

A dark hand shot upward out of the *tuq'mor*, as fast and fierce as a spider. Kira backpedaled, lifting her knees high to take her feet out of grabbing range, but not quickly enough. Rekan clamped strong fingers around one ankle, and Kira knew even before the Klingon hauled back on her leg that she'd run out of options. There was nowhere left to run.

Kira hit the *tuq'mor* canopy full length, her shoulders taking the brunt of the impact, just ahead of the back of her skull. She felt the *tuq'mor* creak and shiver, like a stand of marsh grass under the thrashing of a great wind, and her mind reeled wildly, *I didn't fall that hard? Did I really fall that hard?* Then she heard the thunder, and realized that these stomach-wrenching tremors came from farther away than her own collision with the *tuq'mor*. She struggled to climb to all fours.

At first, Rekan's torso blocked her view of the clearing and the Klingons standing witness on the ground. The *epetai* had dragged herself halfway out of the understory, the scratches on her cheeks and the brilliant blood in her hair only accentuating her fearful wildness. Now, her eyes met Kira's with a flash of purest hatred, and Kira knew in that instant that this battle wasn't between *epetai* Vrag and Kira Nerys—it was a battle between what used to be and what could never be again.

Kira said only, "Listen."

Tremors shook the brush in angry fists. Ash the color of powdered bone drifted up from the *tuq'mor* like smoke, and Kira had to grab at whatever whipping limbs she could reach to keep from being shaken down between the branches. Rekan only knelt where she'd stopped, head lifted, face hollow. She reminded Kira of one of the Klingons' dead goddesses. Even perched and bleeding on the edges of *sylshessa,* her dignity and grace were breathtaking.

Below them, the Klingons did not panic. It occurred to Kira that perhaps they were a people incapable of panic, those genes having been shriven from their species ages ago by warriors unwilling to tolerate such weakness. When K'Taran's *banchory* groaned a long, low bellow of distress, even the youngest of the children merely scurried clear of its thrashing. Then the first of the mounted *banchory* crashed into the open, and the bawling of these lumbering newcomers nearly drowned out the cries of surprise.

Ash-stained primates—the little green-gray lemurs Kira had seen haunting the edges of the camp from the beginning—crowded the backs of the great pachyderms. One of them scampered forward, down its *banchory's* plated rill to crouch on the wide nose-bridge between the mammoth's eyes. The "come hither" curling of its hands and wrists seemed unmistakable to Kira. And, apparently, to one of the children clustered at the base of the *tuq'mor.* The boy took only a single step forward before one of the older women reached out to stop him, stating simply, "*Epetai* says we must stay."

Kira shivered at the helplessly loyal chill that

passed through the family. A few—most of them very young, although some might have been the parents of K'Taran and her rebel adolescents—turned their eyes upward toward Rekan. No recrimination in those stark gazes, no pleas. As though they all stated fact to one another, and their *epetai* simply represented what they already knew to be true.

Duty, Kira realized. *Honor.* It mattered so much to them, they would willingly forsake all else, even survival.

Sinking slowly to her heels, Rekan stared down at her children, and their children, and all the pasts and futures every Klingon House created. "Must honor always be cruel?" she asked softly. Not really to Kira, the major knew, even though there was no one else close enough to hear. "I know in my heart what honor demands of us . . . yet now that we face the final moments . . . I would not see my children die. . . ."

Kira looked down at her hands, not knowing what to say, and sensing the question was rhetorical anyway.

"I would not have love and honor always run in separate ways." The *epetai* straightened, and her voice rang purely, clearly over the roar of exploding comets and the rumble of fidgeting *banchory*. "Go. Take the children—they are this House's future. Put yourselves in safety until the sky no longer burns." When no one moved, she announced, more gently, "Honor commanded only that we remain on Cha'Xirrac forever. Not that we must die."

She turned to Kira as the first of the elders lifted a youngster into one of the primates' waiting arms.

262

"The *Suv'batlh* is ended," she told Kira, very, very quietly. "Go."

Kira touched the *epetai*'s arm when Rekan moved to turn away. "You should come with us."

Rekan stared toward the burning horizon, immobile.

"You can't abandon them now," Kira said. "Your House is going to need you when the comet strikes are over."

The Klingon shook her head, and a ghostly smile brushed her eyes without appearing on her features. "This House is of Cha'Xirrac now. It will need an *epetai* who is of Cha'Xirrac as well." She was silent for a moment, watching K'Taran and her *Suv'batlh* opponent work as allies in herding children onto the *banchory*. Then she caught sight of Kira from the corner of her eye, and smiled with what seemed genuine warmth. "Such a look! There is no shame in admitting that one's service is finished." She gave the major one last nod toward the others as she rose slowly to full height. "I go to Sto-Vo-Kor at peace with the state of my honor," she assured her. "Save your pity for the survivors."

CHAPTER

12

ARMAGEDDON HAD, HORRIBLY, lived up to its name.

The comet storm had started violently enough, with the enormous smoke-shrouded flares of near-surface explosions. Within ten minutes, the planet's atmosphere had congealed and darkened everywhere, giving it an oddly opaque look in the oblivious saffron sunlight. Watching from his command chair on the bridge of the *Defiant*, Sisko realized he was watching the fall of cometary night, a dust-driven darkness whose dawn might not arrive for days or even weeks. But that was just the start.

"The first really big fragment is going in now." Ensign Farabaugh turned at the comet-tracking station, his eyes sober beneath a tidy bandage. "Impact in two minutes."

"Will it explode in the atmosphere?" Odo inquired. "Like the others, only bigger?"

"I don't think so," the young science officer said. "It looks like this one is actually big enough and solid enough to hit the surface. If it does, it could excavate a crater one or two kilometers deep."

"So much for being protected in a cave." O'Brien saw the irritated look Sisko sent him and shrugged. "Optimism is for command officers, Captain. Engineers prefer pessimism, because it saves lives instead of risking them. Are you sure we can't just beam up the away team? We've had a lock on their comms for the last ten minutes, and they've barely moved."

"Not while the Cardassians are on our side of the planet," Sisko said. "Chief, if you want to be pessimistic, why don't you send those comm coordinates to Farabaugh? That way, he can alert us if it looks like a surface impact is going to come too close."

"Good idea." The chief engineer bent over his panel, just in time to miss the enormous steel-colored light that exploded across the upper half of Armageddon's huge eastern ocean. A slowly towering column of fire rose above it, its crenulated ash-black clouds rising so high into the planet's stratosphere that the topmost debris drifted out of the gravity well completely and was lost to space. A collective gasp of horror hit the bridge, bringing O'Brien's sandy head around toward the viewscreen so fast he almost slammed into his console. "God Almighty! Is that anywhere near the away team?"

"The impact wasn't," Farabaugh assured him. "And I don't *think* the tsunami will run quite that far inland—"

"The tsunami?" That was Ensign Frisinger, Worf's substitute pilot, whose fascinated gaze hadn't wavered from the viewscreen once since the comet storm had begun. Sisko hoped he knew his panel controls by touch. "What's that?"

"The shock wave in the ocean that the impact creates," Osgood explained. "High-level explosions don't usually make them, since they displace air instead of water."

Farabaugh was punching a quick calculation into his station. "Looks like the main wave should hit shore starting about three hours from now. The backwash and secondary waves will probably last through tomorrow evening."

"Let's hope the Cardassians don't know that," Sisko said, grimacing. "I don't feel like waiting that long to confront them."

The barrage of high-level airbursts rose to an almost continuous glare of explosions after that, as if the ocean impact had been some kind of floodgate, opening to let all the rest of the swarm pour through. The increasingly ash-choked sky turned each bloom of light a deeper crimson-tinted black, like roses charring in a celestial flame. It was hard, watching from the distant bridge of the *Defiant,* to remember that these silent fireworks represented destruction on a planetary scale.

"Still getting signal back from the away team, Chief?" Sisko couldn't repress the question any longer. A second surface impact had geysered up, this time from the shadowy darkness that he thought represented the main continent. This mushroom-shaped debris cloud rose even higher than the first, high enough that the debris sparked a firefly glitter of auroral light when it burst through the planet's magnetic torus.

"Off and on, between the EM pulses. At least, it doesn't seem to be getting any weaker." O'Brien glanced back over his shoulder. "There aren't any big fragments aiming for those caves, are there, ensign?"

"No, sir." Farabaugh glanced over at Sisko, the pale damp sheen of his face belying his claim of being completely healed. "In fact, there aren't any more big pieces left. The whole storm is tapering off. In another ten minutes, Armageddon should be back to business as usual."

Sisko sat up, his pulse sharpening to battle-ready alertness. "Scan for the Cardassian ship, maximum resolution."

"Got it." Thornton's hand flew across the science station, fine-tuning the resolution on his sensors. There was something to be said for assigning an engineering specialist to use his own instruments, Sisko thought. "Image coming through now, sir. It's the *Olxinder*, for sure."

"I can see that." The Cardassian battleship's sharp-edged silhouette was just rounding the planet's smoky horizon, leaving Kor's patrol and entering their own. Sisko would have bet all the antique baseballs in his collection that the Klingon Dahar Master followed them, and probably at a none-too-discreet distance. "I want to know the instant you get the hint of a shuttle launch, a transporter beam, or—"

"—a scan of the planet?" Thornton glanced over

his shoulder, his quiet face lit with an unexpected smile. "They're doing it now, sir. Sensors seem to be set for native life-signs."

"Can their instruments penetrate into the caves?" Odo demanded. "The Cardassians might cut and run if they find evidence of any surviving Klingons, not to mention Humans, Trills, and Bajorans."

The young engineering tech shook his head. "I don't think they've even got the resolution to cut through the leftover EM furze. They're going to have to go down."

"In a shuttle, too, at least if they know what's good for them." O'Brien saw Odo's questioning look. "You wouldn't catch me trying to transport through that electromagnetic mess."

Sisko grunted. "Then get a tractor beam ready, Chief. Frisinger, make sure we're never out of tractor range—but don't bump into Kor while you do it."

"Aye, sir."

"—to *Defiant*." The crackle of static coming from his chair's communicator couldn't disguise the vibrancy of Dax's voice—or the scientific excitement that ran through it. "Dax to *Defiant*. Can you—?"

"I'm working on it," O'Brien said, forestalling Sisko's unspoken command. "Signal resolution coming up now."

"Link a secure channel to Kor," Sisko said quietly. "He'll want to know that Dax is alive."

"Dax to Sisko. Can you read us yet, Benjamin?"

"Sisko here. What's your situation?"

"Completely secured, Captain." That was his second-in-command, sounding exhausted but just as competent as ever. "All the Klingon refugees are in stable health, and so are the survivors from *Victoria Adams*'s crew—all thirty-one of them. We've managed to save a surprising number of the natives, too, even the big pachyderms. They seemed to have an instinct—"

"It's more than an instinct for some of them." Sisko lifted an eyebrow, knowing Dax was never that rude unless a major scientific breakthrough was bubbling to the surface. "Benjamin, some of the natives are *sentient!*"

"Not just sentient." That was a voice Sisko hadn't heard in too long. Its weary British accent and carefully precise language dissolved a knot of tension he hadn't even realized he was feeling. "The *xirri* are a full-fledged Class-two civilization, Captain: oral history, medicine, long-distance radio communication—"

"The natives have *technology?*" Sisko exchanged startled looks with O'Brien and Odo. If the Klingons had knowingly violated the Prime Directive when they'd chosen this planet for their honorable exile, it was going to be a lot harder to convince the Federation that they now owned half of it.

"The *xirri*'s ability to communicate in radio wavelengths isn't technological, Benjamin." Dax sounded both dazed and delighted by that fact. "It's a biological adaptation, bred into them by reproductive isolation and the stress of cometary impact. As far as we can tell, all the native vertebrates have the same capacity, but—"

Sisko saw the urgent look Thornton cast him and cut ruthlessly across his science officer's explanation. "You can explain all the gory details to me later, old man. I've got a Cardassian *gul* getting ready to tip his hand, and I want to be ready to slap it."

"Understood." There was a muffled grunt behind Kira's voice, as if someone's toe had been stepped on. "Away team out."

"I'm reading a power surge in the circuits around the Cardassians' main shuttle door," Thornton told him, before the crackle of static had even faded from the bridge. "I think they're getting ready to launch an expedition to the planet."

"Shields at full power, cloak controls set for imminent drop," Sisko said. "Set tractor beam coordinates for a kilometer away from the launch door."

"Coordinates laid in," O'Brien confirmed. "Tractor beam fully charged and ready."

"Launch doors opening," Thornton said. The *Olxinder* slowly rotated as she orbited the ash-dark planet, bringing her belly-slit shuttle bay into gloriously clear resolution. "Shuttle deploying inside launch bay."

"Red alert. Quantum torpedoes armed and ready for launch." Sisko didn't really expect Hidret to put up a fight, but you could never tell what a weasel would do when cornered. It would be stupid to be unprepared. "Shuttle position, Mr. Thornton?"

"Four hundred meters and accelerating. Six hundred, eight hundred—"

"Drop cloak and engage tractor beam," Sisko snapped, anticipating the thousand meter mark. O'Brien must have been equally primed for action—the tractor beam flashed out before he'd even finished calling for it, its gold-dust glitter smacking through the silver cometary haze to seize on the Cardassian shuttlecraft.

Sisko felt the *Defiant* rock with an unexpected jolt of backwash inertia, and threw a frown at O'Brien. The chief engineer was growling at his controls.

"If you're going to stay locked even though we were first, the least you could do is match your beam intensity . . . damn arrogant Klingons!"

Sisko's gaze rose to the viewscreen, startled. He could see, now that O'Brien had pointed it out, the mirror glimmer of a second tractor beam, refracting back across the planet's horizon. An instant later, the uncloaked silhouette of a *Jfolokh*-class ship rose above the ashen atmosphere, tracking back along its beam toward the mammoth Cardassian battleship like a fish reeling itself toward the fisherman.

"Hail the Cardassians on an open channel." The corner of Sisko's mouth kicked upward wryly. "And prepare for a three-way conference, Mr. Thornton."

"Aye, sir."

Armageddon's seared image vanished, replaced by a duplicate image of scowling, furrowed faces. Kor's expression, however, was one of pure military ferocity, while *Gul* Hidret's had clearly been plastered over shock and indecision.

"Is this an act of war, Captain Sisko?" he demanded, in what was probably meant to be a preemptive strike. "Are you actually working in league with these Klingon ruffians after all?"

"Yes, I am." Sisko allowed a cold slice of smile to show. "I'm legally required to, *Gul* Hidret, since this is now a joint Klingon-Federation protectorate."

"What?" The Cardassian's scowl lost a little more of its assurance. "When was that treaty signed?"

"An hour ago, in Klingon and Human blood," Kor

retorted. "All it needs now is some Cardassian blood to be complete."

"Nonsense!" Hidret sounded as though he might choke on his own disbelief. "You think to fool me by making such wild, unreasonable claims."

"I admit, you were the one who first suggested this alliance," Sisko said wickedly. "The more I thought about it, the better an idea it seemed."

Hidret shook his head. "I don't believe it. You're going to let this Starfleet officer interfere with your dishonored exiles, Kor?"

"No," said the Dahar Master grimly. "We're going to make sure that my dishonored exiles haven't interfered with the sentient natives whose civilization we just discovered. Of course," he added maliciously, "any little ecological problems they may have caused will pale in comparison with the devastation we just saw you create."

"*What?*" *Gul* Hidret looked like a man whose worst fevered nightmares had just erupted into waking life. "You're lying! There are no sentients on that planet—"

"And how would you know that, *Gul,* if you've never set foot on Cha'Xirrac?" Sisko asked silkily.

"It—it was surveyed by the medical teams scouring this region for the cure to *ptarvo* fever."

Kor snorted. "If you ever needed a cure for the randiness of youth—which I very much doubt—your searches here found no cure for it."

"All you found here," Sisko continued, "was a cheap and easy source of drevlocet. Isn't that right, *Gul* Hidret?"

"Drevlocet that the Cardassian High Command would like to modify to use on Klingons," Kor finished. "Isn't *that* right, *Gul* Hidret?"

The elderly Cardassian grimaced, the wrinkled canyons of his face growing deep and darkly shadowed. "I refuse to answer such accusations in this—this inappropriate setting! I came here in response to a willful attack against the Cardassian people, only to find it was a trap!"

Sisko permitted himself a scowl. "Our diplomats can settle who set the traps in this system, *Gul* Hidret. But the fact remains that this planet beneath us is now its own sovereign state, subject to no external interference in its ecology or its affairs."

"Exactly what I'd be the first to tell you," the elderly Cardassian insisted. "And just as soon as you release my shuttle full of emergency medical personnel, I'll be on my way."

"Good," Kor said. "I hate to break it to you, old enemy, but your ship seems to have a most unfortunate attraction to comets. It would be a shame if one actually penetrated your shields and caused a hull breach." Snaggle-teeth bared in a grin that would have done credit to a crocodile. "And the longer you stay in this area, the more likely that is to happen. Don't you agree, Captain Sisko?"

"Definitely."

Gul Hidret slapped at his communicator controls, breaking the connection without another word. Kor promptly broke into a massive roar of laughter.

"That old *targ*'s going to be swerving around every speck of dust between here and Cardassia Prime, thinking each one's got a photon torpedo buried in it," he decided. "I think I'll follow him halfway back and plant one, just to put him out of his misery."

"Be my guest." Sisko nodded at Thornton and O'Brien to disengage. The *Defiant*'s viewscreen shimmered back to a view of comet-haloed ships, just in time to show their tractor beam vanishing. The Klingons' paler beam twinkled out a moment later, and the Cardassian shuttle darted back into its launch pad like a reef fish diving for cover. A moment later, the battleship's warp nacelles glowed to life and it was gone, shaking them with the nearness of its jump to lightspeed. Kor's ship rippled into cloaked invisibility in that same instant, and Sisko felt a second wash of ion discharge tremble through his ship.

"Alone at last," said O'Brien, sighing.

"Not quite." Sisko lifted his gaze to the sliver of Armageddon's—no, *Cha'Xirrac*'s—darkened skies, seeing the charred but living planet beneath that ashen veil. "We have some new friends to meet, Chief. Let's hope they're a little easier to get along with."

"Than the Klingons and the Cardassians?" Odo snorted. "Captain, I believe that's what Quark would call an ears-on certainty."

Kira had climbed out of the cave system feeling worn, ancient, as battered as the surface of Cha'Xirrac. She'd kept her eyes downcast, preparing for the onslaught of bright light after hours in the womblike dark. Instead, a soft grayness enveloped the world, and the muted features of the terrain sent her memory tumbling backward a dozen years.

Before the Federation came to safeguard Bajor—

before the Cardassians declared the planet raped to a shell and no longer worth the expense to maintain—Kira had walked through this same armageddon landscape under a different name. Rota Province had been battered for forty days and forty nights by every surface-launchable warhead the Cardassians bothered to keep on Bajor. Not atomics—the Cardassians were far too frugal to waste expensive destruction on Bajoran sheep who had no way to fight back or run. They'd shattered Rota with slow-moving conventional weaponry, all because of rumors that the Salbhai resistance cell had taken up hiding among the homesteads and villages of that wealthy province.

Well, they'd gotten Salbhai and her fighters, along with eleven thousand farmers, timbermen, and *peng* herders. The resultant desolation looked exactly like Cha'Xirrac did now—soil blasted down to the bedrock, trees blown down like a children's stick game, the rivers and marshes choked with carcasses, mudslides, and debris. It had been hard to imagine that anything would ever be able to live in Rota ever again. And it was hard to imagine Cha'Xirrac coming back to life after such apocalyptic devastation.

The view had not improved much from the roof of a shuttle. Kira sat, knees hugged to her chest, and watched a distant curtain of smoke ripple against a sky only just now dimming down to the color of natural dawn. No more trees poked their heads above the *tuq'mor* canopy. No more *banchory* crashed their slow, gentle ways through the foliage. Only ash pattered like sand through the brush still standing, tainted with the bitter scent of distant fires.

"Looking for someone?"

275

She glanced down, startled by Sisko's sudden presence. "Not really." The smile she forced on his behalf didn't feel very convincing, and his own amused expression suggested she could have done better. Sighing, she scooted toward the front of the small craft to slide down its nose. "How're negotiations coming?"

"Very well." The captain stepped judiciously aside as she jumped to the ground, neither helping nor hindering her descent. "Actually, there doesn't seem much to negotiate. The *xirri* are still more than happy to share Cha'Xirrac with their Klingon friends, and the Klingons still have nowhere else to go." He gave a little shrug that Kira thought indicated acceptance of the situation, although she wasn't completely sure. "I think the House of Vrag is relieved to have some purpose here. Something to call themselves other than 'exiles.'"

Kira nodded, warding off a thought about how a certain caliber of Klingon would have worn that label proudly, and looked out into the wounded *tuq'mor* again. If she looked very carefully, she could find a few spots of defiant green amid the wreckage.

"It looks like we'll be making several trips with the *Victoria Adams*'s crew," Sisko went on. "I'd rather not stack them in three deep this time, but I also don't want to make any more shuttle runs than absolutely necessary. Our friend George is busy sorting the survivors into shiploads while the Klingons work out the terms of an ongoing scientific study with Dax."

Kira nodded, a bit absently. "He's your secret dignitary—the one Starfleet didn't want the Klingons to get their hands on." When Sisko didn't say anything to refute that, she angled a weary grin up at him. "His name isn't really George, is it?"

Her captain changed the subject as smoothly as if she'd never brought it up at all. "So how is Dr. Bashir holding up?"

"LeDonne says he'll be fine. She's given him something that'll keep him out until we get back to the station." She glanced reflexively back toward the shuttle, even though she couldn't see inside. "She was doing patient triage with him when he was kidnapped. I think she's feeling guilty for not realizing what was happening and doing something to stop it."

Sisko followed her gaze briefly, then somehow ended up scrutinizing Kira with his head tipped slightly toward his shoulder. "And what are you feeling guilty about?"

The question caught her without a ready answer. "I don't know. Nothing." Everything. She started to pace away from him, aborted it, and ended up making a frustrated circle that only put her back where she'd started. "I guess I just don't understand what Klingon honor is supposed to be good for," she finally blurted. "What purpose does it serve to take the best, most noble members of their society and . . . sacrifice them! Why can't there be some middle ground between perfect compliance to honor and death?"

"Because sometimes perfect compliance *is* death." Sisko met her angry glare with a placidity that said he hadn't been making light of her dilemma. "Curzon once told me that he didn't think he would ever fully understand what the Klingons call honor, even if he had a dozen lifetimes to study it. In many ways, I think the Klingons are still learning and refining their own concepts every day. It's part of what makes a culture vibrant and adaptive. But it is a hard thing," he said with resonant seriousness. "A hard taskmaster. It's not our place to say whether or not the rewards are worth it."

Federation rhetoric—noninterference, respect for another culture's ways. Worse yet, it was rhetoric Kira's head believed in, even when her heart ached for want of a better, less tragic way.

"I've often thought honor among Klingons is more religion than social," Sisko continued, leaning back against the shuttle's nose and crossing his arms. "Like fate among Humans, *av'adeh'dna* among Vulcans, and *pagh* among your own people. Honor isn't just a list of rules that Klingons adhere to the way you might a recipe. It shapes them, leads them, determines the character of their souls." He motioned back toward the huddle of Klingons and *xirri* inside the mouth of the caves, and Kira was abruptly struck with the incongruity of that sight. Of the wondrous potential represented by a handful of battered warriors and the small gray-green primates who had adopted them. "Honor led them here to be protectors of Cha'Xirrac—better protectors than any combination of starships or comets could be. They've been reborn, through fire and ice." He smiled a little at the drama of his words. "No rebirth ever comes without loss. *Epetai* Vrag knew that." He caught Kira's gaze up in his own. "Maybe honor required a sacrifice to balance the scales—life for life. You can't hold it against her if she willingly made that choice."

Perhaps not. But Kira couldn't help wishing for a

solution that didn't require bloodshed to water the seeds of new life.

"Dax says the planet will recover," she said suddenly. It was something to hang on to. A memory of Rota Province as it had been just a few months ago, soft and green and scattered with delicate prairie flowers that couldn't have existed in the shadows of Rota's forests. New life, celebrating with a song of colors. Someday, this planet would look like that, too.

"So not just a new life for the Klingons," Sisko commented. "A whole new existence. A whole new world."

"Yes." Kira stood up with sudden decision. "And maybe, if they're lucky, a whole new meaning of honor. One that involves cooperation rather than fighting, and survival rather than sacrifice."

Sisko made a somber noise. "I'm not sure that they'll still be Klingons then," he said. "And, somehow, I think there will always be a Day of Honor celebration on Cha'Xirrac."

"That's all right." Kira glanced back at those glints of water-shielded vegetation, as stubbornly tough as Klingons and as quietly surprising as the *xirri*. "Just as long as it is followed by a Day of Rebirth."

COMING IN SEPTEMBER!

Day of Honor
Book Three:

HER KLINGON SOUL

by
Michael Jan Friedman

Turn the page for an excerpt from Book Three of
Star Trek: Day of Honor

"My name is Ordagher. I am the Overseer of this station. As such, I hold your lives in the palm of my hand."

He paused, eyeing each of the prisoners in turn. When he came to B'Elanna, he seemed to linger for a moment—but only for a moment. Then he went on.

"There was an escape attempt," Ordagher continued. "Like all escape attempts, it was a failure. Still, I cannot permit such things. They are wasteful, and waste is to be avoided at all costs." The Overseer's wide mouth twisted savagely. "I want to know who led the attempt, and I want to know it without delay."

B'Elanna's heart began to beat harder in her chest. This was it, she told herself. She shifted her eyes from one side to the other, curious as to who would finally give her away.

But no one did. In the wake of the "commander's" demand, there was silence. That is, except for the throb of heavy machinery that seemed to pervade the place at all times.

Ordagher's eyes narrowed under his overhanging brow. "I am not a patient man," he growled. "Again, I ask—who led this attempt?"

As before, his question was met with silence. B'Elanna swallowed. How could this be? She wasn't surprised that Kim would stand up for her—or maybe even Tolga, with whom she had established some kind of bond.

But the other prisoners? They didn't owe her a thing.

Nonetheless, they didn't point B'Elanna out. They didn't move at all. They just looked straight ahead in defiance of the Overseer, ignoring their instincts for survival.

What's more, Ordagher didn't get as angry as the lieutenant had expected. He didn't even seem entirely surprised. But then, he was a Nograkh as well.

"You choose to be stubborn," observed the Overseer. He clasped his hands behind his back. "Very well. I know how to deal with stubbornness." He turned to one of the guards who stood behind him.

There was no order. Apparently, none was necessary. Without comment, the guard advanced to within a meter of one of the prisoners. A fellow Nograkh, as luck would have it.

Raising his energy weapon, the guard placed its business end under the prisoner's chin. Then he pushed it up a little, forcing the Nograkh's head back in response. For his part, the prisoner said nothing—did nothing. He just stood there, eyes fixed on oblivion.

Ordagher eyed the others. "Once more, and for the last time, I ask you who led the escape attempt. If I do not receive an answer, your fellow prisoner will die in the ringleader's place."

None of the Nograkh said a word. They seemed content to let their comrade perish for them. Maybe that was their way—but it wasn't B'Elanna's.

"Me," she said, loudly and clearly.

The Overseer turned to her. "You?" he replied, his brow furrowing. Obviously, there was some doubt in his mind.

"Me," the lieutenant confirmed. "I was the one who led the escape attempt." She searched inwardly for a way to back up her claim—and decided some facts might help. "One of your guards tried to rape me, and I grabbed his weapon. The rest just happened."

Ordagher shook his head. "No," he concluded.

"I swear it," she told him. She took a deep breath. "If you're going to kill someone, it should be me. No one else."

She could feel the eyes of her fellow prisoners on her. Tolga's, Kim's. And those of the guards as well. The prisoner whose chin rested on the guard's energy weapon was probably eyeing her, too.

The Overseer considered her a moment longer. Then he tossed his head back and began to laugh. It was a hideous sound, like the sucking of a great wound. Without looking, Ordagher pointed to the prisoner whose life hung in the balance.

"Kill him," he snarled.

Before B'Elanna could do anything, before she could even draw a breath, the energy weapon went off. There was a flare of blue-white light under the prisoner's chin, and a sickening snap.

Then his eyes rolled back and he fell to the floor, lifeless.

B'Elanna's hand went to her mouth. The suddenness of it, the horror and the injustice—it threatened to overwhelm her. She could feel tears taking shape in the corners of her eyes.

The Nograkh had accepted his fate impassively, unflinchingly. He hadn't said so much as a word in his defense. And all for a being he barely knew.

"Take him away," said Ordagher, with a gesture of dismissal. "And watch the rest twice as closely," he told the guards, "or the next neck that snaps will be your own." Then, glaring one last time at the other prisoners, he turned his back on them and left the chamber.

The guards took their spots at the exit. The lights dimmed. One by one, the prisoners drifted to their customary sleeping spots.

But not B'Elanna. She remained where she was, trying to get a handle on what had just happened. Trying to understand what she was supposed to do about it—what she was supposed to think.

The lieutenant felt someone's touch on her shoulder. Numbly, she turned to Kim. He looked white as candlewax.

"Are you all right?" he asked her.

She shook her head from side to side. How could she be all right? How could she just accept what had happened and go on?

Caught in the grip of unexpected anger, she

looked for Tolga. Found him at the other end of the chamber, where he always took his rest. And stalked him like an animal seeking its prey.

As she approached, his back was to her. Still, the closer she got, the more he seemed to notice. Finally, he glanced at her over his powerful shoulder, his silver eyes glittering in the light from the doorway.

"You," she said, her lips pulling back from her teeth like a she-wolf's, her voice little more than a growl.

Then she made a fist of her right hand and hit him as hard as she could. Tolga's head snapped around and he staggered back a step.

She tried to hit him with her left, but the Nograkh managed to grab her wrist before she could connect. And a moment later, his hand closed on her right wrist as well. Finally, he kicked her legs out from under her and pinned her with his considerable weight.

Left with no other weapon, B'Elanna spat at him. "You could have saved him," she rasped. "You could have said something, but you just stood there and let him die for me!"

Narrow-eyed, Tolga took in the sight of her. "Should I have interfered with Manoc's sacrifice?" he asked. "Am I a barbarian, that I should have stained his honor?"

"It was me who should have died," she railed, hardly bothering to struggle. "Me! I led the escape!"

The Nograkh nodded slowly. "Yes. When circumstances allowed, you did what was in you to do. And Manoc did what was in him."

B'Elanna shook her head. "It should have been me," she moaned. "It should have been me."

Tolga didn't say anything. He just watched her expend her outrage and her sorrow. Then he got off her and let her get to her feet.

Kim was standing nearby, ready to try to intervene if it became necessary. But it never had. At no time had the Nograkh seemed willing to hurt her, even in his own defense.

Massaging her wrists, the lieutenant looked up at Tolga. "Why didn't they believe me?" she asked softly. "Why did they laugh like that?"

The Nograkh shrugged. "Ordagher didn't believe a female could lead a rebellion." He paused. "But then, he does not know you as I do."

B'Elanna nodded. Before this was over, she vowed, she would show the Overseer just what a female could do.

Look for STAR TREK Fiction from Pocket Books

Star Trek®: The Original Series

Star Trek: The Next Generation®

Star Trek: Deep Space Nine®

Star Trek®: Voyager™

Star Trek®: New Frontier

Star Trek®: Day of Honor